The Belles of
Solace Glen

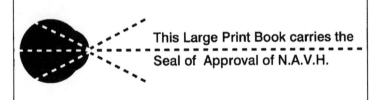

The Belles of Solace Glen

Susan S. James

WHEELER
PUBLISHING

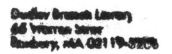

Published in 2004 by arrangement with The Berkley Publishing Group, a division of Penguin Group (USA) Inc.

Wheeler Large Print Cozy Mystery.

The text of this Large Print edition is unabridged.
Other aspects of the book may vary from the original edition.

Set in 16 pt. Plantin by Christina S. Huff.

Printed in the United States on permanent paper.

Library of Congress Cataloging-in-Publication Data

James, Susan S.
    The belles of Solace Glen / Susan S. James.
      p. cm.
    ISBN 1-58724-770-4 (lg. print : sc : alk. paper)
    1. Women domestics — Fiction. 2. Inheritance and succession — Fiction. 3. Large type books. I. Title.
  PS3610.A455B45 2004
  813'.6—dc22   2004054986

FICTION

4/05

To my husband, Jim,
Who made dreams of toys underfoot a reality,
Who made swimming with
tropical fish in February happen,
Who gives generously, inspires unknowingly,
Supports without question,
and loves without limits;
A husband, a lover, a father, a friend,
You make all things possible
— even Solace Glen.

As the Founder/CEO of NAVH, the only national health agency solely devoted to those who, although not totally blind, have an eye disease which could lead to serious visual impairment, I am pleased to recognize Thorndike Press* as one of the leading publishers in the large print field.

Founded in 1954 in San Francisco to prepare large print textbooks for partially seeing children, NAVH became the pioneer and standard setting agency in the preparation of large type.

Today, those publishers who meet our standards carry the prestigious "Seal of Approval" indicating high quality large print. We are delighted that Thorndike Press is one of the publishers whose titles meet these standards. We are also pleased to recognize the significant contribution Thorndike Press is making in this important and growing field.

Lorraine H. Marchi, L.H.D.
Founder/CEO
NAVH

* Thorndike Press encompasses the following imprints: Thorndike, Wheeler, Walker and Large Pr int Press.

Acknowledgments

Boundless thanks to Mary Tahan, who first believed in the quirky little community known as Solace Glen, and her brilliant sidekick, Jena Anderson. To Christine Zika — you signed on the dotted line and made the dream come true. Deep thanks to my parents for giving me the best education they could, in all things, in every way. To the teachers in my life who believed I could — Tim McCorkle, Tommy Samaha, Elizabeth McColl, Elizabeth Keith, James Skirkey, Jonathan Holden, and most especially, Cecil Dawkins.

And a great big HA HA to the teachers who thought I couldn't (who shall remain nameless).

R. Bell / Lucy Hanover Bell
(1755–1800)   (1760–1821)
m. 1781

Richard / Kaye Thomas
(1782–1842)   (1790–1836)
m. 1812

Ferrell / Sara Doddin
(1784–1845)   (1785–1852)
m. 1808

Harold
(1813–23)
Joseph
(1817–30)

Ann
(1815–35)
Richard
(1820–22)

Ferrell / Gretal Stubing
(1828–99)   (1830–1908)
m. 1850

Roland / Florence Openheim
(1851–1908)   (1859–1929)
m. 1878

Roland, Jr. / Katrina T. Chapelle
(1880–1945)   (1873–1940)
m. 1898

Roland, III / Penelope Higgins
(1899–1971)   (1940–71)
m. 1930

Leona Bell Jenner / Jake P. Jenner
(1931–)   (1915–86)
m. 1952

Roland, IV /
(1941–)
m. 1968

Ferrell T.
(1977–)

Lucinda / Joseph Paca
(1787–1850) (1781–1843)
m. 1817

John Bell   Lucy Bell Paca Tanner / Jason Tanner
(1829–1912)   (1800–50)
m. 1847

Lucinda Ann Tanner
(1850–90)

Florie O. Bell
(1884–1939)

Garland Day
(1944–)

Hilda Higgins
(1986–)

Part One

Chapter 1

The ladybugs come in September, right when the first chill sneaks in. They cluster together on the ceiling in the corner of the bathroom, little round faces turned into each other like a ladies' sewing circle. Occasionally, one wanders off as if she's stepping away for an iced tea. "Be back in a jiff," she might say to the others. That's when I make my move.

I pluck the wanderer off and, just as quick, throw her in the toilet. When you touch a ladybug, she gives off a smell, dry and woody, smoky, a candle just blown out. I don't have anything against ladybugs, mind you. I just don't want them taking over. Everything in life needs culling now and then.

I guess you could say that's what I do for a living. I cull. People in Solace Glen, Maryland, have called on me for more than twenty years to come pick through their houses, throw away the trash, put things right, scrub things down. They trust me completely to do the job neat and thorough. I can't stand a dusty baseboard, and they know it. I'll do windows for extra. I'm the only domestic help in this burg. If you want more than once a week, you have to import. Only one

13

of my people ever did — Leona Bell Jenner. Brought in a teenager from Baltimore and she cleaned all right. Cleaned the Bell house out of half the silver and jewelry Leona was saving to give to her niece and namesake, Lee. I could have told her. Stick with who you know. Flip Paxton doesn't cheat people, anybody'd tell you that. I just want enough to pay the mortgage, splurge once or twice a year on something frivolous, and go to Ocean City in the summer to kick up my heels.

Leona apologized, though. "Flip," she said (nobody calls me Felicity and stays on my Christmas list), "you forgive an old woman for being silly, don't you?"

"Miss Leona," I answered, "if all we did was forgive each other for being silly, none of us would get a damn thing done sunup to sundown. I'll be at your place Thursday."

I had left her time slot open, sure she'd see the light, sure that all she'd tried to do was ease my mounting workload and didn't mean any insult or injury. A woman the caliber of Leona couldn't harm a flea. She'd always kept a watchful, protective eye on me almost as intently as she did her niece Lee. I counted her as one of my "mothers," one of the ladies in town who lovingly slipped into the empty shoes of my own mother who died in a car crash with my father when I was eighteen. Between Leona and other women like her in Solace Glen, the blank space my mother left was almost filled, and I couldn't have been more grateful. From the moment I raised my eyes from my parents' grave at the sound of the last "amen," a circle of women surrounded me, all dressed in black, all wearing faces of comfort. And suddenly, to me, Solace Glen became a town with one house, a house of mothers and sisters. When I started my cleaning business, each house I cleaned felt like the house before, each house a connecting room of a large home, a home where love and care wrapped around me whenever I walked through the door.

Two hours was all it took to clean the huge, old Bell house with only Leona to fill the rooms and a cat called Jeb, named after Major General J.E.B. Stuart, the Confederate cavalry hero. Leona said the general not only passed by, he stopped and stayed awhile, and there lay a story. She said she'd tell it to me sometime, and she did. While she was having her heart attack, she got part of it out.

"It makes this house important." She spoke in a raspy whisper, crumpled on the carpet like a leaf of tissue paper left out of the gift box. I had to lean into her face to get all the words. "It makes all of us important. You and me. Solace Glen."

"Solace Glen is already important, Miss Leona." I patted her hand till the ambulance arrived, hoping nobody else in town scheduled an emergency that day. "It's important for its people. Like you."

"Flip," she smiled, eyelids flickering, same as her life, "you are a treasure." She gripped my hand as if I were her last of kin and went on with the story. When the ambulance pulled up, she jumped to the part about the proof.

"You find those letters, Flip. Read them if you want, then give them to my niece. Give them to Lee."

The paramedic twins, Jesse and Jules Munford, went about their jobs and listened to Miss Leona at the same time, their bristly white blond hair shaved so close to their skulls they both looked like eggheads. People would say, "Are you Egghead One or Two?" Whichever one breathed first was Number One. He knew who he was, but nobody else in Solace Glen had a clue.

The Eggheads gossiped the same as they breathed, so I knew Miss Leona's half-told story would rush around town like a flash flood, swirling with incongruous details and wild conjecture.

"Don't you worry," I told that poor woman as they bundled her off, hooked up to God knows what, maple syrup for all I knew. "I'll get those letters right now, hand them safe and sound to Lee, and we'll meet you at the hospital. Everything's going to be fine."

Her face was a satisfaction to me, trusting and content, as if she'd slipped her house key into my apron pocket and run off on vacation. "Thank you, Flip." Her voice trailed away. "You take such care of us all."

I think back now to that moment. Things might have been so different if the Eggheads hadn't heard any part of Miss Leona's story. I would have found those letters, probably not read even one, and handed them over to Lee Jenner at the Historical Society, where nothing ever happens. As it was, I read all three letters so I would know the facts, something the Eggheads never had a grip on.

Those letters changed everything. Funny how something buried so deep in the past can suddenly break through this earth and grow tall, branches sweeping out to scrape one, offer shelter to another.

Chapter 2

Lee Jenner lived on Center Street smack in the middle of downtown Solace Glen, though calling Solace Glen a town is stretching it. The rust red brick of her two story home, brick almost as old as Frederick County, Maryland, exhaled a fine crimson dust even on wet days, and the iron-lettered marker above the little green door let visitors know the house was built in 1794. A peeling picket fence outlined the square yard, and at the entrance gate hung a ten-year-old sign that read in faded green letters, "Solace Glen Historical Society. Contributions Welcome."

With nothing but time on her hands after college down the road at Hood, Lee took the old house her Uncle Jake left her and made it into a sort of tourist attraction, open whenever she felt like it, which wasn't often. She majored in history at Hood (an education I would have given an arm for) and liked the idea of taking that pile of crumbling brick and elevating it above its station in life, buying antiques in New Market, furnishing the downstairs the way it might have appeared two hundred years ago, years before J.E.B. Stuart even rode into town. But Lee also had a quirky, artsy style (she said it was "the Jenner-inner") that her poor Aunt Leona would fret about and Lee would laugh about. A prime example is when she paid a visionary artist from the Maryland Institute to create a make-believe early nineteenth-century woman and plopped her in a chair with a wooden bowl on her lap as if she was shelling butter beans.

Lee called the make-believe woman Plain Jane, but I never thought she was. Her hair rang out tomato red and her mouth wore a wicked tilt to it that made you wonder what those early American women had up their sleeve.

People got a lot of mileage out of Lee's big doll, and the public mention of Plain Jane's name gave Leona the vapors. Dancing to her own drum, Lee didn't care what people thought. She kept to herself more than most, earning a reputation (according mostly to Marlene Worthington) as "rude when approached," and "too smartie pants for her own good." But I loved Lee like a sister, sharing our "mother," Leona. We considered each other best friends. She was thirty-two, ten years younger than me, let me borrow books any time, always had coffee and Danish out when I came to clean, took seriously any advice I doled out, and had the most wonderful, vicious sense of humor.

"We need a name for Marlene," she said, just a week before Leona's heart attack. The first fall breeze of mid-September flowed through an open window. I flapped a dust rag around Plain Jane, wondering to myself how that visionary artist envisioned the doll's black eyes, which I only then realized were dyed condoms. What would Leona think?

Lee bit into a Danish and wiped a sticky finger across her jeans. "Marlene Worthington. Marlene Worthington. Saint something." She mulled it over. "Our Lady of Vicks VapoRub."

"She does stink of it," I agreed, moving away from Plain Jane's soulless black eyes. "One time I saw her out in public with two wads under each nostril. Looked like she needed an operation. Her mother would have been mortified, dear woman."

Lee nodded. We both adored Louise Lamm, another of my "mothers," who languished away from cancer, losing a little bit more of herself every day. I felt even closer to Louise than Leona. She'd almost filled the roles of both mother and father to me ever since the car crash took my parents and I had to start up a business to support myself.

"Poor Louise," Lee sighed. "She's got enough to think about without having to wipe her daughter's big troll nose."

"You're right about that." I didn't want to get weepy, even in front of my best friend, so I picked up a can of cleanser and headed upstairs to Lee's midget bathroom. Everything in her house could be measured by the inch. Shoe box windows, cramped ceilings, rabbit hole doors. The people who lived back then must have come from Oz. Lee herself stood five foot five, no more than 110 pounds. She wore her long auburn hair swept up in one of those toothy, tortoise shell dime store clips. Her face claimed the name Jenner — jaw set in concrete, a wide, courageous mouth, nose straight as a paring knife, and hazel eyes that always carried a question in them, never satisfied with any answer.

"I like 'Our Lady of Vicks VapoRub,'" I called downstairs to her. "That's a good one."

"Take a book when you leave," she called back, and I heard the kitchen door open and close. She'd gone outside to the garden, I guessed, to work on the historical herb plot. I scrubbed her munchkin tub. Maybe, instead of a regular scarecrow for the herb garden, she'd get a visionary nineteenth-century man to carry on with Plain Jane. Maybe his eyes could be IUDs.

I glowed at how artsy I'd become, and pictured Leona, dying of embarrassment. Little did I know that a week later, she'd simply be dying.

I knocked once on the door and went right in, as usual. It was Thursday morning, two days after Leona's funeral. Lee sat at the antique pine farm table on a painted chair beside Plain Jane. She sat so still, for a second I thought both were made-up women, that she'd gotten a bosom buddy for Plain Jane.

"Brought back that book I borrowed." I laid it gently on the table. "Thanks."

She cocked her head to view the title. "*Straight On Till Morning.* So what did you think of Beryl Markham?"

The hazel eyes held some luggage under them, a sign of traveling, no rest stops.

"I'd say she got around." I drew an old milking stool from under the table and planted myself at her feet. "How you been, Lee? Like I have to ask. You look awful."

"I feel awful." Lee never minced words. "I just lost my only remaining family. Leona was good to me. She was so good after Daddy, then Momma died."

Her voice choked on the last few words and she took a deep breath, prepared to dive low. I reached for her hand, conscious of the taint of disinfectant covering my fingers, and barely brushed her skin, the way I might dust one of Leona's dear little heirlooms. I almost said, "You've still got the Bell's," but fortunately I caught myself. Leona's brother, Roland Bell, and his twisted crew could hardly be called family. His was the one disconnected room in my house of Solace Glen; his home was the only place that didn't feel like home.

"Tom Scott says she left me almost everything. I'm supposed to meet with him in a few days to go over the will." The dip of Lee's mouth said it all. "Flip. What am I going to do with that big house and this one, too? It's not like I'm married and have a pack of kids. It's just me and cranky ole Jeb now."

The mention of Jeb, Leona's worthless cat, reminded me of my mission, a mission I hadn't accomplished as fast as I'd told Leona I would because Leona's own timing had left me shaken. I hadn't expected her to die before I could call Lee. I hadn't expected her to leave at all. "I've got something for you, Lee." I drew my rough, smelly hand away and pulled the velvet bag of letters from the carryall. "This was Leona's last request, though I didn't know it at the time. She told me where to find them, and now I'm handing them over to you."

"What is it?" She fingered the blue velvet. "A tiara?"

I took the yellowed pack from the bag. "Letters."

"What kind of letters?" She leaned back and studied the three envelopes tied with red ribbon, not touching, letting curiosity grow.

"Love letters."

The dip in her mouth turned up. "Leona and Uncle Jake?"

"No. . . ."

"No, paper's too old. Somebody in the family way back?"

"I don't know. Leona didn't tell me who the woman was."

"Well, you've read them, haven't you?"

"I read them. Leona gave me permission."

"Don't get nervous. I wasn't pointing a finger. You're just being so mysterious."

"So was Leona. Maybe she didn't know who the woman was in the letters. Maybe she did and wouldn't say. Could have been a cousin, a friend, a visitor staying in the Bell house. But Leona's mother told her the man who wrote the letters was J.E.B. Stuart, even though the signature on all three is K.G.S."

She reached her hands behind her head and pulled the clip out. The auburn hair fell long and glossy over one shoulder.

"Well?" I shoved the letters closer to her.

The hazel eyes questioned that stack of yellow paper like it might rear up on the table and give a speech.

"Why," she looked at me hard, "would Leona tell you to give me some antique letters as a 'last request'? What's so important about these pieces of paper?"

"Why don't you read them and tell me. You're the historian. I'll come back later to clean." I rose from the milk stool. "Leona said something else kind of curious. She said the letters were handed down only by the women in the family. From the beginning, the Bell men were kept in the dark."

When my hand gripped the brass doorknob of the front door, I turned and told her, "Leona had those hidden in a waterproof canister inside a plastic bag stuffed in the arm of an uphol-stered chair under a sheet in the corner of the attic. She wanted those letters hidden, but she didn't want them destroyed. The rest is up to you."

My fingers twisted the knob. "And Lee," I hated telling her this part, "the Eggheads heard enough of the story to make you miserable the rest of your life."

I could swear when I shut the door, even Plain Jane looked alarmed.

Chapter 3

Roland Bell, Leona's miserable brother, owned the only restaurant in town where he peddled decent, home-cooked food and held the town patent on cheapness. You sat down at a table without any flourish from a menu-toting hostess. You picked up the list of specials, hand-written and photocopied that morning, right at the table. You made your choice and wrote it down with a pencil and a pad, also supplied at the table. You handed it to whoever passed by wearing a red Roland's Café and Grill T-shirt, and you didn't wait more than fifteen minutes for your steaming-hot meal to arrive.

Paper napkins, but real plates and flatware. The plastic flowers changed with the seasons, four times a year: white carnations, yellow tulips, orange mums, and red poinsettias. If you left a tip of more than fifteen percent, Roland, never one to squander a buck, thanked you in a prosecutorial manner and might lecture you on the Great Depression next time you walked in. I never got that lecture.

The Jenners and the Bells were kin only by marriage; Leona Bell married Jake Jenner whose brother, Henry, was Lee's father. But Lee never thought of the Bells as family, except for her Aunt Leona, because Roland, his wife Garland, and their two children, Hilda and Ferrell T., stopped acting like family. They acted more like she didn't exist, which came to suit Lee just fine. When Leona and Roland's parents died, the big house — the Bell house — was left to Leona, not her younger brother; he got the money. Leona and Jake moved out of the 1794 munchkin cottage and set up digs. Roland nearly blew a gasket.

"I'm the only son! I should inherit the big house!" He'd tell anybody who would listen how he'd been terribly mistreated, how Leona must have exerted undue influence, gotten his parents drunk or read up on hypnotism so she could snap her fingers from across a room and they'd start signing legal documents by the truckload.

"Thank God he wasn't a twin," is what Leona used to say behind his back. While Jake lived, he never spoke an ugly word about his cheap, whiny brother-in-law. I don't know how, though. The rest of the quirky, artsy Jenners could hardly contain themselves. Lee's mother and father, Marie and Henry, used to take turns imitating Roland and his scaredy-cat wife, Garland.

Marie, who for too short a time was one of my "mothers," would hunker down behind a lamp and squeak, "Oh, Roland. I'm so ashamed. I forgot to wash your socks by hand in lavender water and gold dust the way you like."

And Henry would pounce up on an ottoman, hands on his hips and sneer, "Woman. That's probably why my parents left Sister the Big House and we're stuck here in this Victorian monstrosity of only fifteen rooms. If you'd done what you were told and washed those socks, we wouldn't be in this fix."

I count Henry and Marie as my first customers. They did everything in their power to help get my business going. Called their friends, raved about my detail work. Slipped a fifty in my apron pocket that first New Year's Eve, which was a lot of money to an eighteen year old who'd suddenly found herself alone. "Have a happy," Marie whispered and kissed me on the temple, the way my mother used to do. Then Henry poured me my first glass of French champagne, and we had an early toast to Auld Lang Syne. He sang in a magnificent Welsh voice. A few months later, when he passed so quickly from pancreatic cancer, we knew Marie couldn't last long in this world. Never strong alone, she lived the next couple of years as though split in two, desperately longing for her missing half. She drank herself to death, leaving Lee, only ten years old, without parents, same as me — one reason we bonded so close. Lee, at least, had her Uncle Jake and Aunt Leona and went to live with them. I rejoiced at the good care they gave her, but harbored envy, too. The drunk driver who took my parents left no family in their empty place. Leona swept Lee under her wing and cared for her like another mother, not wild and crazy like Marie, but solid and sympathetic, which was what she needed.

As good as God made Leona, He still gave her a sufferance. Roland made Leona miserable all her life. Lee told me from the time she moved in with Jake and Leona, Roland would appear at least once a month to whine and pout about some piece of furniture or doodad. He'd pick up a china bunny and claim his daddy or momma told him he could have it after they passed. Sometimes he would burst into tears. Sometimes he would throw a temper tantrum. You never could predict Roland's reaction to anything, but you could always count on his greed. The will gave everything in the house to Leona, lock, stock, and barrel, but she felt a little guilty about getting all that stuff, so she played along and gave in to Roland's whining, going as far as to feel sorry for him. The visits increased after Jake died. Still, Leona never said no to her brother.

By the time her heart gave out, Leona had given more than half her belongings to Roland. His fifteen room Victorian overflowed with sofas, chairs, tables, rugs, porcelain, crystal, silver, art work, and linen — a lot to keep clean. I noticed, though, the Bells had little in the way of books and family photographs. As long as his house spilled over with impressive knickknacks, Roland could look down at the rest of us. That's how he measured himself against others — with a yardstick of touchables.

If he'd known how valuable the Bells' library was, though, he might have asked for the written word up front. As it happened, most of the books went with Lee when she moved to the 1794 house, and over the years, she added to the collection. Books gradually replaced walls in the little Historical Society, giving Plain Jane and her butter bean bowl an unexpected air of dignity. But to Roland, a book was something you kept your accounts in, tallying up at year's end. His fist closed tight around money and the stuff crammed in his house, but Roland's grasp around the important things in life went undetected. Under normal circumstances, Roland never would have wanted those letters I handed to Lee. Letters, books, family photos — that was just the worthless junk you threw in the trash at the end of the day.

The Eggheads, however, specialized in colorization of normal circumstances. Leona hadn't been buried two weeks, and they sat blabbing over lunch at Roland's Café and Grill about her last words to me, the story of the letters. You never heard such distortion of truth.

Roland got an earful, along with everybody else in town.

"She never told me about any letters," he said, casual, matter-of-fact.

Small hints give way to an awful truth. The trembling of a coffee cup, the touch of purple in a cloud, a faint dip in pressure, a few raindrops, creeping water. All little things that lead to people asking what if. What if the Eggheads had kept their mouths shut? What if the half-story Leona told hadn't filtered its way through every living soul who passed through Solace Glen?

Roland rang up a customer, slid a peppermint across the counter, wiped a cotton cloth over the cash register. "You're awful quiet, Flip."

My usual table hovered behind the cash register, out of the mainstream against a wall in the corner, a table most customers wouldn't want or even notice. The nicest table, of course, the one by the center window, invariably berthed the town cop, Officer Palmer Lukzay, who claimed the dubious honor of being Roland's only friend. He received all his meals on the house, the only person who ever did.

"What do you want me to say, Roland?" I turned my gaze toward Lukzay, then in the opposite direction where I could see the Eggheads straining in their seats, wanting to hear the parts they didn't know, but wouldn't admit to not knowing.

"I don't want you to say anything. I'm just curious if what Jesse and Jules say is right." A curiosity that sounded like an accusation.

"Right?" I dotted my mouth with a napkin, anxious to switch the subject. "Eggheads don't know right from left. Remember the time Pal nearly severed his left arm off chopping wood for Miss Fizzi? Eggheads came and got him, took him to the emergency room, found out they'd slapped the tourniquet on the wrong arm. Lucky he didn't die."

"Flip Paxton!" One of the Eggheads shot up, I don't know which one, stabbing a fork in the air. "That was our first job, and there were extenuating circumstances the average layman wouldn't understand."

"Yeah," I said, "like how the two of you ever graduated from high school."

The other Egghead sprang up. "OK, Flip, Miss Smartie Ass, why don't you stop trying to change the subject and answer Roland about those letters. We were there. We heard it all. Don't you go acting like we're a couple of liars."

"Who said anything about lying?" I concentrated on my Swiss steak.

"You insinuated that what we said wasn't right."

"That's true, Flip, you did." Marlene Worthington, Our Lady of Vicks VapoRub, sashayed up to the cash register to pay her check. She handed Roland a ten and leaned both elbows on the counter as if she might camp out awhile, as curious about the letters as everybody else. But then, anything you could sell for money intrigued Marlene.

"This town is lucky to have you as a moral compass, Marlene. We all breathe easier with you around." I waved a hand in front of my nose.

Roland gave Marlene her change. "The gist of it is this, Flip. If Leona had some valuable letters, historic and all, then as her next-of-kin, I should get them."

He looked to Officer Lukzay for official confirmation. The cop nodded officiously enough, brushing cornbread crumbs off his bushy, gray mustache.

"How do you arrive at that? And, I might add, Officer Yes Man over there is no attorney-at-law."

Lukzay squinted sternly at his cornbread as if it owed him a juris doctorate.

I shoved my plate across the table, eager to make an exit. "Leona gave those letters to Lee while she was still alive. They're not part of the estate. Anyway, as far as I know, the will hasn't been read yet. Has it?" I couldn't believe I'd asked Roland such a blunt and personal thing. I scrambled to pick up my stuff.

Roland plopped a peppermint in Marlene's outstretched palm. "Not that it's any of *your* business, but Tom Scott's reading the will tomorrow. Guess I'm in it or he wouldn't have bothered to inform me."

I threw a five and two one's on the table. I couldn't reach the door fast enough to get out on the sidewalk. Roland was right. None of this was any of my business, and if Leona hadn't had her heart attack on my cleaning day, I wouldn't be worrying myself into a fever.

"Flip!"

33

I screeched to a halt, my clumsy plastic carryall banging against the well-toned thigh of the man in front of me. It was Tom Scott, followed by his ever-present black Lab, Eli.

"Flip," he removed his hat even though it was beginning to rain, a cool, late September rain. "I've been talking to your answering machine for two days."

"Oh, sorry." I set the carryall down. I loved Tom's low, husky voice. "Sometimes I forget I have that thing."

"Sometimes I wish I could forget I have one, too." His smile could grace the cover of any magazine, an off-center Harrison Ford grin. "We are reading Leona's will tomorrow at my office, around two. You should be there."

"Me? Why?" Maybe he wanted a dust-up after everybody left.

"Because you're in it," he said, putting his hat back on. "Don't be late."

I nodded, too shocked to protest that I am never late, thank you very much.

I picked up the carryall, shuffled down the street to my horrible diesel car, and climbed into the driver's seat. I turned on the ignition, punched at the radio, and sat there, stunned, listening to WFIB's Screamin' Larry announce the jazz lineup for later that evening. John Coltrane. Dinah Washington. Ella Fitzgerald. Tim Weisberg.

I could only think of two things: I would have to reschedule Louise Lamm, and Roland Bell was going to have a fit when the woman who scrubbed his toilets showed up at Tom Scott's office.

Chapter 4

I telephoned Louise Lamm around eight o'clock that night. When someone doesn't have long to live, you're never sure when is a good time to call. With some folks, no time is right, but with Louise, any time suited her fine. She appreciated the attention because her worthless daughter, Marlene, barely gave her a nod. Everybody in Solace Glen tried to make up for Marlene's deficiencies, bringing Louise little bouquets and casseroles, cutting the grass, painting her porch. The Circle Ladies at the Episcopal Church even pitched in and got her a VCR, rotating movies every week, and books, too.

"You see the local news?" Louise admitted to being a news addict. She would watch the Farm Report if that was the only thing on.

"Nope." I unloaded a bag of groceries consisting mostly of three pints of Ben & Jerry's Cherry Garcia and a vat of skin cream for my horrible hands. "Somebody's cat stuck up a tree? Or maybe Roland's Café burned to the ground, nothing saved but the plastic mums and a peppermint?"

"You're close. The Café got honorable mention, but the big story was the Eggheads blabbing to a TV reporter about secret Confederate spy letters turned over to the Historical Society, which will put Solace Glen on the map."

I didn't want to break any confidences, so I simply said, "Things must have really popped after I left the Café. Who else made the news?"

"They showed Screamin' Larry and Pal and Joey Sykes. Larry was eating, of course. Pal and Joey looked like they'd come straight out of the hood of a Ford at the Crown station. Those two were hanging on every ridiculous Egghead word, eyes the size of hubcaps poking through the oil and grease. Marlene's face made its television debut for about three seconds. She was sucking in her cheeks trying to look skinny."

"Yeah, well," I scooped into my ice cream, "hope springs eternal. Any Circle Ladies get their five seconds of fame?"

"Just Tina Graham, and she looked mortified. You know how TV always makes you look fatter than you are, and Tina's no condensed version. Poor thing doesn't need any more hard knocks to her terrible self-image."

I made a noise of agreement, cheeks filled with ice cream. Tina, a golden-hearted gift to the Circle Ladies, had battled the bulge all her fifty-eight years, attacking every fad diet in the book with true conviction that this would be the one to turn her into a Barbie doll. Over the years, she'd probably lost as much weight as she'd gained because the pounds always seemed to end up in the same place. She had a beautiful face, though, and could have been a Lane Bryant model if she'd ever wanted to.

We talked a little more, as we usually did two or three times a week, trading stories about the rich and famous and people we knew. We never considered our conversations gossip, just part and parcel of the national and local news, as Louise liked to say. For twenty-four years, talking to Louise was the closest thing I'd had to talking to my own mother. I rescheduled her cleaning so I could run over to Tom Scott's office the next day. Louise showed real interest in my surprise invitation to hear the will, and thought maybe Leona bequeathed me a piece of jewelry or a soup tureen, something she'd kept from Roland's greedy paws.

"Yeah. That'd be nice. I'd like something to look at and remember her by." I fixed myself a Working Girl's Martini — a lot of rocks, a lot of olives, a lot of cheap gin. "But whatever she left me, I'll tell you this, Louise, and mark my words." I took a swig. "Roland Bell will try to get it."

Chapter 5

At two o'clock the next day, on time as always, I crept into Tom Scott's law office determined not to look at Roland Bell if I could help it. I spotted Lee, crossed over, and sat down beside her on Tom's nice leather couch. As a rule, lawyers have better office furniture than doctors.

"Hey," I said, patting her hand, a little nervous. "Do we have to sign in or anything? I've never been in here but to clean."

I threw Ferrell T. a glance (the T. as much a mystery as the name Ferrell). Tom, for reasons known only to himself and God, hired Roland's useless son as his secretary. Most men, like Tom, made my palms feel clammy, but Ferrell T., like the Eggheads, brought out some sassiness in me, since none of them had hit thirty yet, and I felt I at least had more brains than all three put together. Despite his lofty airs, so much like his father, Ferrell T. couldn't intimidate me the way Roland always had. There he sat, a lumbering hulk, looking like a circus bear behind a desk. He must have looked the same to his teachers back in high school. Margaret Henshaw, our ever-so-correct English teacher, told me as much one day when I was cleaning her house. I was fussing out loud to myself about how Tom could put up with a guy who twanged rubber bands at Eli's bad hip when he thought nobody was looking. Margaret chimed in that Ferrell T. had every appearance of a dolt, but whatever filled his head, ninety-nine percent of it was devious. She said every time she used to turn around, he was up to some no-good prank, like switching the smart girl's homework with his and setting cigarette fires in the bathroom trash cans. I guess Tom would have hired Ferrell T.'s sister, Hilda, but she was still in high school and a bigger idiot than her brother. Kind-hearted in her own fashion, the most she could do was wait tables at the Café. Even that taxed all her brain cells.

"Hey, Ferrell T.," I called, "we supposed to sign in?"

Ferrell T. pushed up his black-framed glasses, which were always slipping halfway down his greasy nose. You'd think somebody in his mid-twenties would have grown out of that bad skin, but Ferrell T. still struggled with the worst kind of zits. It didn't earn him any sympathy in my book; the bad skin merely enhanced a repulsive personality.

He shifted in his chair from one cheek to the other. "Of course not."

He launched the first volley so I shot back. "Don't speak to me in that tone of voice, like I'm stupid and you're God's gift to Mensa." I knew that'd confuse him. "Don't know what

40

Mensa is? Ever pick up a book, Ferrell T.? Or is *Hustler* the closest thing to the ABC's you've ever seen?"

"Mensa?" He touched a finger to his bow tie. "Why would you come in here talking about female stuff? You're so weird."

Lee and I exchanged a look. The top of her lip quivered and she bent down to bury it in the heel of her hand. I reached for a magazine, *Forbes*, not something the average domestic subscribes to. I hid behind it and checked out who else got invited.

Roland and Garland sat in two matching armchairs, legs crossed in the same direction, ankles jiggling up and down in the same rhythm. I could feel Roland staring at me and Lee while Garland fussed with a tassel on her pocketbook.

I thought the five of us filled the room until a little whimper came from the corner behind the Bell's. I strained my neck and spotted Wilma Fizzi, head bowed, a lace hankie covering her nose. The sweetest, godliest, most well-respected example of senility in Solace Glen, Miss Fizzi never made a move in life without asking herself the question, What would Jesus do? Then she'd try to one-up him.

"Miss Fizzi?" I flopped the magazine on Tom's expensive looking coffee table and crossed the room, careful not to make eye contact with Roland. "You OK?"

She nodded, face still turned into her lap, and patted my hand when I placed it on her

41

shoulder. It felt like touching a dress on a hanger, no flesh and blood beneath, only the outline of bone holding up a piece of fabric.

"Leona was one of my best friends." Her voice broke into the handkerchief, shoulders trembling.

I knew Leona had paid close attention to Miss Fizzi, making sure her heat stayed on in winter and that she had plenty of fresh garden vegetables in summer, as anyone might do for an elderly neighbor. But apparently their friendship ran deeper than I'd imagined.

I crooked a finger at Lee and she immediately moved toward us. I noticed she avoided eye contact with Roland, too.

Lee kneeled down in front of Miss Fizzi, reached up, and gripped their four hands together. "Miss Fizzi," she whispered, sincere and dignified, "Aunt Leona was like a mother to me, and I think you were like a mother to her. So I guess that means you've got a granddaughter." She kissed Miss Fizzi's wrinkled hands and buried her head in the old lady's lap, a thirty-two-year-old little girl. With that, the colors in the room changed.

Miss Fizzi's shoulders stopped shaking. She sat up straight and the bloodshot eyes rested on Lee kneeling at her feet. "Get up, child. You'll mess your pretty skirt. And I was really more like a big sister to Leona than a mother. Heavens, don't make me older than I am."

Lee tugged on Miss Fizzi's arm and said,

"You come sit over here with us," and Miss Fizzi followed like a lamb.

For all my good Christian feeling about Lee and Miss Fizzi, I bristled when Roland spoke.

"Miss Fizzi," he couldn't hold it in, "you and Flip here on some business? Because if you are, Lee and us were here ahead of you. May be awhile."

Miss Fizzi drew a blank. For all she knew, she and I did have some business together.

"Ferrell T.," I said, using a tone you'd employ with a five-year-old, "why don't you tell your daddy what Miss Fizzi and I are here for."

Roland turned and glared at his numskull boy. "Well, boy?"

"They're in the will, Daddy."

"What will?" He still didn't get it.

"Leona's will, of course."

Roland's mouth dropped. "Leona? My sister, Leona? My dead sister, Leona, who just died two weeks ago?"

I fixed my eyes on the ceiling as Roland leaped out of the chair. "Why in hell would she leave anything to a crazy old lady and a god-damn maid, for God's sake!"

Miss Fizzi shrank into the sofa, assaulted by the obscenity. Lee and I wrapped an arm around her, in tune with each other.

"Oh, Roland, sit down," said Lee, tired.

Garland popped out of her chair, a little late following Roland's lead. She watched him, clutched her pocketbook, held her breath.

43

"I can't believe it," huffed Roland. "I just can't believe it. She must have been influenced. You must have gotten her drunk or drugged or both."

"Neither," I retorted, feeling brave with Lee beside me. "Miss Fizzi jumped on her back and I pulled a knife on her. Butcher's knife. About this long."

"Merciful heavens." Miss Fizzi's hand touched her heart.

I figured any second Roland would order Ferrell T. to phone the police, which could have meant trouble because Miss Fizzi would confess to anything. The pure in heart are always willing to take on the sins of the world — Jesus and Miss Fizzi two cases in point.

"I wouldn't put anything past you, Flip Paxton," Roland growled.

Garland curled her lip. She was doing a fine job of mimicking her unfortunate choice in husbands. "Uh-huh," she said, which was the most she said all day.

Roland moved a step closer to me. "I never trusted you," he hissed, voice growing louder. "I never trusted you with my sister's things, *my* things, and I flat out told her so many a time."

I focused on Roland's hands, dangerously close to making eye contact when the door swung open and Pal Sykes ambled in covered in axle grease. The big, white teeth shined, framed by blackened skin.

"Howdy, howdy," he croaked, happy as a cartoon character.

Roland twisted around. "What the hell are you doing here?"

Pal stopped in his tracks and beamed. "I'm in the will!" You'd have thought he'd won the Lotto.

"Oh, good God," moaned Roland, collapsing into the armchair. Garland dutifully wiggled backward and slowly lowered her bottom into the chair beside him.

"Well, congratulations!" I started laughing so hard, so relieved at the break in tension, that pretty soon Lee was laughing with me and Miss Fizzi, too, although she couldn't fathom what was so funny.

We wriggled around in this undignified manner until Tom poked his head around the corner and requested we all come in. Ferrell T. grabbed a yellow pad and herded us into a conference room that doubled as Tom's law library. I'd always thought the books made the room, spines of blue, red, and green lined up together with the gold lettering. Books like that inspire confidence, which I suppose is why lawyers have them.

Tom asked that we take a seat, and we formed into two opposing camps: Roland, Garland, and Ferrell T. on one side of the table, Miss Fizzi, Pal, Lee, and I on the other. Tom sat at the head with his faithful dog, Eli, stretched out at his feet. He opened a blue paper and spread it out — Leona's will. "I'll just get down to it and separate the chaff from the grain."

"Or the sheep from the goats," chirped Miss Fizzi, rolling with the Bible verses.

Roland mumbled something to himself and Garland chimed in with a responsive purr. Ferrell T. started scribbling notes on the yellow pad, a good little secretary.

"Lee," said Tom, "as you and I previously discussed, Leona left you everything but a small trust and a few personal property items that she devised to the people in this room. You and I have been over the exact provisions, and an appraisal of the personal property items has been rendered. Therefore, unless anyone cares to protest . . . ," he paused and glanced Roland's way, "those items may be disbursed immediately."

"You mean Lee gets the house?" Roland blurted, slamming his fist on the table. At the same moment, Ferrell T. stabbed a period on his legal pad so hard the pencil point cracked.

"Yes," said Tom, firm and quiet in a tone that hinted there better not be any more uncontrollable outbursts. Even Eli threw Roland a dirty look. "Lee inherits everything but the items we're about to discuss."

Roland snaked his arm back into his lap and shut up. Ferrell T. tossed the broken pencil aside and whipped a pen from his shirt pocket.

Tom turned to Lee and she nodded, expressionless.

"Now then," he said, and let out a big sigh as if sitting took a lot out of him. He flipped a

46

couple of pages and started reading. " 'To my dear friend, Pal Sykes . . .' "

Pal's grease-streaked face lit up. "Whutn't she sweet?"

" 'I leave my 1972 Cadillac . . .' "

Pal gasped.

" '. . . because he has always admired it and I know he will take such fine care of it.' "

"Oh, my Lord." Pal clapped his charcoal hands together and wrung them out. "Whutn't she sweet? Whutn't she sweet? Wait'll I tell my little Joey!"

I smiled. Pal's half brother Joey, barely seventeen, towered over Pal by a good five inches. He had come to Solace Glen two years before, when their father went to jail down in Georgia. Because of that, and a seventeen-year age difference, Pal treated his half brother more like a son.

Tom slipped an envelope across the table. "There're the title and the keys, Pal. She's all yours."

"I'm happy for you, Pal," said Lee.

Roland snarled, "Well, isn't this just the damn *Wheel of Fortune*. All we need is some bimbo handing out the goods."

Ferrell T. snorted and smirked.

Tom snapped the pages of the will like a cracking whip. Roland shut up again, and his useless son tried to imitate Tom's professional demeanor without success. " 'To my dear friend, Wilma Fizzi.' " He stopped, daring Roland to say something, anything, but all he got was silence. " 'I leave two thousand dollars a month to be taken out of the trust established in paragraph seven above and to be administered by my niece, Lee Jenner, as stated above. This monthly sum will continue for the lifetime of my dear friend, Wilma Fizzi, and will, I hope, grant her peace of mind regarding her mortgage, utilities, and groceries. Whatever is left, I hope she will take a nice trip every now and then and think of me.' "

Roland started gagging so hard he had to get up and hang out the window. Garland grabbed a paper cup of water Tom had thoughtfully put at each place and handed it to her husband.

"You OK, Daddy?" Ferrell T. turned and glared at Miss Fizzi as if she'd tried to physically catapult Roland out into the street.

I patted Miss Fizzi on one shoulder, Lee handled the other. "Your worries are over, Miss Fizzi," I said, happy as a clam.

"You deserve a nice retirement." Lee absolutely glowed.

"Whutn't she sweeeet!" Pal could hardly contain himself. This was the most excitement he'd seen that didn't involve transmission fluid.

"Damnation," coughed Roland. "Damnation."

Miss Fizzi sat awhile, letting the news sink in. Finally she said, "Leona was the kindest woman I ever knew, and I will do my best to make good use of her resources. With your help, dear." She grasped Lee's hand.

Tom cleared his throat and went on. " 'To my dear friend, my treasure of more than twenty years, Felicity Ann Paxton, . . .' "

I cringed.

". . . and I apologize to her for using her legal name, but this is a formal document and Tom says I have to for the first mention. To Flip, . . .' "

I relaxed again, settling my gaze on the green carpet.

" '. . . who was always there for me, always listened, always gave good, common sense advice, always gave comfort even in her own sorrow, and always lifted my spirits in times of darkness, I leave one of my most cherished possessions, . . .' "

I could feel Roland's eyes burning into me.

" '. . . one of my mother's most treasured possessions, . . .' "

My face flamed. I could not look at him.

" '. . . the Bell family Bible.' "

My pupils twanged from floor to ceiling to Tom Scott to Ferrell T. to Roland Bell. I watched as Roland's fist closed tight around the paper cup he held. It crumpled and dropped to the floor. Ferrell T. stopped writing.

"The Bell family Bible," Roland repeated, hoarse. "The family Bible?"

"Allow me to finish the paragraph, please," said Tom evenly. He continued. " 'I leave this Bible in your care, Flip, knowing your deep appreciation of books, your love of this commu-

49

nity and its history, and your own aloneness since the loss, so many years ago, of your family. May this old book, with its words of wisdom and inspiration, its pages filled with Bell family mementos, give you what I believe you long for most.' "

After trying so hard to avoid him, I could not tear my eyes off Roland, his gray face, gray hair, gray eyes.

"And what is it you long for most, Fe-lic-i-ty Paxton?" He swaggered to the conference table, anchored both hard hands on its surface and leaned toward me.

I sat, a lump on a stump.

"Well, I know," he whispered low and eerie. "I know what you long for most." He reared back and boomed, "You want to steal what is mine! You want what is rightfully mine! Mine and my children's inheritance!" He flung a pointed finger in Ferrell T.'s direction.

Lee's hand reached for mine.

"Sit down, Roland," Tom Scott rattled the will slightly, moving one finger across the page, his free hand touching Eli on the head to stifle the rising snarl. "If you wish to legally contest any portion of this will, you better let me know. You're next on the list."

"You mean there's something left? For little ole me? Her own brother?" Roland flopped into his chair, a sulky teenager. Ferrell T. picked up his pen, aiming it at me like a javelin he wanted to throw.

" 'To my brother, Roland Bell, and his family, I leave the remaining Bell family portraits, the ones I still have in my house.' "

"Great," spat Roland. "I get stuck with a bunch of dingy paintings that aren't worth a plugged nickel."

Tom's jaw twitched. " 'I also leave the houseplants, Garland has such a green thumb, and the Bell sterling and china.' "

He quit reading and folded the will up.

Roland's narrow mouth leaned to one side, eyebrows crossed. "That's it?"

"That's it," replied Tom. "Lee, I suspect you can work out with Roland and Flip when to pick up these items. Miss Fizzi, we'll be in touch soon. Pal, the car is parked out back."

Pal took on the appearance of somebody miraculously healed. "Thank you," he said, backing out of the room. "Thank you, thank you, thank you, thank you."

"I'll see you later, dear," Miss Fizzi pecked Lee on the cheek. "I think I have a hair appointment." She nodded good-bye to me and Tom, avoided Roland and Garland altogether, and wafted out of the room.

"I guess I ought to be going." I spoke to Tom and Lee, my back to the Bell's. "Lee, I'll see you this week when I come clean and we can . . . you know, do the Bible thing."

"I'm really glad Leona left you the Bell family Bible," Lee squeezed my arm. "She showed it to me once. I only glanced through it. There's a lot

51

of local history between those pages: pictures, letters, dried flowers, and little poems. The past really does come alive."

"Letters?" Roland jerked his chair back and stood up. "More letters, Lee? Like the ones you got from Flip right after my sister died?"

Lee's nostrils flared and she faced Roland head-on. "What of it?"

"Those letters are stolen property! They were stolen by her." He pointed a long finger at me. "And I intend to get them back and prosecute to the full extent of the law! Everybody get that? Ferrell T., you still writing stuff down? You get that?"

Ferrell T. nodded furiously and kept his head low.

"Prosecute your heart out, you greedy maniac. But I tell you this right now." Lee raised her own finger at Roland. The blood rushed to her face, and the temperature in the room rose with it. "You will not succeed. You will lose. You have taken all you are going to take. I will hand over to you exactly what Leona wanted you to have and no more, Roland. You hear me? No more! Don't even think of coming around the house every couple of weeks like you used to, pointing at this, that, and the other thing and carrying stuff away. Leona was too good. She should have told you to go to hell ages ago." She lowered her finger and held both hands at her sides, fists tight. "You come get the portraits and the sterling and the china on Friday. If you don't, I'll pack it all up and leave it out on the street. Is that clear?"

Roland appeared to hang in midair, measuring the weights on either side of him. Suddenly, his whole demeanor changed. The gray of his skin turned to a childlike pink. His shoulders relaxed and he slowly sank back into his chair, smaller, a beatific expression on his face. "I guess I owe everybody an apology," he said sheepishly. "I don't know what got into me. My dear Leona's death came as such a shock." He pointed at the will in Tom's hands. "These words are her last wishes on earth and she obviously meant to be generous to the ones she loved. Who am I to question that? I don't want to make trouble. Tom, Lee, I'm not going to contest the will. I may not agree with all of it," a momentary glint flashed in the placid eyes, "but lawsuits are nothing but a waste of time and money."

That was it, then. The cheap side of Roland won out over the insult of not inheriting everything.

"Flip," Lee spoke to me, voice even as a lead pipe, "if you stop by my house after work, I'll make sure you get the Bell family Bible tonight. OK?"

"No problem." I was ready to leave, for sure. I ducked down the hall, stopped, leaned against a door frame, and took a deep breath.

In the quiet of Tom's office, I heard Roland's voice, wheedling and whiny. "But there's room for a little negotiation, isn't there, Lee? Surely, you'd agree — I got my rights. What would you take for those letters, for instance? They're only paper. . . ."

Chapter 6

The night after Lee handed it to me, I sat down with the Bell family Bible, publisher's date 1898, and took the first step down a road that would lead me to a place I had no idea existed. I'd decided to keep the Bible hidden way up on top of a kitchen cabinet, shoved against the wall inside a big basket, protected by plastic and covered with Spanish moss I'd bought at a garden shop. Better safe than sorry where Roland was concerned.

The damn thing must have weighed eight pounds. I studied the inside cover. A family tree stretched across the paper, spilling onto the next page. Years and years of prominent Bells, going back to R. Bell, the first to land in Maryland in 1778, during the Revolution. He found somebody named Lucy Hanover to marry him three years later, and they had their first child, a boy, the next year. Six more children followed that boy, four of them dead by the time they turned six, a common tragedy before the progress of medicine caught up with the progress of disease. The three who lived — Richard, Ferrell (mystery of the name solved), and Lucinda — all married, had children, survived into their sixties, and were buried here in Solace Glen.

The writing of the entire chart changed three or four times with the generations, though the same hand wrote all the early part of the family history. I could picture a little wife of a Bell sitting down in 1898 with her new Bible she got as a wedding present and painstakingly drawing her new family tree, maybe from the memory of her husband's relatives, maybe from an older Bible on its last legs. Something to leave her children so they'd know their roots.

I knew so little of my own. Grandparents on my father's side seemed but a dull memory; I only knew the names of my mother's Baltimore parents. Beyond that, the branches of my pitiful family tree hung bare and fruitless. If my parents had lived, I would have learned more of the Paxtons once I reached an age where such things intrigued me. But my parents didn't live; I would never know. I hated that the older I grew, the larger that void within me stretched, replacing the contentment I should have earned by now with a stifling restlessness and loneliness.

Leona knew how much I envied people with an orchard of family trees, so she gave me hers to tend. That must have been why she left me such an inheritance, why she chose me as the gardener.

I closed the Bible and lugged my grove of Bells back to the top of the kitchen cabinet, safe from one of their own, safe from Roland Bell.

By mid-October, the tension between Roland and those of us unfortunate enough to inherit from a Bell cooled to a steady simmer. Roland couldn't stand the thought of paying good money to the cleaning woman who'd cheated him out of the illustrious family Bible, so he dumped me, something of a relief given my state of anxiety. The note read: "Miss Paxton. Due to circumstance, your service is no longer required. R. and G. Bell." Not that Garland signed it herself. I imagined Roland told her she'd have to vacuum her own floors now, on top of her non-paying job at the Café. No skin off Roland's back. He could brag about the money he'd saved.

Fall appeared without much fanfare. Foliage changed color in the blink of an eye. I'd drive down Center Street in the early morning and the sugar maples lining the sidewalks flashed by in the mid-October sun like a parade of bright orange school buses. The chilly air required a sweater at the start of the day, but by ten o'clock, I'd peel off the extra layer and do my business in shirtsleeves.

"What's Plain Jane going to be on Halloween?" It was Thursday, my regular cleaning day at the Historical Society.

Lee glanced up from her coffee mug, considered Plain Jane, and twisted her mouth. "A car mechanic or a prostitute. She can't decide."

I deposited my carryall on the floor and reached for a Danish. "Why not both?"

"That's an idea. I could dress her in a white jump suit zipped down to her navel with her name sewn on the shoulder in flame red, and she could wear black, vinyl stiletto boots." She dipped her nose into the coffee mug. "So, aren't you curious about what Roland wanted to do?"

"About what?"

"About the letters."

We hadn't discussed Roland's reaction to Leona's will until now, and I hadn't wanted to pry. I licked icing off my thumb. "Did he offer to buy them?"

Lee smirked. "Roland spend a nickel he doesn't have to? No, he wanted to trade."

Now it was my turn to smirk. "And what, pray tell, was his generous offer?"

"Half price meals at the Café. For forty-eight hours. Tuesday and Wednesday only."

We burst into gales of laughter, and it felt so good. I snorted, "He may as well have offered to steal them."

Lee drew a deep breath. "Yeah. Tom Scott told me to watch my back."

Behind my smile, a shiver iced my spine. Tom possessed both brains and common sense. If he'd told Lee to be careful, the rest of us had better mind our p's and q's. I pictured the Bell Bible on top of my kitchen cabinet and wondered if the hiding place was good enough.

"Where'd you put Leona's letters?" I glanced around the room for secret spots. "Somewhere safe, I hope."

"Don't you worry about them." Lee reached over to Plain Jane, unbuttoned her high neck collar a few inches and drew out the velvet bag of letters. "Jane's bosom buddy."

"Ooooo." I had to hand it to her. "Even Roland isn't weird enough to look there."

"That's what I thought. Anyway," she stood up and stretched, "I've been too busy dealing with renting the big house to worry about the letters."

"Renting the big house?" I blinked. "I didn't know you were looking for anybody. I thought you might change your mind and live there yourself."

"Oh, please. Abandon Plain Jane? Keep Jeb, the spoiled cat, in the manner to which he's grown accustomed? He'll just have to get used to the smaller things in life."

"Well, I can't say I blame you. I couldn't picture you anywhere but here. This house suits you."

I didn't say it suited her because she was single with no kids. She wouldn't have said such a thing to me, either. The difference between us was I'd almost accepted my lot in life, dusting the pictures of other women's children and picking up the dirty clothes of other women's husbands. In the back of my mind, on the smallest shelf, I still held onto the hope that there was somebody out there for me, but as the years passed, the hope faded. With my endless work schedule from age eighteen on, the most eligible men I met consisted of vacation drunks on the make in Ocean City. Any other single man I lucked upon turned out too old, too young, too stupid, or not single enough. So I dusted and cleaned and traded what wishes and dreams I had for the happy dreams of friends. Lee wanted the Cinderella dream, the whole enchilada, and she possessed the beauty and brains to snare a prince, but she was also old enough to understand we don't always get what we want.

"Yeah." She glanced around the room, so cozy and familiar to her. "It'd depress me to move right now. If I rent the big house, I can always change my mind at the end of a year's lease. A history professor from Hood's going to live there."

"You met her?" A new resident always tweaked my curiosity. The last newcomer we'd welcomed to Solace Glen was Miss Fizzi's awful grandnephew, Suggs Magill, who moved into her basement apartment three years ago. He proved himself so surly and antisocial, we'd snatched up the welcome mat before he could plant a dirty boot on it. No need to knock yourself out for somebody who's only going to spit in your eye.

"It's a him, and I haven't met the man. He came through a real estate agency in Frederick, but he's stopping by this morning to say hello to his new landlady. Moves in tomorrow."

"Where's he been living?"

"How should I know?"

I picked up a rag and started wiping down the pine table. I worried about Lee. "Well, what do you know about this man? He's going to be surrounded by a lot of nice family heirlooms. He could run off with everything for all you know."

"The agency checked him out, Flip." She batted the hazel eyes. "He's only a murderer and a serial rapist. Not a thief, thank God."

"All I know is what I read in the papers."

"Then you ought to read more optimistic papers." She stared out the back window. "I'm going to plant more rosemary this spring. Maybe some extra basil."

A thought struck me. "Who's going to tend to Leona's roses?" She'd spent half a lifetime mothering her flower garden.

"Oh, my gosh. I hadn't even thought about that." A knuckle rapped on the door and she jumped. "Damnit. I need a doorbell."

"You need a lot of things," I mumbled, wiping the table, keeping an eye on the door she opened wide to a stranger.

The man hesitated. "You are Mrs. . . . . Miss . . . Ms. Lee Jenner?"

"Lee." She whipped a hand out. "I'm Lee Jenner. Come in."

He had more than six feet on him because he had to tilt his neck to one side in order to get through Lee's front door. He stepped into the house and stood, waiting for further instructions as a gentleman should. I stopped pretending to clean and took a good look.

Not movie star handsome, but his face might turn a few heads. Regular features; strong cheekbones; a firm, if slightly lopsided mouth; long, thin nose; deep-set eyes that looked like layers of blue scraped down to the barest color; brows straight as a shot across a high, intelligent forehead; rust-colored hair; a few wisps of gray combed back off his face. My guess — early forties. Good shape. Probably a runner.

Also, probably married, gay, or divorced with baggage.

He caught me inspecting him, nodded, and turned to Lee. "I'm Sam Gibbon," he introduced himself, voice deep and smooth with an accent I couldn't quite place. "But I expect you know that."

"She only knows what she reads in the papers." Good thing I was there to say that.

Lee flung me a dirty look, and I slapped the dust rag at Plain Jane a few times, arching an eyebrow at Sam Gibbon.

The high, intelligent forehead creased at the sight of Jane. "Are her eyes made out of . . . condoms?"

"Why, I'm not sure," said Lee, puzzled. "Flip, show the professor your eyes."

I gaped, fuming.

"You know, I believe they are. Are they Trojans, Flip?" She crossed her arms and one ankle as I grabbed the carryall and stomped upstairs. I could have killed her, embarrassing me like that.

"Former friend of yours?" I heard Sam Gibbon ask.

"That's Flip Paxton, our local caregiver. If you want," her voice carried upstairs, "she'll keep house for you."

He must have nodded because she called out, "Yeah! He'd like you to come by every . . . once a week? . . . every other week! Got that, Flip?"

"Mmmmm," I mooed downstairs, suddenly wishing I was the one who owned the Historical Society and Lee was the one who mopped floors.

"What day is good for you, Ms. Paxton?" he called up.

I remembered Roland's open space. "Friday mornings!"

"Done deal!" Lee sealed the contract and I heard Sam Gibbon wonder how expensive I might be.

"Oh, twice a month cleaning is part of the rent," she answered.

That's when I knew she liked him. And wanted me for eyes and ears.

Chapter 7

Sam Gibbon wasn't the only new face in town. The day after he moved into the Bell house, Solace Glen experienced a major storm — Hurricane C.C.

At the Crown station, where the sign above the door read, THE ONLY GAS IN TOWN YOU CAN PUT IN A CAR, Pal Sykes handed out Styrofoam cups of coffee with one hand and directed Joey how to pump gas with the other. His only help in this endeavor rested on the iron shoulders of Suggs Magill, Miss Fizzi's silent, surly, bullish nephew, a man the exact opposite of Pal in every way except mechanical skill. Pal handled the customer contact; Suggs rarely emerged from the garage.

The Crown stood kitty-corner between Center Street and Dorsey, perched on a triangular lot so if you drove up from the Center side, you had to exit onto Dorsey and vice versa. Unless you happened to be Cecile Crosswell.

The first time C.C. drove into the Crown and honked her silver BMW for Pal and Joey to come running and fix her up, we knew Solace Glen was in for some push and shove. I'd just pulled up to the diesel pump, so I saw the whole mess.

C.C. sat on her horn for a good sixty seconds until she couldn't take the terrible lack of service any more. The car door flung wide, and this creature emerged dressed to the nines and reeking of the perfume counter at Sak's.

"My God!" she exploded loud as a firecracker. "My Gaawwd!"

This religious exclamation enticed Pal out of the garage, wiping his oily paws and blinking like some forest animal that hadn't seen the light of day all winter. "Ma'am?" he chirped. "What can I do for ya? Didja want some gas? Joey! Where is that boy? Probably round back sittin' in the Cadillac again." Pal loped over to the BMW to check if it read "Unleaded Only."

"*If*," C.C. flung her brunette coif around and clapped her hand across her bosom, "it would not be too much t-rou-ble." Then she hurled Pal an expression that could have drawn blood.

The moment C.C.'s car registered full on the gauge, she slapped a ten and a twenty in Pal's dirty palm and started to back onto Center like a bat out of hell. I watched all this thinking, that's none too smart, somebody's surely going to be coming the other way. Sure enough, somebody was. Screamin' Larry from WFIB 102.7, Frederick's Defiant Jazz station, drove up in his Big Orange Volkswagen Beetle with the Syracuse University sports logos plastered all over it — ten for basketball, fifteen for lacrosse, thirty for football, and who knows how many more. Never played a sport in his life, but the coaches used to beg him to come to games just to scream.

This is who C.C. nearly creamed in her pretty BMW.

After a horrific screech of tires from both sides, the dust cleared and the two vehicles sat nose to ass, with Screamin' Larry wiping a jelly doughnut off his face. C.C. sat ramrod straight and glared into her rearview mirror. Larry cleared a little jelly path for his nose to breathe and sized up the situation: brand new BMW, obviously a newcomer or a visitor unaware of Solace Glen road protocol, Northern Virginia, maybe, or worse, D.C. He didn't have to be at the station until nine p.m., six more hours.

He turned off the ignition, opened his dinner pail of KFC, and started the picnic.

C.C. tapped her manicured claws on the steering wheel. Finally, after a whole two minutes, she steamed out of the car, stationing herself by the driver's leather seat, arm draped across the top of the door like it was her best friend. "*Ex-cuse* me. I need to get out. Please back up."

She pronounced each word as if she'd found herself in a foreign country where none of the natives spoke English, especially obese men in orange Beetles. She bobbed her head in a take-no-prisoners fashion and slid back into the BMW.

Larry was having a fine time with his picnic.

He'd gone through a breast and a cup of mashed potatoes.

Other motorists and pedestrians began to notice this roadside drama at the Crown. Marlene dawdled outside the cleaner's across the street. I caught a glimpse of the Eggheads and Officer Lukzay staring through the picture windows at Roland's Café and Grill. Lee coasted to a stop at the Center Street stop sign and idled, windows rolled down. Tina Graham and Margaret Henshaw, window shopping at Solace Glen's pitiful retail offerings, lingered in front of Connolly's Jewelry Store.

C.C. did not budge. Nobody in front of her, a clear exit. But she came in Center Street and was hell bent on going out Center Street. End of story.

Screamin' Larry tossed a chicken bone out the window and helped himself to a biscuit.

C.C. reemerged from the BMW holding up typed directions with a map, same stance. "Ex-*cuse* me . . . sir. I have a very important appointment with my decorator. I drove in from that street and that is the direction I need to go. Now. My husband, Leonard — Leonard Crosswell? THE attorney? Well, he and I have just bought the O'Connell estate. . . ."

At this point, the audience snickered at her hoity-toity reference to that old barn as an "estate." But like any good actress worth her salt, C.C. let the reaction pass and moved on with her lines.

". . . and I am sure you would agree that it is in the community's best interest for you to back up and let me get started renovating an important local landmark, and then you can get on with whatever it is you do." She thumped her map, repeated the same sharp bob of the head and climbed in the BMW, her foot gunning the engine ever so slightly. Maybe she figured she'd get lost if her wheels touched any street except Center, but her head problem was now Larry's.

Screamin' Larry popped open a carton of coleslaw, amused by C.C.'s entire performance. His amusement tripled when a car pulled up behind him. He grinned at C.C., strands of coleslaw sticking out of his teeth, and pointed a finger behind him, shrugging his massive shoulders.

C.C.'s jaw dropped. "How many jackasses are there in this town?"

The jackass who pulled up behind Larry was none other than Wilma Fizzi.

Screamin' Larry doubled over, heaving. Miss Fizzi would wait in line for days, a good sheep, no complaints. He peered into his rearview mirror. Miss Fizzi smiled back at him and fluffed her hair up with a knitting needle, lighting his candle something fierce. This called for dessert.

The crowd, growing steadily, waited in anxious anticipation. C.C., our new neighbor, could make or break the welcome mat, have crab cakes and spiced shrimp on her doorstep next week or end up wondering why the Christmas carolers always skipped her house.

The BMW backed up, slowly, slowly, the rear fender barely kissing Larry's front bumper. No doubt C.C. thought this creeping adagio would intimidate the dumb local yokel into backing up. When he realized what C.C. was doing, however, Larry fired up the Big Orange. C.C. gradually applied the gas. Larry leaned forward, gripping the steering wheel, licking the last of the apple tart off his lips. The Beetle pushed against the BMW. After all those years of watching the action, Screamin' Larry had at last found his athletic niche.

The BMW, however, owned more horses, a fact not lost on C.C., who apparently could care less if her insurance company had to mend some scratches. Larry's Big Orange Beetle bumped into Miss Fizzi's Oldsmobile station wagon. The crowd moaned, "Awwww." Joey Sykes came running from somewhere behind the Crown station and screeched to a halt, bug-eyed at the excitement. Here and there, some-body called, "Hang in there, Larr!" "Give it the gas, boy!" Michael Connolly from the Jewelry Store yelled, "Miss Fizzi, wake up! Whatchoo think Jesus would do?"

The startled face gleamed pasty white as Larry's Big Orange Beetle again rolled into her wagon. Lips mouthing the Lord's Prayer, Miss Fizzi grabbed the gearshift, searching for re-verse. Her corrective shoe stomped the gas pedal and the Oldsmobile lurched forward forcing Larry into a Beetle sandwich, squished in front, rocked from the rear.

C.C. floored it.

The Beetle shook so hard, it looked like a big, round jackhammer pounding into Center Street. Screamin' Larry did his best to hold on, arms wrapped around the steering wheel, a crazy, murderous glint in his eye. I wouldn't want to be C.C., however this turned out.

Finally, Miss Fizzi had all she could handle. Her tiny hands grasped the air, pupils rattling wild around the whites of her eyes, settling on the two faces that stared out the window at Roland's Café. The Eggheads. She slapped her palms against the driver's window and mouthed the words, *Hellllp meee,* and the Eggheads leaped into action. Chairs turned over, plates bounced off the table, paper napkins tucked into their collars flapped like white flags as they raced out of Roland's leaving the immovable Lukzay in their dust.

The crowd yelped, "Hoorah!" A tourist, grabbing an oyster stew at Roland's, wriggled through the commotion and aimed his camcorder. At this point, even Suggs Magill emerged from the Crown garage, in time to see the Eggheads attempt to rescue his great-aunt. He could have at least helped but, true to form, Suggs stood stone still looking mad at the world and the Eggheads, in particular.

The Eggheads galloped to the wagon and

halted, studying the situation. The Oldsmobile rocked back and forth, engine roaring, gear stuck. Miss Fizzi bammed on the window.

The Eggheads conferred, blond heads locked together. Suddenly one started pacing back and forth, waving his arms at Miss Fizzi, chanting, "OK, OK, OK," in an apparent effort to calm her down. The other one bolted off, pants on fire, into the Crown station. Within seconds he bolted out again carrying a tire iron, Pal skipping along behind him, calling, "Jesse/Jules, Jesse/Jules! Whatchoo doing with my iron? I was using that iron. That was my daddy's iron."

The Eggheads now had weaponry.

One yelled at Miss Fizzi to get out the way while the other one raised the tire iron quarterback-style and made a play for the window full steam, leaving Miss Fizzi just enough time to dive for cover before the tire iron rammed through the Oldsmobile. The crowd murmured, "Oooooooo." Egghead No. 1 withdrew the weapon while Egghead No. 2 reached in, pulled up the lock, and opened the door. He dragged the shocked Miss Fizzi out of the car, flung her fragile little body over his shoulder, and took off running, the winning touchdown in the big game. The crowd roared. The tourist with the camcorder got it all.

Meanwhile, the Oldsmobile, without Miss Fizzi in it to occasionally stomp the gas pedal, no longer lent Larry the added force needed to defeat Cruella Deville in the BMW. The Big Orange edged back against the wagon, and the two cars gave way to C.C. With a smirk of red lips and no looking back, the newest addition to Solace Glen neatly shifted gears and sped away.

"I'll be." Marlene, eyes wide, grinned like the Cheshire cat. She and Larry always took delight in each other's misfortunes.

"Praise God no one was killed." Miss Fizzi wobbled around in front of Roland's while her surly nephew, Suggs, shrugged in her direction and retreated back into the garage. One Egghead fetched her an iced tea; the other one proudly inspected the smashed window of the Oldsmobile. Officer Lukzay, still seated at the window, sipped his free coffee.

Pal and Joey pulled Larry out of the Beetle. Larry stood up; chicken bones and biscuit crumbs tumbled off his chest and lap. They walked to the front of the Big Orange, shook heads, shuffled to the rear, shook heads. Larry glanced in the direction C.C. disappeared. His eyes narrowed as he stroked his overgrown beard.

"You gonna press charges, Larry?" Pal rubbed a finger across the new indentations in the tail of the Volkswagen. A Syracuse lacrosse sticker floated off.

"No," said Larry. "I'm gonna take care of this myself."

My eyebrows shot up. The last time Larry announced he was going to take care of something himself — involving a notorious slumlord — the town ended up having to pay for a whole new gas line. Nobody got hurt, and those who suspected Larry considered the act a civil service since the slumlord picked up and slithered elsewhere. (An astonishing fact, Larry held dual degrees in music and chemical engineering and would use either discipline to accomplish his streaks of revenge.)

I capped off the diesel and screwed the lid on my tank. The crowd dispersed. Pal and Joey swept up the glass by Miss Fizzi's car, Joey chattering excitedly in his high-pitched falsetto. Larry drove the Big Orange next to a pump and filled it up. Marlene hung some dry cleaning in her car and puttered off. Lee pulled away from the stop sign and headed home. Margaret and Tina resumed their stroll. Michael Connolly steered his wife, Melody, back into the store, both of them handed something to talk about the rest of the day besides the usual bad business complaints.

I climbed into the car and hurried to my next appointment. On the way, I turned on the radio, WFIB 102.7. Larry's prerecorded voice screamed a commercial. "The DEFIANT jazz station," the radio boomed, "that DEFIES country. DEFIES classical. DEFIES rap. DEFIES, most especially, bluck! the Oldies."

I wondered what Larry would play that night on his show. I'd bet anything the whole town would be listening.

Chapter 8

Sam Gibbon knew about roses. He greeted me in the garden, intent on rewinding a hose around a rusty container, a pair of pruners dangling off a belt loop of his old jeans. He wore a faded red chamois shirt and weathered boat shoes with hole-ridden socks that used to be white. I studied his eyes, so watery blue, slightly crinkled — eyes I'd started to imagine lately in daydreams. He glanced up from the hose and smiled. I quickly looked away.

"I forgot you were coming today."

That pretty much summed me up. Forgettable. My hair, a nondescript brown, never got more interesting than a tight ponytail and hadn't seen a pair of scissors in six months. No make-up and a washed-out complexion probably appealed to him, too. At least I had flat mouse ears and a long neck, my only good features.

I hoisted the carryall, practically another limb on my body, and headed for the front door. "It's been two weeks. Guess Lee forgot to remind you."

The words flew out so fast, he stumbled over them. "How well do you know Lee?"

I paused at the front door and wiped a rag across the brass knocker, hiding my frown but not my curiosity. "You two getting to be good friends?" Lee had become uncharacteristically close-mouthed on the subject of her new tenant. At her last cleaning, I couldn't pry a word out of her with the most obvious hints.

"Now that's a question my mother might have asked about a new buddy on the block."

"OK, I'll try to be more sophisticated." I spit at the doorbell and rubbed it clean. "Taken her to a pig roast yet?"

Sam rhythmically swung the hose, eyes dropping to his feet. "Garsh, Miz Flip. I haven't known her a month."

"You're absolutely right." So maybe they weren't an item yet and I had a chance. I squinted at the drab face reflected in the knocker. "I should never have asked such a sophisticated question." Then I shamed myself by lying, "I'm just looking out for Lee."

Sam slit his eyes at me and laughed. "I guess I should expect this sort of thing — probing, personal questions. Small town. Not that many singles under fifty. Any newcomer is suspect."

I swung the carryall onto my hip. "Yeah, not many singles around here under fifty. *We're* a definite minority."

I zipped inside to work on the house, worried I'd been too forward. When I finished a couple of hours later, Sam was attacking the yard with a rake.

"I didn't know history professors came out of their ivory towers long enough to do manual labor." I set the carryall at my feet and watched him rake. He appeared comfortable enough.

"Oh, we poke our poor, strained eyes out the tower door occasionally on the chance a beautiful maid and her Rebel general might come riding by."

My eyes twitched. Which maid did he mean? "You been talking to Lee about those letters?"

"No," he quit raking and leaned against an oak tree. "She's been talking to me."

That really straightened my spine. "You? Why you?"

"I guess she figures I'm some sort of expert." He grinned a sexy, disarming grin that made me wonder if I was jealous of Lee or protective of her. "I haven't actually *seen* the letters, but she described the contents to me. Our friend J.E.B. got around."

I didn't return the grin. If he knew Leona had entrusted those letters to me while she was dying, then his little joke fell flat, but maybe he didn't know. "Well, *I've* seen the letters."

He snapped to attention. "You, Flip? I had no idea." He observed the serious frown I wore. "I'm sorry — I just realized Lee said they were her aunt's last request and . . . you delivered them, didn't you?"

I replaced Sam on my pedestal, but still worked my way through the conversation with a caution flag raised. It bothered me that Lee

76

would discuss the Bell women's secret with a virtual stranger, but maybe it was her way of breaking the ice and getting to know him better. "Just what has Lee told you?"

"Not much." Was he lying? "She's mostly asked me questions, like somebody thinking out loud." That did sound like Lee. "She's wondering who to have look at them to check out their authenticity. If they're not by Stuart, why go farther? They could be written by anybody."

"But they refer to members of his family by name. . . ."

"Really? She didn't tell me that."

Should I have? I kept quiet, my protective instinct tuned high.

"Anyway, I told her I know somebody who can authenticate them."

I bet you do, and I bet *you'd* have to be the one to take them to your so-called expert.

"She can drive them down to D.C. or FedEx them. He's at the Smithsonian."

"Oh." Sounded plausible enough. "You're sure *nice* to take such an interest in our little slice of history."

Sam shrugged good-naturedly. "History's my bag, what can I say. Gives me a chance to get to know Lee."

That really set my antenna zooming. I picked up the carryall and slowly walked to the car. Sam fell in beside me. I quickly ran through an idea and cleared my throat. "If getting to know people around here is important to you, *some-*

times . . ." — like never — "Miss Fizzi throws a little Halloween tea party and some real nice people drop in. . . ." — like *me,* her cleaning lady — "and you'd get a chance to mingle." Or change the course of your entire future forever.

Sam nodded enthusiastically. "Great! I'd love it! Is there something I can bring? I'm not familiar with the local standards."

"Sam Gibbon." Flirting came as easy for me as nuclear physics. "You've lived here two whole weeks, you have all those big books stacked up in every room, you're a big college professor, and you can't look around and see how high our standards are?" I gave up, embarrassed at how stupid I sounded and tossed the carryall and mop in the car. "Wear a shirt that covers your chest, pants that cover your rear, and shoes that cover your feet. Exposed opinions are acceptable."

He stuck his chin on top of the rake. "So I should dress how I want and say what I will."

"Only if you wish to impress the ladies," I replied, sweet as a jonquil, giving it one last shot.

He watched me go, chin balanced on top of the tool. I glimpsed him in my rearview mirror, lost in thought, a tiny, faraway smile slowly spreading across his face.

Now what the hell was I going to tell Miss Fizzi?

Chapter 9

Louise Lamm kept a picture of Marlene on her dressing table taken on Marlene's sixth birthday, around the time Mr. Lamm died. She posed in a stiff yellow crinoline dress, new white patent leather shoes, and an Easter bonnet that sprouted tiny pink and purple pansies. The color in the photograph had faded over the years, the same way Marlene's love for her mother had.

I hated dusting that picture. Louise kept dozens of other pictures, too, little monuments scattered all over her bedroom to the daughter she used to cater to. Baby pictures in sterling silver frames, buck-toothed elementary school pictures in brass, high school pictures of Marlene wearing red lipstick and white pearls, framed in floral fabrics. As if Marlene had only lived to age eighteen. No pictures of her beyond that time existed in Louise's home.

The story ran that when Marlene went off to college in southern Virginia thirty years ago, she met a boy right off the bat and Louise hated him. She told Marlene the guy was nothing but a redneck out for only one thing, and it wasn't Marlene's winning personality. Louise refused

to pay for Marlene to continue a second se-
mester at that college unless she ditched the
boyfriend. Marlene declined the offer.

Everybody thought that, without means,
Marlene would slouch back to Solace Glen and
sulk until she got that boy out of her system, but
she suddenly grew a backbone and ran off with
him. This happened in the early seventies, and
Marlene imagined she was experiencing free
love, but all she had really latched onto was a
freeloader.

The boyfriend took every penny of her
meager college savings and dumped her, leaving
Marlene crying in Santa Somewhere, Cali-
fornia. She had no choice but to call Louise and
beg for travel money to fly east. Louise slapped
her back in that woman's college fast as you
could spit, and Marlene eventually graduated
with a degree in Social Embarrassment. Their
mother/daughter relationship never recovered,
and Marlene's resentment gradually rivaled,
then outdistanced, Louise's mortification. She
returned to Solace Glen, lived with her mother
only until she could afford to rent a place of her
own (thanks to Louise who bought the local
flower shop for her to run), and began to treat
her mother with such disrespect and disdain, it
made the whole community sick.

Sooner than later, Louise showed the strain of
having her only child reject her. Before she got
sick, before the cancer set in, she tried everything she could to make amends with her un-

grateful daughter. She started buying things: a new car, landscaping for the ugly shack Marlene rented, expensive vacations, fancy clothes, jewelry. Anybody could have told Louise she was wasting her money. Marlene took and took and took; Louise gave and gave and gave.

There are people in life who are natural born takers, and no matter what you give them, no matter what you do for them, no matter how hard you try to win their affections, you are fighting a losing battle because all they really care about is numero uno. So much time and attention was lavished on the child Marlene that the girl thought the world owed her something and the woman knew for sure it did. Marlene grew from spoiled brat to snotty snit to obnoxious teenager to arrogant, cold-hearted bitch. And Louise watched wide-eyed, horrified, and disbelieving.

Finally, Louise realized nothing she did and nothing she bought could patch the holes that had erupted during Marlene's rebellious college years. So she simply stopped. She told me she would wait, she'd done enough; now Marlene would have to make her own move toward reconciliation.

I could have told her how that plot would play out. Zilch. Nada. All she wrote.

Marlene never called her mother on the telephone. Never visited. Never wrote a note. Never asked anybody to look in on Louise to check how she was getting along. She even married a man

81

and didn't tell her mother. Nobody knew anything about Marlene's husband except his name was Worthington. They never lived together and divorced within a year. She probably paid some illegal English alien who jumped ship to marry her so she could ditch the Lamm name.

So Marlene and Louise lived in the same town, attended the same church, knew the same people, shopped in the same stores, ate at the same restaurant. Bloomed off the same family tree. Yet, the two barely made eye contact. Marlene lived her life; Louise lived hers. People came to appreciate the family dynamics, would ask one to a party, not the other. Next party, they'd switch off. If Louise and Marlene showed up at the same event, the room tended to split into two teams. I'd gravitate to Louise's side; the Fifth Commandment means something to me. It was Louise, two weeks after my parents died, who hemmed my graduation dress and saw to it that I carried a dozen red roses just like the other girls. In that sea of faces that ran together in the high school auditorium, hers was the only one I saw when they handed me my diploma.

Louise put down the book she was reading, *The Shell Seekers*, and stretched out her legs on the ottoman in front of the rocker. "So how are all Leona's heirs and heiresses this Monday morning?"

I slapped a dust rag at a Marlene exhibit, age ten. "Everybody's holding their own, including me."

We shot each other a knowing look.

Louise took a sip of orange juice. "Pal's car hasn't been vandalized?"

"Nope. Even if it were, he'd never believe anyone from his own hometown could be involved in hurting a beautiful old Cadillac."

"Miss Fizzi doing OK?"

"You mean except for the fact she's got Suggs as a nephew?" I forced a thirteen-year-old Marlene to face the wall, giving me the illusion of punishing her.

"Isn't he awful? I heard he didn't lift a finger to help her get out of the car with that mess between C.C. and Larry."

"Yep, it was a despicable thing to witness. You'd think he'd be more appreciative, a thirty-year-old man living rent free in her house the last three years. But, at best, he treats her like she doesn't exist and, at worst, acts like her kindness is unbearable punishment. Makes you wonder where he sprang from because he's nothing like Miss Fizzi."

"Nobody's like our Miss Fizzi." Louise took a possessive view of Solace Glen's residents. "And how are you? And Lee?"

I rolled my eyes. "We're big girls. I've got the Bell family Bible well hidden and Lee has those Civil War letters in a *very* safe place."

"Well," Louise sighed hard, "all I can say is you and Lee better . . ."

"Watch our backs?"

Louise nodded. "Exactly."

"That's what Tom Scott thinks, too." As soon as I said the words, I bit my tongue.

Louise dropped the book. "Tom said that? Tom's worried?"

"Oh, you're out of juice." I didn't want her blood pressure skyrocketing. "It was just talk. Matter of fact. Casual."

"But Flip," Louise slid her legs off the ottoman and straightened her back, "if Roland is serious about getting everything Leona gave away, he'll do anything. Anything. You can't trust him, and do not underestimate him. He's volatile, mercurial. Tom's right about him."

I gently pushed her back into the rocker and lifted her legs to the ottoman. "Read your nice book and quit worrying about that idiot Roland."

"He's not an idiot," she protested. "A greedy Scrooge, yes. An illiterate materialist, yes. But he's not an idiot. I repeat, don't you underestimate him."

I patted her shoulder, so thin and bony, knowing she spoke the truth. "I won't. I promise."

"Good." She breathed easier and caressed the jacket of the book in her lap. "Now tell me about Lee and this new young man in town."

"Sam Gibbon. I was just over there two days ago." I felt the red flood my cheeks. "Cleaning." People were already saying his name next to Lee's, even though those blue eyes had floated through my mind more than once.

"I'd like to meet him. So would Miss Fizzi."

Unknowingly, Louise had just solved my dilemma. "Miss Fizzi wants to meet him?"

Louise closed her eyes, drifting off. "This weekend, Flip. You arrange it. You're so good at arranging. You take such good care of everybody."

I took a mohair blanket from the foot of the bed and ballooned it over her outstretched legs, two matchsticks.

"Tea," she murmured. "Or lunch." Her head slowly drooped to one side. I could hardly catch the words. "I'm tired. You decide. You decide for me."

Before walking out the door, I leaned over and whispered in her ear, "I'll talk to Miss Fizzi about a tea on Halloween. Don't you worry. I'll take care of everything."

Chapter 10

I never understood why Tom Scott hired any-body to clean his office; it was never the least bit dirty. The man was a housewife's dream. I'd never even stepped foot in his old, stone house outside of town where he lived with his younger brother, Charlie, who traveled the exotic places of the world as photojournalist. Tom always said it wasn't worth my time to clean his home, but I suspected he valued his privacy more than just about anything, except Eli. I also suspected he dust-busted his office before I arrived to clean because I never saw any evidence that Eli shed. Highly impossible for a black Lab. Nevertheless, every Wednesday, come hell or high water, I climbed the narrow oak steps to his second-story office above Marlene's Gift and Flower Shoppe, loaded down with scrub sponges and disinfectants, prepared to do combat with the dirt, grime, and filth of the twenty-first century.

He always said the same thing when he saw me, his voice as smooth as the red silk ties he wore. "Ah. Flip. My heroine."

As if I came galloping in on a white horse to sweep him and all his dustballs up and trot off into the sunset to Tahiti.

I always said the same thing back to Tom. "I'll start with the john, if you don't mind."

Tom hovered in his early fifties but looked younger. Despite the youthful good looks, he got a kick out of quoting eighteenth-century writers like Swift and Pope, and his jokes usually flew over everybody's head except Margaret Henshaw's. He made a good lawyer, but I pictured him more as a suave English professor in a distinguished old British college, peddling a rattling bike around campus in his gym shorts, black gown flapping in the breeze while the lusty coeds whistled at his legs. He stood a feather under six feet tall with graying coal hair, hawk ebony eyes that could spot a flea on a black dog, and a sharp nose able to savor a fine wine and smell a deal gone sour at the same time. When he smiled, ice melted two states away.

Tom was another one with an orchard of family trees. He counted two governors and a State Court of Appeals justice among the branches, but his was the last branch, and we'd all given up hope he or Charlie would pick a wife and continue the Scott name. Tom — because of his love of privacy, and Charlie — because he could never touch his feet to the ground long enough to make a footprint.

I always felt ill at ease with Tom. Inferior. He constantly asked questions, much worse when I was younger. Back then I didn't know any better than to answer. By the time I hit thirty, though, I started saying, "Mmmm," when he asked me something I considered none of his business. A smart guy, he took the hint.

I finished the bathroom, spotless before I cleaned, spotless after, and started on the conference room. Tom sat at the long table, poring over a pile of red books and looking sexy and scholarly at the same time. Eli raised his intelligent head when I entered, matching his master's scholarly expression.

Tom pulled his wire-rimmed reading glasses off, rubbed the bridge of his nose, and leaned back in the chair. "I hate custody cases," he moaned.

"Who doesn't?"

His mouth barely twitched into a grin and he shook his head. "How's it going with you, Flip? You enjoying the Bell family Bible?"

"Makes a good doorstop," I lied.

The hawk eyes flew at me, formed an evaluation, relaxed. "I'm sure you've put it in a safe place."

"He'll never find it. He'd have to burn the whole house down to destroy it."

Tom shifted in his chair and stared out the window. From that view, we could see Pal's newly shined Cadillac behind the gas station. Pal worked away, scrubbing hubcaps with a toothbrush and beaming at his brilliant reflection. Twice he had to shoo Joey away from the driver's door. No way was he letting a seventeen year old with a new driver's license behind the wheel. Suggs slouched against a soft drink machine, wiping a dirty rag over an engine part and shooting Pal sly, envious glances. It wasn't in his makeup to feel happy for anybody's good fortune, especially Pal's. Pal churned through each day with the energy of a four year old and expected the same from his employee — go, go, go, work, work, work. Too bad garage work formed Suggs's only employable skill. No doubt he pictured himself in quite different surroundings — the kingpin of a Las Vegas casino with glitzy showgirls draping each iron shoulder. But the road from here to there lay buried under reality.

Tom chewed on his lip. "I hope Pal's careful, and you . . ."

"I know, I know. Watch my back."

He stood up and did a couple of shoulder rolls. "To tell the truth, it's Lee I'm most worried about. Roland is . . . unpredictable. I wonder if *I* shouldn't act as custodian of those letters."

I rested my back against the windowsill, one question on my mind, one on my lips. "You think Roland would go after those letters Lee has?"

"He's curious enough about them."

"Aren't you?" That was the question on my mind.

Tom's eyes crinkled. "Jesse and Jules made it sound like they're worth a fortune. Something about J.E.B. Stuart and a woman?"

Lee obviously hadn't told him. "An expert needs to see them."

He eyed me and I could see the questions lining up in his brain, little soldiers ready for their marching orders. I zipped across the room and attacked a bookshelf with a dust rag while he stood by the window watching me, cradling his chin, scuffing the carpet with the toe of his shoe. A few minutes later, I announced the room was fit to do business in.

"Flip," he said, as I was sauntering out, "who is Sam Gibbon?"

"Sam Gibbon? Why?" The words squawked out of my mouth so high-pitched, he must have guessed who my daydreams centered on.

But Tom only answered my question with a question. "He's renting the house from Lee, isn't he?"

I lowered my voice and spoke slowly. "If you already knew, why'd you ask?"

He scratched his cheek. "Just wondered. I'd like to meet him."

"Oh. I see." A devious thought struck me. "You know, Miss Fizzi and Louise are having a tea Halloween afternoon to do just that. I arranged it." Thoughtful me. Unfortunately, my great idea had backfired in my face. When I called Miss Fizzi to set up an intimate little tea for four — her, Louise, Sam, and me — she'd started winding up like a spin toy over what an incredible opportunity this would be for her and Louise to find a husband for Lee before

Christmas. So now Lee was the main event.

I studied Tom. "Why don't you drop by? Sam will be offered up as the entertainment and Lee is going to serve as the sacrificial lamb. Or maybe it's the other way around, I forget."

He perked up. "Lee will be there, too?"

I studied him harder. "First you say you're worried about Lee, mention Roland, and ask about Sam. Are you worried about Lee and Roland or are you more worried about her and Sam?"

The hawk eyes zoomed in on me. "What about her and Sam?"

"Mmmmm," I lifted one eyebrow at him.

"*Is* there a Lee and Sam?"

"Mmmmmmm," I said, slow as melting butter, lifting the other brow. "Gotta go."

So that's how it was. That's how it was.

Later that night, I took down the Bible from its hiding place again, feeling guilty I'd neglected it for so long, knowing these were Leona's people and she'd wanted me to tend to each one. I made up my mind to do just that.

I reread the names of the first three Bells born in America who survived their childhood — Richard, Ferrell, and Lucinda. The oldest son, Richard, married Kaye Thomas in 1812, and by 1820, they had four children who, sadly, all died before age twenty. Only one sibling lived long enough to marry, in 1834, and she died within a year, probably from childbirth fever. The child must not have survived, either, because that whole branch of the family broke off, nothing but blank space beneath the four names with their birth and death years.

I thought of Tom Scott and pictured his name, birth date, and date of death inscribed in the Scott family Bible. Underneath, the same blank space. It made me sad.

Somehow, I couldn't imagine my own name and the empty space beneath because I owned no Paxton family Bible, no special book handed down generation to generation. Granddaddy Paxton lay sleeping in the Presbyterian graveyard with my grandmother and parents; my mother's parents died by the time I turned two. So, whenever I pictured my own death, I saw only a few lines of print in the local newspaper — thin, crisp paper collected by the Boy Scouts, tied in bundles, and recycled.

The second Bell son, Ferrell, married Sara Doddin in 1808. They produced one offspring, another Ferrell, born twenty years later in 1828.

Think of waiting that long for a child. Poor Sara. She must have been knitting baby booties for other women, for her nieces and nephews, for twenty long, heart-wrenching years. She probably gave up hope and accepted the pity of those other mothers. Probably prayed a lot and listened when the family preacher told her it was God's will she live life barren. Maybe he even hinted she was being punished for some silly thing she carried out as a child: pulling her sister's hair or refusing to share an apple with her little brother. Nobody would have blamed her husband. Anything related to hearth and home fell squarely on the woman's shoulders.

Then one day, at age forty-three, the miracle happened. Out of the blue, God answered her prayers with a single nod of his head. He gave Sara a son in 1828, the year John Quincy Adams sat as president and Webster published the first *American Dictionary*.

I breathed a sigh of relief for Sara (my own mother gave birth to me at age thirty-eight) and ran my finger parallel across the page to discover what happened to the last sibling, Richard and Ferrell's sister, Lucinda.

Lucinda made her appearance in 1787 and married late, at age thirty, in 1817. Her husband's name was Joseph Paca. She bore him two children: a boy, John Bell, in 1820, and a girl, Lucy, in 1829.

John Bell Paca never married and died in 1861, no doubt a war casualty. I wondered which side he fought on, with J.E.B. Stuart or against him. If you claimed Maryland as your home state back then, the coin could land on either side. I'd strolled around Gettysburg many a Sunday afternoon and the Maryland state monument tightened my chest every time. Two wounded soldiers, one in ragged Yankee blue, one wearing torn Rebel gray, helping each other, leaning on each other. Both wanting to go home. The words on the statue read, "Brothers Again. Marylander's All."

Poor John Bell. One of many who didn't make it home to his momma and daddy and little sister in 1861. No wife, no children. A blank space beneath such sheared numbers.

Chapter 11

A few days before Halloween, I took my lunch break at the regular time at the Café. I nodded at Garland who twitched her nose like a rabbit on the run and dipped back into her hole, the kitchen.

Hilda traipsed over, red T-shirt tight as a tick. The high school proved lenient about letting her work during her own cafeteria time. I took a hard look at Hilda. She'd done an awful job of painting her face, as usual. The mascara hung off her lashes in black, spidery clumps. The sides of her round face and the heavy flesh of her lips looked like a child had dipped his thumb in ketchup and conducted an experiment across her. I couldn't help but think of the Bell family Bible and Hilda's illustrious background.

I handed her my order as she attempted to engage me in conversation.

"In gym class yesterday . . ."

"I can't remember. Do you graduate high school this year or is next year your time?"

"Next year," she answered quick and hustled lickety-split back to the kitchen.

Hilda's sensitivity on the subject of her two

extra years in high school was common knowledge, a fact I counted on whenever small talk with her seemed too large a cross to bear. She struggled with math; she struggled with science; she struggled with gym class. And for what probably seemed an eternity to Hilda, she struggled with Margaret Henshaw. Whenever Margaret graced the Café, Hilda automatically sank into a deep slouch.

I drew my pocket atlas out of the carryall and settled in to contemplate New Mexico and Arizona. Each week, I'd plan a trip to a different part of the planet. Sometimes, the trip might include more than one place. I figured if I ever got the chance to see Arizona, I might as well throw in New Mexico, too. I pictured myself in Albuquerque, hanging out of a hot-air balloon swigging champagne and singing "We May Never Pass This Way Again" at the top of my lungs. These little imaginary vacations kept my hopes up that one day I might actually go someplace besides Ocean City, Maryland. I easily, if unrealistically, pictured myself the happy counterpart to Charlie Scott.

I was enjoying the hell out of myself when the front door of the Café swung open and Marlene Worthington swished in with who else but the already infamous Cecile Crosswell. For the past three weeks, Screamin' Larry's hint of coming catastrophe took the form of song dedications to "the red-lipped babe in the silver BMW," songs like "I'm Painting the Town Red." Not a good omen. It came as no surprise to me after the Battle of the Beetle that Marlene had sought out C.C. and now sported a new best friend.

I scrunched down behind the pocket atlas.

Marlene searched out a table by one of the picture windows on either wing of Officer Lukzay's permanently reserved table, as chic as it gets at Roland's Café and Grill, and the two of them slithered into their seats for a power lunch. C.C. sported a lime-green suit with black piping while Marlene put on a pretty good show in a beige cashmere sweater Louise picked up for her one year in Bermuda. Her heavy black corduroy skirt hid a multitude of sins.

Hilda appeared with my liver and onions. Waiting on my table as often as she did, she'd learned that when the pocket atlas came out, a DO NOT DISTURB sign might as well be dangling around my neck. She quietly put the plate down, refilled my tea glass, and wandered off again, reminding me she did have a decent streak.

Five minutes hadn't passed when the Eggheads tramped in with Pal, disrupting the peace. Pal rarely left the Crown station for lunch, preferring to share a pitiful Spam sandwich and some chips with Joey, but every now and again he stepped out "for the sake of public relations," he said. The three feuded in a loud conversation with each other on the merits of Lawn Boy versus John Deere. They did this all the time. One would choose some particular consumer

97

product and rant and rave about how great he thought it was, and the other two would get equally steamed up about a competitor's product. The problem was they watched too many commercials.

I sawed at the liver on my plate. Tom Scott and Ferrell T. strolled in while I downed the iced tea, Tom explaining in a patient tone something about trusts, Ferrell T., Mr. Paralegal-in-Training, nodding as if he understood every word. I gobbled a final bite, scraping the ittiest bit of onion up with the meat, and was about to leave when Lee popped in.

She glanced across the crowd and spotted me, raised a hand and skipped over, pretending not to see Roland at the cash register. Nearly two months of time had lapsed since Leona's funeral. When I'd stopped by to clean her house that morning, I'd noticed a definite change for the good in Lee. The peach in her cheeks reappeared, her hazel eyes sparkled, her auburn hair gleamed, the set of that Jenner jaw showed confidence and positive thinking.

"Hey, guess what?" she plopped into a chair.

"What? You get Plain Jane a playmate?"

"No," she picked up my empty tea glass and slid a piece of melting ice into her mouth. "I'm going to use Sam Gibbon's big, fat rent check to buy you a hair cut and some new clothes."

"Very funny." I slipped a stray strand of mousy hair behind an ear. "So . . . is it only business between you and Sam Gibbon?"

Mischief shined in the hazel eyes. She opened her mouth to speak. That's when the door swung open and Screamin' Larry bellowed, "After you, beautiful ladies, stealers of hearts!"

Louise Lamm, having a good day, and Miss Fizzi bustled into the Café, blushing and giggling into their kidskin gloves.

"Isn't he the cat's pajamas?" said Louise to Miss Fizzi, who nodded and mewed, "Mercy, yes."

Trotting right behind, Melody Connolly and Tina Graham gave their favorite radio personality huge grins.

Larry bowed and scraped the four of them to a table against the wall and proclaimed he hated to kiss and run. He pecked each one on the hand and lumbered across to his regular seat in the center of the room. Melody, never without an impeccable piece of jewelry from the family store, twisted her fingers around a dark necklace of jade beads and fondly watched Larry take his leave. Tina, too, basked in the light of his attention. Larry was probably the only man in the world to ever kiss her hand.

Larry's appearance offered the lunch crowd a whole new option of entertainment besides talking to themselves, and gradually the place grew quiet. For the first time, he and C.C. occupied the same air space since the Battle of the Beetle. His radio song dedications to "the red-lipped babe in the silver BMW" ran with such frequency, nobody could miss them.

So there Larry sat, not twenty feet from the object of his personal obsession.

The place bulged with customers yet nobody said a word, clinked a glass, or bent to retrieve a stray napkin. Larry, however, ran a finger over the menu, humming "Satin Doll," tapping at the food items he wanted, scratching away on his order pad. A demented Paul Prudhomme.

Everybody participated in Larry's lunch order. Every eye in the Café followed the movement of his hand as he wrote. Every ear attended the notes of "Satin Doll" as he hummed. Every face searched for Hilda to come snatch the order from Larry's fingers so the first scene of the drama could begin. Even Roland laid bony elbows on the counter and focused full attention on Larry.

After Hilda trotted off with Larry's order, nobody breathed. Any moment, he would glance up and see C.C., a sitting duck, in open view at the window.

C.C., as one might expect, wore the air of a woman bored out of her mind. Her lunch companion had clammed up when Larry blew in. Marlene's pop eyes bounced from Larry to C.C., C.C. to Larry, anxious for her to see him or him to see her and all hell to break loose.

C.C.'s idea of hell, however, was slow service. In a loud voice tailored especially for restaurant personnel, she squawked, "Does anybody work here? I'm famished!"

Marlene's mouth unhinged and she whispered loud enough for everybody to hear, "Why are you calling attention to yourself? Don't you know that's Larry sitting over there?"

Hearing his name, Larry glanced up from chomping his fingernails and spotted Marlene. Then he saw C.C.

C.C. scowled at the room. "You mean that person who's been playing songs for me on the radio?"

Marlene pumped her head up and down.

"Which one is he?"

Larry stood, a towering man.

"Is that him?"

Marlene scooted her chair backward, prepared to leap out of harm's way. "Yep. That's the man you pushed your car into."

C.C. squinted at Larry. "He was in my way." She dipped red nails into a purse, pulled out a gold cigarette case, drew one long, skinny tobacco stick out, and lit it with a long, skinny sterling silver lighter.

I saw Roland open his mouth to recite the no-smoking speech, think better of it, and clamp his lips tight.

"You there," called C.C., spewing a thick, gray cloud that slowly drifted in Larry's direction.

Larry glimpsed over both shoulders, stuck a simper on his face, and pointed a finger at his chest.

"Yes, you," said C.C., irritated at his antics.

He took two steps forward.

You'd have thought he wore a holster with a .38 and growled, "Draw, cowboy." Chairs scraped the floor, women gasped, Roland ducked behind the cash register. Marlene reared back in such a panic, she toppled over and nobody cared.

C.C. exhaled more inconsiderate second-hand smoke. "If you find it funny to play those stalking songs on the radio to me, and we all know you mean me because I am the only one in this dump who owns a silver BMW — which had to be expensively fixed, thanks to you — then I can assure you, I do not find it funny, mildly amusing, or remotely clever." She tapped some ash on the floor. Roland gawked but kept quiet. "My husband, Leonard . . . Leonard Crosswell? Perhaps you've heard of him if you read the *Post* or the *Times*? I'm assuming you can read. Well, Leonard is a very high-profile Washington attorney."

"Yikes," shuddered Larry and moved two steps closer.

"You could find yourself out of your little radio job if you continue to harass me in this manner. That is all I have to say to you." She swiveled her brunette hairdo around, completely finished with Larry and completely ignorant of the maniac she was dealing with. "Now, where is that waitress? I have an appointment." I hadn't seen a gleam like that in Larry's eye since the gas line blew up. He spoke three words and took three steps: Listen. Here. Babe.

The newest addition to Solace Glen was about to become its only homicide victim when a terrible crashing noise stopped Larry in his tracks and scared everybody out of their seats. "What the hell was that?" C.C. glared at Larry as if he bore responsibility.

Larry tore his eyes off her and stared out the picture window over Officer Lukzay's half-finished lunch. Everybody stared with him.

"Oh, mercy," whimpered Miss Fizzi. "I hope that nice young man isn't hurt."

The Eggheads took that as their cue to rush outside and lend expert assistance. Pal rose in his seat, curious.

"Who?" called Marlene from the floor. "Who is it?"

"Not so much who as what," announced Larry. He turned sly, gleeful eyes on C.C. "Pal's big . . . heavy . . . Cadillac. Looks like he lost control. I am so sorry, Mrs. Crosswell, on your recent loss." He peeked out the window again. "Your *total* loss."

Pal gasped. "But . . . but I'm here, Larry. That couldn't be my car. Unless . . ."

C.C. followed his gaze and started coughing and hacking and stomping out her cigarette and gathering her designer purse and clutching her throat. "That idiot!" she gagged. "Not again! That stupid boy! I just had that car fixed! Can't anybody do anything right in this hellhole?!"

She flew out of the Café, denying herself the pleasure of Roland's liver and onion special and us the pleasure of her company. The door of the Café banged open and everybody stood and strained their ears to hear the street-side drama. Pal raced after her.

With an attentive audience, C.C. lurched ahead of the Eggheads and screamed into the demolished Cadillac. "What-is-wrong-with-you?! Can't you drive?!" She got no answer and barely paused. "Don't you have anything to say for yourself? How could you manage to hit *my* parked car and nobody else's!"

Pal yelled explanations at the back of her head, complete bewilderment in his eyes. "I don't know, Miz Crosswell! I don't know! I'm telling you I just fixed the brakes! I don't know how this could happen! Joey! Are you OK?"

"Imbecile!" C.C. did an about-face, grabbed hold of Pal's shoulders, and shook him hard before crunching her high heel into his sneaker and whipping out a cell phone. She marched away.

The Eggheads guided a white-faced Pal to a sitting position on the curb and got busy attending to Joey, alive but covered in blood. I felt so bad for Pal, I wanted to cry.

Roland, however, displayed a different reaction, focused only on the Cadillac Pal inherited from Leona. His chuckle became a loud cackle as he bent over, pointing a long finger at Pal. "Perfect! Serves him right." He twisted around and looked Lee straight in the eye. "Isn't that just perfect! One down, Miss Jenner — and I didn't have to lift a finger."

Chapter 12

Although none of us had known Joey Sykes very well or for very long, we'd known Pal for almost as many years that made up Joey's precarious life. For days, the boy teetered on the edge, in a coma at Frederick Memorial Hospital. The Circle Ladies rallied around Pal in his shock and helplessness, making sure he received proper nourishment and rest during the vigil.

I put in my two bits around day four, sitting at Joey's bedside while Pal tried to grab a nap on the cot they'd brought in. He mumbled to himself all through the fitful sleep, "It's my fault. Car keys on my desk. Wasn't a good driver yet. Never checked the speedometer. All my fault."

I wondered. In his fluster at the scene of the "accident," Pal blurted out that he'd just fixed the brakes on the Cadillac. Did he do a bad job of it? Not likely for someone of Pal's skill and experience. Did someone tamper with the brakes? For what reason? Or maybe, like most people believed, Joey simply drove too fast and lost control.

At any rate, Officer Lukzay was conducting an "investigation" in between free meals at

Roland's. I had little doubt he'd turn up nothing, if he even bothered to glance under the hood.

The next day, the day before Halloween, the doctors told Pal that Joey had slid out of the danger zone, but might be in the coma for days, weeks, or months. Pal breathed a sigh of relief and got back to work, content to visit his brother in the evenings until he finally woke up. So on Halloween morning, Pal reappeared at the gas pump, throwing himself into his work with the usual energy, vigor, and irrepressible good humor. I felt awful that now his only work companion was the uncompanionable Suggs Magill.

I edged my car past the Eggheads and sidled up to the diesel pump. They were at it again, arguing over which brand of motor oil could save the free world, Pennzoil or Quaker State.

"There is no comparison," one said to the other, and that one barked back, "You don't know what you're talking about."

Behind me, Pal, no doubt happy to engage in familiar and distracting conversation, dragged a third brand of oil into the mix. Just as I was about to add Oil of Olay as a fourth choice, a horn blew. I didn't need to turn around to know who it was.

"Coming, Miz Crosswell," Pal squeaked. A regular fire ant, he crawled over her second BMW, shining and polishing, doing what he could to make up for Joey's unforgivable driving. "This is a mighty fine car. This your husband's car? How's the house going?"

"Slow," she huffed. "Too damn slow. And yes, as if it's any of your business, this is my husband's car. I hope your insurance company doesn't drag its feet."

I gaped. This woman really did take the cake. Pal merely nodded in response, never violating his standard of customer service.

"Patience, patience," drawled a man's voice. "Mr. Sykes fortunately uses a very reputable company. *You* won't suffer any loss over this."

I focused in on the black BMW. C.C. sat in the driver's seat, checking her lipstick out in the rearview mirror. Beside her, a man leafed through the *Wall Street Journal*, elbow stuck out the window so he'd have more room to turn pages, tortoise shell glasses perched on his long, fox snout, white hair smooth as silk thread, a cashmere camel coat, bright yellow and navy tie. Quite the dapper gentleman.

"I am devoid of patience, Leonard," she snapped. "At least that's what you always tell me."

"And I'm right," was all he said, deadpan. He never slid her a glance or cracked a smile, the way couples do when they share a little on-going, private joke.

Suggs appeared, a jumpsuited apparition, and eyed the two of them with the usual silent envy and anger he directed at everyone in his path.

107

He held the familiar rag and piece of equipment in his dirty hands.

I topped off the diesel and started to open the car door.

"You there! Flip Paxton!"

I toyed with the notion of ignoring her, but tacked a polite smile on my face and strolled over, taking my time. "Ma'am?"

Before she could tell me what she wanted, Leonard fired a question. "Flip Paxton?" He hardly glanced up from his paper. "Isn't she one of those people Marlene was talking about? An inheritance, wasn't it? Valuable letters from the Civil War period?" Then he mumbled, "Might fit into my collection."

I bristled. "I doubt you'd fit into mine."

The fox snout rose out of the paper. Iron eyes strafed me over the tortoise shell frames.

"My schedule, of course. And I wasn't the one to inherit the letters. I received a family Bible."

He tipped his head, the only hint of interest. "Right, it was Lee Jenner. Miss Jenner owns the letters."

As if he were telling me astounding news I didn't already know.

He snapped his paper to the next page. "Old family Bibles have a small following." His eyes returned to the *Wall Street Journal*, but I could tell his mind lingered elsewhere.

I turned to face C.C. "You rang?"

She cocked her head and jutted her lower

108

teeth, trying to get a fix on the attitude. "Yyyyes, I heard from my good friend, Marlene Worthington, that you are the person to speak to about house management. Now, mind you," she rattled on, "we have a little ways to go before the house is finished, but my contractor assures us it will be in move-in condition before the end of the year."

I twisted my mouth. "That is fast."

"Maybe for some. Not for me." She patted a flat chest. "Leonard says I'm impatient as a flash flood. Anyway, I wanted to line you up as soon as possible, arrive at some understanding, so that when the property is finally done, we can have a smooth transition as far as cleaning and so forth."

God only knew what she defined as the "so forth" of life.

She suddenly jerked her head down and rooted around in her handbag, ripped a fifty out, captured Pal's filthy palm as he scurried by and plunked the bill into it. She pulled a linen hankie out of her Chanel suit jacket like a magic trick, wiped her hands off, and dropped the dirty cloth inside the Gucci purse.

"Well. Have to run. Leonard has a train to catch."

She brushed my arm with her fingertip, as if that gesture sealed the bargain.

I stood there, dumbfounded. I'd hardly said ten words, and the woman took it for granted I would work for her.

Pal appeared beside me, eyes large over the fifty-dollar bill. He waved as the Crosswells zipped away in their luxury vehicle. "She left me a tip. Must be her way of helping out with Joey. Itn't she sweeeet?"

I took a good, long look at Pal. He'd said the same thing about Leona at the will reading, a woman the polar opposite of C.C. To someone like C.C., a fifty-dollar bill zipped out of her purse as often as her lipstick — a mindless, insignificant habit.

Pal grinned, apologized, said he had work to do, excused himself, and skipped off into the garage, motioning Suggs to hop to it.

I recalled the Parable of Talents, the story preachers make constant use of to compel us to take advantage of the special gifts God gives each individual and not waste those gifts.

I decided then and there: Pal's special gift from God was the ability to see no evil.

Chapter 13

Because of the usual Halloween hoopla, my workday ended earlier than usual. I drove past houses decorated with craggy mouthed pumpkins and paper witches. Sheets with ghostly faces flapped in the autumn trees. I decided to make a quick stop at Connolly's Jewelry Store and buy myself a pair of hoop earrings, something to set off my mouse ears at Miss Fizzi's tea party. Not that a couple of fake gold hoops would have Sam Gibbon swooning to his knees, but they might make me easier to look at.

Melody Connolly put down the glass cleaner that practically served as another limb and cheerfully gave me her full attention. A compact, spry woman with a boundless get-up-and-go attitude that could outmatch Pal's, Melody ran the Episcopal Ladies Circle with the common sense, efficiency, and community spirit of her Jewish heritage. Somewhere along the line, she'd drifted away from the religion of her birth, and marrying an Irish Catholic, she told us, had been the final straw for her staunchly Orthodox parents. Her family shunned her. I couldn't fathom parents cutting themselves off from a child, or a child — even an adult child — losing family when there's been no death. Melody had her orchard, but a NO TRESPASSING sign barred the way.

"I gave up a nice inheritance and much more for love," she'd tell any young couple shopping for engagement and wedding rings. Then she'd yell over to her husband, Michael, "For you! For love! For this!" And her hands would sweep across the jewelry store.

"Oy vey," Michael would chirp, and they'd both break into gales of laughter. They shared the same laugh — loud, infectious, pure from the heart.

Melody almost fit into my list of mothers, but she, like Tina Graham, hadn't hit sixty yet. They made my list of sisters, though.

"Flip! What brings you by?"

"She's getting engaged," called Michael from the back office.

Melody turned on me with openly astonished brown eyes. I didn't know whether to be insulted by her astonishment or flattered by her belief.

"Yeah, that's right." I plopped my ugly pocketbook on the shiny glass counter. "But I can't decide between Screamin' Larry or Mel Gibson."

"Mel's taken," Michael responded.

Melody's wide eyes drew narrow and she threw her husband a nasty look he no doubt could picture as he worked in the back room office.

"That man. What can I do for you, sweet pea?"

I smiled and shook my head. Melody's mantra — what can I do for you? When she wasn't fielding the Episcopalian flock's problems, she was delving into the needs of Catholics, Methodists, and Presbyterians. For such a small package, she spread herself wide.

"Gold hoops," I answered. "Nothing too gold."

She nodded knowingly and went for the gold-fill case.

"So tell me," Melody and Michael loved to gossip even more than Louise, "who does this C.C. person think she is and what's this I hear about Lee having such important historical letters?"

"History belongs in museums so we can all stare at it." Michael could participate in any conversation from any point in the store.

"Don't interrupt, Mr. Gift-of-the-Gab. I should talk." Melody waited for me to answer both questions. Her curiosity never limited itself to one subject at a time.

Before I could open my mouth, the door opened and the October chill wrapped around my neck. Tina and Margaret walked in, both talking over each other. They made a funny pair, one so wide and the other long and straight as the pointer she rapped on her chalkboard.

Tina glanced around the store, checking that Michael worked in the back. She clutched both

113

hands to her massive stomach and yanked up. "Damn pantyhose. They're about to cut off my circulation."

Margaret clicked her tongue in disapproval and scurried away from Tina. "Where are your social graces, for heaven's sake."

"I lost them in your class." The two had known each other all their lives, though Margaret had five or six years on Tina. The first year Margaret taught English at Solace Glen High, Tina sat in her senior class. Margaret handed her a C for her final grade, and Tina still held a grudge. She'd been a B student all her life. Lord, Lord, she'd cluck, how could her good friend Margaret have blackened her good name that way. They'd feuded good-naturedly ever since.

I, myself, held Margaret in high regard. I'd worked my bottom off to earn an A in her class and still felt the need to work for her approval. Probably the reason she'd never made my list of "mothers" owed to the fact I did hold her in such high esteem. She seemed unapproachable, somehow, as if she'd sting my knuckles with her pointer if she didn't fancy how I dusted.

Margaret lingered over the pearl necklace display and called to Melody, "Go on and help Flip. We're just browsing."

"Speak for yourself, old woman, *I'm* not browsing." Tina smoothed her dress. "I'm going to buy myself something big and gaudy to wear in Florida when I go visit my parents."

114

Margaret's eyebrows tilted up but she kept her opinion to herself. From the back, Michael's voice could be heard. "Big and gaudy is nice."

Melody leaned forward. "So, Flip? You were saying about this C.C. person?"

Margaret and Tina moved closer in unison.

"Well," I started fiddling with the earrings in front of me, "you know what they say about first impressions."

"They're everything," Melody's index finger punctuated her statement.

"Everything," agreed Tina.

I held a pair of hoops against one ear. Too small. "All I know is, she's shown more compassion for her wrecked BMW than for poor Joey Sykes lying in a coma, *and* she's hired me to clean her new digs. I hardly got to say a word about it."

"Unbelievable," murmured Margaret. "Pushy."

"Charge an arm and a leg," advised the voice from the back.

I picked up a second pair of hoops, wondering if I should reveal my doubts about how "accidental" Joey's car crash was, but decided against it. I stuck to concrete gossip. "And . . ."

All three bent their heads closer.

"I met Mr. C.C. this morning at the gas station."

"You did!" Tina's blue eyes fluttered. "What's he like?"

I could tell she wanted to hear the worst.

"Oh, I'd say they deserve each other. Pretty

smooth. Sophisticated dresser. Looks like the sort who's raided a few hen houses."

"A ladies' man, is he?" Melody hated men who thought they were God's gift to women. Her own husband couldn't have been more humble in that department. "He didn't try anything with you, did he, darling?"

"Oh, yeah," I held the hoops to my ear. Too big. "I wowed him with my refined manner and movie star teeth. He especially lusted after my jug of Clorox."

"I've always admired it," Michael said.

"Is he as rude as C.C.?" Tina picked out a pair of earrings and handed them to me. When she wasn't doing secretarial work for Frederick County, she moonlighted at Sally Polk's Salon, selling and applying makeup. She'd always wanted to give me a makeover. Earrings were a start. "C.C.'s about the most bitchy person I've ever met in the world."

"Watch your language, you're in a public place," Margaret chided. "And given the fact all bitches are female, you could have condensed your sentence."

I held the earrings up to my ear. Perfect. "No, he's not rude like her. He's more . . . dismissive. But I'd bet anything he can turn on the charm when he wants something. I bet he turns it on full force for Lee."

"Lee?" Melody's forehead wrinkled, then the light dawned. "Oh! Does this have something to do with her historical letters?"

Tina and Margaret drew even closer to me. Michael appeared in the doorway, deft fingers polishing a silver bracelet, jade eyes glued to me. I really didn't like gossiping about Leona's letters, I considered them so private. But the cat was slowly creeping out of the bag. Anyway, I excused myself, the subject really centered on Leonard Crosswell.

"Yeah, in a way. Leonard — that's Mr. C.C.'s name — let it spill that he collects Civil War documents and that Lee's letters might fit into his collection."

"Presumptuous," huffed Margaret. "Lee would never give up to a stranger something Leona left her. Her morals are too high."

High morals can't pay the bills, I thought, *and Leonard probably had a ton of disposable income to throw at Lee.* But I responded, "You're right. I'll take this pair, Melody. Thanks for the help, Tina."

Tina glowed from any compliment. She busied herself searching for something big and gaudy with Michael's help while I paid for the hoops and said I had to hurry home and change for tea at Miss Fizzi's. They pressed for details, but I squirmed out of the store quickly and headed home.

Standing in front of my bathroom mirror, I found it impossible to attach the gold hoops to my ears. Thoughts of Sam Gibbon made my palms so sweaty and shaky, it took forever to do the simplest thing.

I appraised the final product in the mirror and frowned. The hoops did nothing for me; my lipstick covered everything but my lips; bobby pins stuck haphazardly out of my glamorous bun as if a satellite landed on my head.

Happy Halloween. Perfect day of the year for me.

Chapter 14

In Solace Glen, a guest at an afternoon tea party could arrive empty-handed and nobody would think a thing of it, but most people toted along a small tray or plate of something. I stepped out of the car and carefully lifted a tray of ham salad sandwiches from the back seat, balanced the tray with one hand, and smoothed down my dress with the other. I wore my usual autumn number, a navy blue corduroy jumper with navy pumps and a rust sweater trimmed in black. Not an outfit to either merit astonishment or get me thrown out of a public place, as Margaret might say.

"I didn't know you had legs."

Sam Gibbon strolled up smiling, swinging a small, Halloween-theme gift bag from the candy store.

I dipped my head involuntarily at my legs, mostly shrouded by blue corduroy, and realized he'd never seen me in anything but khaki work pants and an apron the size of Baltimore.

"Sure I've got legs." I stood staring at him with his perfect smile in his handsome tweed jacket. I'd never known a man to get better looking every time you saw him. Finally, I took a step toward Miss Fizzi's house and stumbled out of one navy pump.

Sam grabbed my arm and herded me toward the front porch. "After our talk last week," he spoke in a conspiratorial tone, "I've decided to make an indelible impression on the entire female population of this town, being a new single under fifty, you understand, and you could help immensely by pretending to be madly in love with me."

I jerked my arm away, open-mouthed, sure I'd been discovered.

"OK," he wasn't even looking at me, "then I'll pretend to be madly in love with you. That'll have the same effect."

I wrapped white knuckles around the tray of sandwiches. "Is this about me asking 'probing, personal questions'?"

"Something like that." He rapped gently at Miss Fizzi's front door. When we heard footsteps, Sam whipped an arm out and hugged me into his side. "Darling." The door opened and both Louise and Miss Fizzi stood there, fresh pink lipstick stretched into wide, welcoming smiles that iced on their faces when they saw Sam's long arm wrapped around me like a python.

"Hello, hello," chirped Sam, cheerful as a kindergarten teacher greeting his first class.

I could practically see the little film winding through their heads, The Story of Lee's Heartbreak, how a handsome, middle-aged college professor rode into town, won her affection, then dumped her for the town domestic who, sadly, was probably beyond her childbearing years, unlike the fertile Lee.

"Don't get all excited," I said, extracting myself from Sam. "He's fooling around. Doesn't mean anything."

I brushed past them and headed for Miss Fizzi's parlor, face on fire.

Sam called after me, "Babycakes, does this mean the elopement's off?"

My eyes popped. Poor Miss Fizzi would believe anything.

"It is a pleasure to meet you, Sam," she said, but it sounded more like a question.

"Come in, come in!" Louise started chattering about the weather, how it'd been warmer than usual this year.

"El Niño," replied Sam.

"Oh, you speak Spanish," twittered Miss Fizzi. "I used to know Spanish. Or was it Swedish? Started with an *s*."

They entered the parlor together, Sam towering over the two ladies on either side, the apex of an odd pyramid. I excused myself abruptly, mindful of the glance Sam hurled for leaving him with two women he'd never met but who'd already mapped out his future.

I waltzed into the kitchen and bumped into Lee drawing cookies from the oven.

"Those should impress him," I snipped, feeling a little miffed at her presence until I saw what she wore. I slapped a hand on my hip. "What are you doing dressed like that? Looks like you've been playing in the mud."

"What are you doing wearing a dress? Is the Queen coming?" She brushed a hand across the seat of her jeans. Caked mud fell off. Over her pants hung a plaid flannel shirt streaked with dirt and pocked with dead leaves. "Do I look that bad? I'd forgotten this thing, this *tea* was today and by the time I remembered, I rushed right over."

I snapped the collar of her shirt. Bits of dried marigold floated to the floor. "Have Miss Fizzi and Louise seen you?"

"No, I came in through the kitchen a minute ago." She sighed and brushed hair off her face. "Well, too late. I'm not running all the way home to change. What's the big deal, anyway?"

I lit into her. "You know what the big deal is! Miss Fizzi and Louise want to marry you off to Sam Gibbon. They're going to throw a hissy fit when they get a load of you."

She took a step back. "What are you so hostile about? Maybe it's you they want to marry off, ever consider that?"

No, Lee, I wanted to say. *You're the golden girl, not me. Never me.*

Louise entered the kitchen with a festive grin, took one look at Lee and muffled a scream. "Lee! You look like a street urchin! And that nice young man dressed so sweetly in his tweed jacket, the perfect gentleman." She shot me a disapproving face, as if I'd been trying to seduce an innocent bystander right out there on the front stoop.

I shoved both hands in my sweater pockets and scrutinized the magnets on the refrigerator as if I might purchase one.

"Is Sam by himself in the parlor with Miss Fizzi?" Lee peeked over Louise's shoulder.

"Yes." Louise couldn't hide her displeasure. The Big Plan was about to blow up.

Lee turned to me, mouth twitching. "I wonder what they're talking about."

My mouth twitched back at her. "Calculus. Astrophysics. Sex."

Louise tapped her foot and spoke between clenched teeth. "Stop it. Both of you. You're talking like a couple of wild teenagers." She drew herself up, suddenly taller than her five feet three inches. "The two of you may serve tea. I will go into the parlor and await our other guests."

"What other guests?" Nobody'd told me about other guests. Then again, I hadn't mentioned my invitation to Tom.

"The other men, of course. Miss Fizzi felt Sam might be more interested if he believes he has some competition." She blew out of the kitchen.

Lee fell into a chair. "Oh, no," she groaned. "You *know* who she's talking about."

I nodded, grim-faced. The pickings were pretty slim.

When we somberly carried the tea finery out to the parlor, Louise and Miss Fizzi were howling as loud as tornadoes while Sam took over the room, acting out a story. He barely noticed us as he played a dozen parts. We set the trays on the coffee table and slid into our seats as silently and quickly as if we'd entered Carnegie Hall in the middle of a Horowitz concert. When he delivered the last line, we stomped our feet and applauded, and Lee and I gave him a standing ovation, a cup of tea, and a chicken salad sandwich.

"What an entertaining fellow you are," praised Miss Fizzi, wiping tears off her powdery cheeks. "You must be a wonderful teacher."

"I don't know about that." Sam stirred his tea. "That was my one and only parlor story. It's all downhill from here."

I studied Lee's face. She liked Sam. Liked him a lot. If she had felt any embarrassment about her clothes, you couldn't tell. Sam possessed an easy, natural manner that pulled us out of ourselves, as if we'd boarded a raft with Sam at the till and all we had to do was sit back while he steered us gently downstream, telling funny stories along the way.

I could see the good impression he made on Louise and Miss Fizzi. Miss Fizzi constantly threw a glance of approval at Louise who tossed one after another at me. And we all three slid eyes at Lee, measuring her interest. Especially me.

Sam had traveled a good bit, which easily kept my attention. I was enjoying his account of getting lost in Wadi Rumm when the doorbell rang.

"Oh, *Lee*," Miss Fizzi smiled like the cat with feathers in her mouth, "who could *that* be?"

"I'm afraid to guess." She chomped into a cookie.

I sat closest to the hall so I hopped up and opened the door.

Screamin' Larry bowed low, dressed elegantly in brown sandals, red sweatpants, and a matching WFIB 102.7 sweatshirt. "Flip."

"Larry."

He lay one hand across his heart. "I have answered the call."

I stepped aside and Larry tramped in, his huge frame filling half the entrance hall.

"I heard there was gonna be food."

"Naturally you'll be paid. In the parlor."

Larry dipped his head at me and headed straight for the coffee table, scooping up a fistful of sandwiches before addressing the others. "Thanks for inviting me," he mumbled and swallowed his fist. "I haven't eaten yet."

"You poor dear," clucked Miss Fizzi.

"He means in the past ten minutes," Lee sniped. "Hey, Larry."

"Lee."

Making Sam believe Larry's intentions lay anywhere beyond the spread on the coffee table would be a hard sell.

"Sam," Louise stepped up to the challenge, "I'd like to introduce you to a *special* friend of Lee's."

As Lee's eyeballs fell into her lap, Sam stepped forward, extending a hand for Larry to shake. Larry turned away from the food long enough to wave two greasy fingers in the air. Sam gave the fingers a firm, polite shaking and made a stab at normal conversation.

"Glad to meet you. I believe I've heard you on the radio."

"You BELIEVE?" Larry bellowed. "If you'd heard ME, you'd damn well know it!"

Sam retreated a few feet. "Now that you mention it, it was definitely you."

Larry stood proud and smiled wide, pink wads of ham salad decorating his teeth. I thought he might start singing or initiate name-that-tune to really show off, but thank God the doorbell rang again.

"Now, *Lee*," a look of incredulity covered Miss Fizzi's face as if Lee was pulling eligible bachelors out of the woodwork, "who could *that* be?"

"It's your party," sniffed Lee, already exhausted from so much male attention. "You ought to know."

I leaped up, the good domestic help, and opened the door to Pal, one Egghead on either wing. The Eggheads still sported their mint green work uniforms. Pal, I was heartened to see, wore a smile and a fresh brown garage shirt

126

with his name stitched over one pocket and the Crown Petroleum symbol patched across the other.

"Hi, Flip," they all chimed in their best party manner.

"Hi, boys. Welcome to the *Dating Game*. Chow's in the parlor."

The humor zipped over their shaved heads, and all three marched into the house single file, members of a band unit about to perform the half-time routine.

Miss Fizzi waved at them in gleeful schoolgirl fashion and beamed at Sam, certain the sheer quantity of Lee's suitors would impress him into an immediate proposal of marriage.

Louise again offered the introductions, emphasizing what *special* friends they all were of Lee's. The three managed to act proper for about ten seconds before descending on the food with Larry.

Miss Fizzi courteously inquired after Joey's health, and in between bites, Pal explained the unknown as best he could. "So they don't know when he'll wake up or what his . . . his 'mental state' will be like when he does. I can't figure for the life of me why he couldn't stop the car and why he'd be going so fast." His thin chest heaved. "I got a quick look at the Cadillac down at the garage yard where Officer Lukzay had it towed. It's totaled."

I made a mental note to ask dear Officer Lukzay the status of his "investigation" and noticed Sam edge away from the crowd to go stand by Lee.

"Praise God Joey wasn't totaled, too," said Miss Fizzi, putting an end to upsetting subjects. Then she batted her eyes at Sam, "Isn't this lovely?" — ecstatic at how well her plan was working.

I didn't think it was so lovely. Even in my best corduroy dress, I couldn't compare to Lee in her mud-caked jeans. Sam started up a quiet conversation while the ladies glittered, Lee's special friends devoured the coffee table, and I sulked.

Somehow, I don't know how, Suggs suddenly appeared. He must have stolen up from his basement apartment. For such a stocky man, Suggs possessed the unusual talent of wafting in and out of places. He hadn't gone to the trouble of changing clothes, that would be too social, but had at least managed to wash his hands. Without a sound, he moved to a chair in the corner with a napkin full of cheese biscuits and hunched down to feed himself.

Miss Fizzi eventually realized her nephew had joined the party — invited or not — and frowned at his attire. When Louise spied him, her face went sour. Neither lady introduced Suggs to Sam as a *special* friend of Lee's.

Not five minutes had passed when the doorbell rang again, but this time both Louise and Miss Fizzi wore only question marks. I got up and slouched to the door.

"Hello, Flip. I took you up on the kind invitation." Tom Scott stepped into the house to escape a light rain shower and suddenly wrinkled his forehead, staring at my dress. "Did you take the whole day off?"

"Halloween's a national holiday, isn't it? Welcome to the celebration."

"Tom? Is that you? You didn't bring that dog, did you?" Miss Fizzi called from the parlor. "Come in and join my little soiree."

"A soiree is an evening affair," corrected Louise. "This is an afternoon tea party, dear."

"Tom knows what I mean," said Miss Fizzi, tickled pink to add another man to the mix. She'd probably left him off the list in the first place because she considered him too serious to qualify as a *special* friend of Lee's. Everybody knows there's no fun in lawyering.

Tom motioned me to go ahead, ladies first, and followed me into the parlor. I slid back into my chair, a creaky Victorian upholstered in cranberry velvet. All the furniture in Miss Fizzi's house fell under the heavy Victorian variety, dwarfing her and most visitors.

Tom smiled politely at Miss Fizzi and Louise. "Eli's at home reading Shakespeare." He caught sight of Sam and crossed the room, arm extended. They shook hands and said each other's names. When he spotted Lee, his eyes softened like gelatin, a change so subtle I doubt anybody noticed but me.

"Ah. Lee. Good to see you." He nodded in a short, businesslike manner.

Miss Fizzi crooned, motioning Lee to pour a cup of tea. "We were just having a little get-together to meet Mr. Gibbon, and he's been entertaining us so. I can't remember a more enjoyable afternoon."

"Well, that's fine," said Tom, taking the cup from Lee a bit shakily, "that's fine. Are you from Maryland, Sam?"

Here come the questions, I thought. You may commence your cross-examination now, Mr. Scott.

"Eastern Shore." Sam gobbled down a sandwich no bigger than his pinkie. Louise probably whipped those up. "Tilghman Island."

"Tilghman Island?" Pal had probably never heard of it. "That on the Eastern Shore?"

"Eastern Shore," croaked one Egghead with food in his mouth.

"Eastern Shore," the other Egghead bobbed his head up and down like a dashboard dog ornament.

Larry grunted and scarfed down a row of sugar cookies. Suggs slowly chewed on a biscuit. Exhibiting his normal horrible personality, he glared down at the carpet.

"Ah," said Tom, "lovely place. Some development going on down there, am I right?"

"Yes. The residents are more or less split in their opinions."

"Are you antidevelopment, then?"

"No. I'm anti–stupid development. My father was a waterman, owned his own skipjack. My

130

mother taught high school history. They taught me to appreciate the wisdom of the past and the beauty of the present. I guess that means change is unsettling to me."

That speech constituted the most background information any of us had been able to wheedle out of Sam Gibbon. Lee crossed her legs and leaned forward, hugging a mud-caked knee and jiggling her ankle up and down.

The motion distracted Tom for a moment before he said, "Change isn't easy for any of us, past a certain age."

"Tom," Lee teased, "you self-conscious about your age?"

Before he could answer, I blurted, voice harder than intended, "You self-conscious about yours? Because you're the freshest chickadee here."

She frowned at me, eyes quizzical. "I mean, change is unsettling to me, too."

She looked straight at Sam, a little too bold for my taste. He didn't utter a sound, but something passed between them that had a strange effect on me. For the first time in my life, I didn't want the best for Lee. I wanted the best for myself.

My cheeks burned and I had to turn away from the two of them. Tom abruptly stepped to the window and stared outside. His eyes squinted the way I'd seen them do when he'd been reading for hours. His mouth tightened as it sometimes did when he struggled with a difficult case, searching for issues and answers.

He told me once that the hardest part about being a lawyer is determining exactly what the right issues are. If I miss the heart of the case, he said, it doesn't matter what answers I find because I will have wasted so much time barking up the wrong tree. If I don't pose the central issue precisely, I lose and people suffer. I told him it sounded pretty simple to me and if being a lawyer boiled down to figuring out the right questions instead of the right answers, this was a screwier world than I thought.

I could only imagine the questions flying though Tom's mind as he stared out the window, and the one question he wouldn't want to ask: Have I waited too long?

Sam cleared his throat and jump-started us onto a new subject. "Lee was just telling me, speaking of the wisdom of the past, that you, Flip, inherited a family Bible from the aunt who left her the old letters."

This perked up the Eggheads. They stopped mowing through appetizers long enough to stammer, "Letters? Leona's letters?"

"Lee," Tom turned around, composed and courteous as ever, "are you going to have an expert evaluate them? I hear," he glanced at the two shaved heads hovering over the coffee table, "you might have a valuable piece of history on your hands. Flip might, too, for all we know."

Par for the course, I only warranted a footnote.

As soon as he said valuable, the Eggheads started to shake and shimmy. "See? See?" They nudged Pal and poked fingers into each other. "See what we told you?"

Larry snorted and reached an arm between them to get at the onion dip. Suggs quit chewing on his third biscuit and actually showed interest in the conversation.

Lee's forehead wrinkled and she huffed, "Thank you for bringing it up, Sam and Tom. I'm glad everybody's so engrossed in my business."

Nobody, apparently, cared about mine.

"So you gonna give 'em to an expert, Lee?" Pal never was one to take a hint.

Sam poured himself more tea. "I told Lee I know somebody at the Smithsonian who would love to take a gander at anything bearing J.E.B. Stuart's name."

"But the signature isn't . . ." I began, but Lee rattled her cup, tossing me such a scornful look, I immediately clamped down.

"It is J.E.B. Stuart! It is!" Cheese bits flew out of the mouth of one of the Eggheads. True to form, neither one could contain himself and started spouting a sermon of misinformation.

"Leona said so. Said he'd stayed in the house during a major campaign. Antietam, it was. Or was it Sharpsburg?"

"Same thing, moron. I believe she said General Lee was staying at the house, too, along with Longstreet and, and . . ."

"Grant. Didn't she say something about Grant?"

"Yeah, that's right. Her dying breath. It's all in the letters, all ten of 'em. And there was women."

"That's right! A network of spy women recruited from right here in Solace Glen. Right out of the Bell house by J.E.B. Stuart and General Lee and General Grant."

They twinkled at each other, thrilled with their combined version of impossible events.

Tom's jaw twitched. "Now that certainly is a history worthy of expert interpretation."

Nobody said much more after that. When the food ran out, so did Larry, Pal, and the Eggheads. Suggs had managed to evaporate into the atmosphere some time before without anyone noticing. They'd added nothing to the conversation or the gay social atmosphere Miss Fizzi and Louise had shot at and missed. Sam and Tom drifted out soon after with a promise to fish the Monocacy.

I folded plastic wrap on two lone celery sticks and stuck them in the refrigerator for Miss Fizzi to nibble on. Lee washed out the teapot, cups, and saucers; Louise dried. Miss Fizzi sipped a sherry.

"What an interesting character that Sam is," commented Louise. "So well traveled. So educated."

"So handsome. So polite," added Miss Fizzi. "Bilingual, too."

"What do *you* think, Lee?" Louise prodded her in the side with an elbow.

"Let's see," said Lee. "We have well traveled, good education, good-looking, good manners, and knows one Spanish word." With each item on the list, Louise and Miss Fizzi got more excited. "Yep." Lee popped the stopper out and the water slurped down the drain. "When's the wedding?"

"I don't know, dear," said Miss Fizzi. "Before or after he elopes with Flip, I suppose."

"Ohhhhh," Lee wiped her hands on a towel, checking me out. "So we're rivals?"

"Miss Fizzi is teasing." I pretended to be extremely busy opening and closing a drawer.

Miss Fizzi sipped away, ignoring me. "All I know is, you two girls need to work it out between yourselves."

"We could arm wrestle," I suggested.

Lee shrugged. "Or have a bathing suit contest."

"Or a wet T-shirt competition."

"Or a spitting tournament."

"Hush, both of you," Louise snapped. "You wear me out." Her tone contained enough edge in it to shut us up.

"It is getting late," said Lee. "I walked so I can't offer anybody a ride."

I offered Louise a lift right away, but she'd driven, too. "We'll talk later," she whispered in the hall, out of Lee's earshot.

Miss Fizzi escorted the three of us to the door and happily waved good-bye; in her mind, the little tea party a great success.

I drove home, listening to Larry's tape-recorded announcement of the Saturday night jazz lineup. George Winston. Earl Klugh. Billie Holiday. Diane Shurr. I couldn't wipe the scowl off my face.

Usually, Halloween launched me into a holiday mood that lasted straight through New Year's. My favorite part of the evening was flinging open that door, mouth wide, eyes round as pumpkins to spout, "Oooooo! Look at yooooooou! Aren't you the scariest bunch of Raggedy Ann's I ever saw! Here's a whole bag of chocolate bars and jelly beans!" That's the fun of Halloween. Like Christmas, it's an overload holiday, centering on children.

I pulled into the driveway and trudged to the front door, trying to work myself into the Halloween spirit before the trick-or-treaters arrived. The moment my fingers touched the knob, my stomach lurched. The door stood cracked. Someone had been inside my house.

I yelled through the screen, "Hello! Anybody in there?"

Nothing but silence. I walked slowly in.

A tornado might have done more damage, but I doubt it. Tables and chairs lay overturned. Drawers gaped. Paper cluttered the floor. Books torn from shelves. Pillows strewn across the floor. Everything from eye level down blown apart. Whoever tore apart my house kept his focus low.

I froze, breathless, as if movement might animate the chaos. Gradually, my breath returned. My fists clenched and unclenched. This was no Halloween prank. I walked in angry, long strides through the living room into the kitchen, knowing exactly where I needed to go.

I flicked on the kitchen light and zoomed in on the kitchen cabinet. The basket still sat on the roof of the cabinet, undisturbed, shoved slightly toward the wall as I'd left it. I shimmied onto the counter, reached up and pulled it down. The Bell family Bible lay safe and sound hidden under the Spanish moss, a baby Moses in its cradle. I stroked the Bible and remembered who Moses was: God's own tool in His plot to restore an inheritance.

Part Two

Chapter 15

The Monday lunch crowd hadn't filtered in yet. I walked quickly to my table behind the cash register, picked up the daily menu, and scribbled out an order on the notepad, my heart pounding.

I hadn't slept the Saturday night before; the mess in my house took care of that. I even considered skipping Sunday morning services and opting for TV church, but that's like having a side dish instead of the main course. God knows, I tried like crazy to concentrate on those high Presbyterian ideals and not on the hate building, spreading, seeping from every pore as I sang "O Come, My People, to My Law" and glared at the back of Roland Bell's neck two pews away. Who else could have been so brazen to try to steal back an inheritance? I could still hear his bizarre cackle over Joey's mysterious "accident." Anger clouded my vision, and I could barely read the words on the page. *A testimony and a law The Lord our God decreed, And bade our fathers teach their sons, That they His ways might heed.*

The whole time Reverend McKnight conducted the service, delivered the sermon, accepted our tithes, and benedictioned us out the door, I simmered, plotted, and calculated. By the end of the service, as McKnight glided down the aisle to the front door, I knew what I had to do.

Hilda finally showed up, busting out of her red T-shirt, make-up the same old clown face. She'd decided to play it safe and avoid conversation.

"Hilda," I gave her the notepaper that trembled in my hand, "is your daddy in today?"

The slightest encouragement and she burbled.

"Oh, yes, he is. He'll be back at the register in a minute, but would you like me to get him for you? I can look in the kitchen, and if he's not there, I can go upstairs to the office. He might be there if . . ."

"No, no. That's all right. I'll see him when I pay up." I whipped the pocket atlas out.

Hilda's lips dutifully clamped and she left me alone.

A trip to the Caribbean was just what I needed. After the house salad with blue cheese dressing and a pork chop with baked apples and green beans, all of which I barely touched, my trip measured out in the month-long range because I couldn't decide which islands to skip. *What would the exotic Charlie Scott do*, I wondered.

By the time I'd neglected a full meal and traveled half the Caribbean, the Café brimmed with customers, about a dozen strangers plus the usual staff and patrons: Louise and Miss Fizzi (Miss Fizzi proud to pay the bill herself), Tom and Ferrell T., Garland floating ghostlike through the kitchen, Hilda waiting tables, the Eggheads arguing over brands of flashlight batteries, Marlene and C.C. — the Ladies Who Lunch, Lee picking up a sandwich at the take-out counter, Screamin' Larry, in a wonderful humor since C.C.'s BMW took a dive, and Tina with Melody, both admiring Tina's big, gaudy peacock brooch. The only ones missing were Pal, who practically worked nonstop now; Margaret, holding court at the high school; Michael, waiting for Melody to bring him back a plate of something; and Sam, disappearing Mondays through Thursdays to Frederick to teach American history to young, nubile, good-looking college girls. Suggs, of course, never stepped foot in the Café; that might require him to speak.

And there, walking through the door like he owned the place, was Officer Lukzay. Before I launched into Plan B, I'd have to give Plan A a stab. I waited for the beer-gutted old grouch to sink into his chair, took a deep breath, and walked over.

"Officer Lukzay, I have a crime to report. But first," I presumptuously sat down across from him, "I'd like to hear how your investigation of Joey Sykes' 'accident' is going."

The bushy eyebrows met and he crammed a napkin into his collar. "You say the word like you don't believe it was an accident. What's that expert opinion based on?"

"The fact that the brakes didn't work and Pal had just fixed them."

"How do you know that dumb, juvenile hick thought to apply the brakes? I saw him myself come speeding down the hill into town like a bat outta hell. Car's totaled."

"Look out the window. You see any skid marks? And none of us heard a terrible screeching, did we?"

Lukzay rubbed the ends of his mustache and chortled. "You're a regular Nancy Drew."

I leaned into the table. "Can't you do something as simple as have the brakes checked? Or are you trying to protect somebody?"

The chortle froze in his throat. "You watch your mouth, missy. I'd be careful of who I accuse of what if I were you. Now why don't *you* do something simple like tell me what crime you have to report."

"My house was broken into Halloween night."

He snatched the menu Hilda handed him on the fly and opened it, creating a barrier between us. "Too bad. Kids these days do crazy things for fun."

"This wasn't a prank."

He huffed, "Another expert opinion from Miss Drew," and briefly lowered the menu. "I'll look into it. When I have the time."

Plan A dissolved in a heap. Officer "Look-away" went back to his menu — so much more important than any crime committed against the town maid — and I went back to my table to fetch my sweater. No sooner had I thrown it on than Roland reappeared behind the cash register to stand sentry over his kingdom. Routinely, I would pay the check at my table, sliding the meal dollars under the salt shaker and the tip money under the pepper. Not today. I filled my lungs with one long, deep breath and slowly exhaled. Time for Plan B.

Roland reached for the bill, smiling, more money in the bank, until he saw it was me at the register. He froze, scrawny fingers suspended in midair. The smile dried up.

I raised my head, screwed courage to the sticking place, and lightly touched one of his fingertips with the bill for $5.95.

"Not gonna grab it, Roland?" I snatched the bill away and turned up the volume so the whole audience could hear. "What's that? My meal is ON THE HOUSE?"

That was a conversation-stopper.

One of the Eggheads yelled out, "You giving Flip a free meal, Roland? What's the deal?"

Roland unhinged his jaws to bark but I jumped in first.

"He certainly is giving me a free meal!" I yelled back. I glared hard into Roland's shocked face, the vision of my wrecked house the only thing anchoring my feet to the floor. "He *owes* me. Don't you, Roland?"

"What the hell . . ."

Before he could finish, I called out, "Miss Fizzi, everything OK with you?"

"Yes, dear, fine." I'd thrown her a loop.

"Just wanted to make sure all your belongings are OK." I never took my eyes off Roland. "There's been a little trouble in the neighborhood lately."

"What kind of trouble?" One of the Eggheads wanted to know.

"A break-in."

"Who?" somebody asked.

"Me," I said. "Saturday night."

Roland snarled, "Tut, tut. What's that got to do with me?" He threw Lukzay a look as if to say, arrest her and her big mouth. Lukzay sneered back at me.

A knee buckled, but I called out loud and clear. "Lee, everything OK at your house?"

"So far," she replied, in sync with the situation.

I drew a bead on one of Roland's two pupils and aimed every syllable, willing my voice not to shake. "It had damn well better stay that way." I leaned across the counter and added for his ears alone, "And if anybody else's property gets torn up, totaled, or destroyed, anybody who happens to be in Leona's will, that is, we'll all know where to point a finger." I wadded up the bill and threw it at his feet.

Screamin' Larry burst into applause and pumped a fist in the air, always eager to encourage conflict, sports, or otherwise. "Yes! Bravo! Huzza, huzza!"

Roland glowered. "That'll *still* be $5.95, Miss Paxton!"

I ignored him and walked out, astonishing everybody, even myself. I had publicly accused Roland Bell of breaking and entering, destruction of property, and being a damn liar without aid from our local police or giving Roland a case for slander.

My only thought was, *Had I gone too far?*

That night, needing some comfort, I opened the Bell family Bible again. I ran my hands over the pages that contained Leona's family tree, touched the branches, slowly stroked the names of the people I'd thought about so far, wondered about, imagined what they looked like, how they talked, the clothes they wore.

Leona knew this comfort all her life, always knew the worth of her stock, knew the long ago names of the people she sprang from. Just as a living family is supposed to lend support and give you a sense of self-worth, a written history can do the job as well. Sometimes even better because a flesh-and-blood family can be tough to take at times, the way Roland bothered Leona all her life. Still, having a family history at all, written or walking like the Bells', beat living alone with only a paltry photograph album. The fading pictures of my mother and father did nothing but emphasize my own fading. Leona probably expected the Bell family Bible to put some color back in my life, to help fill the empty spaces. In a strange way, she was right.

Sara and Ferrell's only child, another Ferrell, born in 1828 after twenty years of waiting, married a German girl, Gretal Stubing, in 1850 when he was twenty-two and she, twenty. The German influence in central and western Maryland runs high. Lots of German names — people, towns, landmarks, streets. As far as I could tell, Gretal counted as the first instance of Germanic breeding in the Bell family. They probably needed it. I pictured Gretal Stubing Bell, a hard-working rural girl, hands hard as horseshoes, nagging Ferrell to get out of bed and go milk those cows so she and baby Roland, born 1851, could have fresh milk over their oatmeal at breakfast. I bet he did what she said.

Ferrell lived seventy-one years, dying before the turn of the century in 1899. He was thirty-three when the Civil War started, thirty-seven when it ended, so he probably enlisted. Maybe he and his cousin, John Bell Paca, enlisted together. Maybe they fought on opposite sides. Maybe a bullet from Ferrell's gun ended up in John's heart or liver. Not probable or likely, but stranger things have happened. I wondered what life offered up to Gretal at home in Maryland with a ten-year-old boy during the war. That child grew up fast, no doubt, performing his daddy's chores.

Gretal died in 1908 at the age of seventy-eight. In that time, she witnessed twenty-two states enter the Union and lived through a war that nearly destroyed it. The year she was born, Sir Walter Scott wrote *Letters on Demonology and Witchcraft*; the year she died, H.G. Wells published *New Worlds for Old*.

Most of us don't appreciate the changes we live through. We can barely recall most historical events, things that occurred twenty years before, as if our memories were news magazines stacked high in a corner, never opened or referred to after that first, brief glimpse.

Gretal Stubing Bell and her generation might have been different. I don't know. She lived through a major war and the industrial revolution. Horse and buggy to Model T. On her deathbed, she might have lain back on the pillow and sighed, "O Lord, the sights I've seen! The sights my son will see!"

I'll never know, but I'd like to think she did. I touched her name lightly with one finger, then Ferrell's, then John Bell Paca's. Their names, scratched in ink so long ago, couldn't completely fill the empty spaces, replace the family I'd lost or become the family I'd given up hopes of ever having, but somehow those names, now in my keeping, did give a kind of comfort. That alone was more than I'd ever asked for or come to expect.

Chapter 16

Even though Louise lay pale and listless, propped up against her bed pillows, she felt talkative.

"No need to change the sheets this morning, Flip. I actually had the energy to do it last night."

I quit fiddling with a dusty picture of Marlene, age twelve, braces in her mouth and jodhpurs on her bottom. "What are you doing wearing yourself out like that? You know I do it every Tuesday. Plus," I shook a finger at her, "you've been going out too much lately, gallivanting around with Miss Fizzi."

"Well." She examined her hands, so small and white, as if surprised they belonged to her. "I've a right to enjoy myself. But after lunch yesterday, I had a feeling I wouldn't want to get out of bed today, so I went ahead and did the sheets."

I frowned. "You been to the doctor lately?"

"Doctors don't help any more, Flip," she said wearily. "But I take comfort in knowing I can slip away peacefully in my own home. Now, tell me what gave you the courage to make such a scene at the Café yesterday. Everybody thinks you've gone plum crazy, including Roland."

"I must have because there's no other explanation for me getting in his face."

"You certainly got the town talking."

"Then I accomplished something." My face turned serious. "Roland's the one who's gone crazy, Louise, wrecking my house the way he did." I didn't tell her my suspicions about him tampering with the brakes in Pal's car.

"Are you *sure* it was Roland?" she whispered, as though somebody might be hiding under the bed, listening.

"If he didn't do it himself, he hired somebody. That would be just like him — pay a few bucks to some drug addict off the street in Baltimore to rip apart a woman's belongings. And for what? A Bible that normally he wouldn't shake a stick at. He's sure never read one."

"Flip," she pursed her lips a moment, "do you think he might go after Miss Fizzi? Or Lee?"

I chewed on my cheek awhile, not wanting to upset her, already sorry I'd conjured up images of rampaging drug addicts. "I can't for the life of me think what he could do to Miss Fizzi, the way things are set up, with a trust and all. He can't get at the trust. Lee . . . I don't know."

Honest enough words, but as soon as I said them, I wanted to rake them back in. Me and my big mouth. Louise started to whimper, wringing her hands, shaking her head.

"No, no," I tried to soothe her. "Don't misunderstand me. Lee is a strong, independent person. Don't go getting all upset over something that's not going to happen. And she's got plenty of good people watching out for her."

"Like who! She lives alone except for a big, weird doll and a useless cat, for God's sake!"

"Well, Sam, for one." I hated to admit it. "And Tom."

"Oh, Tom," Louise rolled her eyes and chuckled. "He's as good-looking and sophisticated as James Bond, but not exactly prone to kicking doors down."

Tom might surprise you one day, I thought. I swiped at a ladybug kissing Marlene's face, age fourteen.

"Sam, though." Louise smiled as sly as a coyote, obviously cheered by this particular theme. "Sam's a different story. You know he's been calling her on the phone."

"Oh, yes," I replied, too sharp, "and I'm sure he'd turn into Superman for Lee if he had to."

"Oooooo," she shook a finger at me. "I spy a green monkey on somebody's back."

"I don't have time for green monkeys." My shoulders drooped. "I'm tired. That's all. I've had a full three days."

Louise eyed me quietly. "You need some recreation, Flip. Why don't you take a day off and go to Baltimore? Get some nice seafood. Have your hair done while you're at it." She scowled and tilted her head, "And buy yourself a new wardrobe. We're all sick to death of seeing you in the same things."

"Gee, thanks." But suddenly, I wanted nothing

more. "You're right." I jammed the dust rag in my carryall and hoisted it up. "If you don't mind, I'll clean your kitchen and be gone. I might even call and cancel my appointments for tomorrow."

"Good for you! Get the hell out of Dodge."

She was absolutely right. I needed to get the hell out of Dodge.

Nothing inspired my mood like throwing on a dress, taking my one credit card out of the sock drawer, and heading for the big city. Admittedly, such an adventure didn't crop up every day. But once or twice a year, besides my normal vacation to Ocean City in July, I would go a little nuts and treat myself. If I made the one day special enough, it could feel like a long weekend holiday.

I lolled in an overstuffed chair in the safari bar at the Harbor Court Hotel, staring out of the huge picture window at the sunset water view. The *Clipper City* sat moored to a dock while motor boats and water taxis scurried behind her through the waters of Baltimore's Inner Harbor. Little lights began to twinkle in the twilight.

Checking into a fine hotel for one night with room service, maid service, dining service, and bar service could turn any maid-in-waiting into a pampered queen. I loved drinking champagne out of the tall flute glass, watching the tourist boats shuttle back and forth. I loved the bartender keeping a protective eye on me, sending the waitress over now and then to see what they could get for me. More cashews, ma'am? Is this bottle of Taittinger cold enough for you, ma'am? Would you like an appetizer with that? Caviar? Shrimp? Crab cocktail? Would you like a bellboy to take those expensive-looking shopping bags to your room?

I sat on the ugly, worn, black handbag I'd owned practically since high school, hiding it from view, the pocket atlas inside. When I felt looped enough, I'd take the atlas out and go to Brazil. In the meantime, Baltimore, Maryland, suited me just fine.

Even though I'd arrived in a nice enough dress, I decided to really splurge and buy something I'd never owned: a suit. I found something half price, a little designer number at the Gallery, and I couldn't stand not to wear it immediately. So there I sat in the safari bar showing off a sea green silk suit, short skirt, long jacket, a new shell-pink blouse underneath. I'd even bought a pair of pointy shoes and gotten my hair done, figuring Christmas tips would cover the difference. No handbag, though. I had to draw the line somewhere.

Of all the ridiculous things to pop into my head at that moment — swishing bubbles around in the glass, appreciating the color of light on the water, admiring the pointy toe of my new shoes — I thought about Roland's Café and whether I'd ever be able to eat there again.

Half of me said yes, Roland couldn't turn away a dollar to save his life; half of me said no, he could not forgive what I did or said in front of all those people. With Roland, forgiveness never figured into the equation.

I shifted a hip to one side of the chair and slowly pulled at the old handbag. The strap stuck and I tugged harder.

"Flip? My goodness. It is you!"

My arm jerked at the sound of Tom's voice and the ugly purse flew like a startled crow, into his face. Tom reached to his bruised nose with one hand and retrieved my handbag with the other.

I sprang up. "Are you all right?"

He held the bag out for me, dabbing the space between his eyes. "Fine. Fine. Funny thing. Nothing to worry about."

He blinked a few times and focused.

"You sure your eyes are OK?" They fluttered uncontrollably.

"No," he said. "I'm not sure I see what I'm seeing. Flip, you are a vision. I mean, you are . . . stunning."

I reached for the handbag and maneuvered it discreetly behind my hip. "I clean up good as anybody."

"Much better, I'd say." He smiled that magazine smile. "Hope you've recovered from your break-in. That's an unsettling thing, even as a Halloween trick. Did you report it to Lukzay?"

I nodded mutely. Why spoil one of my rare

evenings of luxury whining about lazy Officer Look-away? Stumped for conversation, I examined the bubbles in my glass.

Tom leaned forward and gently took my elbow. "And the blush is very becoming, too. Sit down, sit down."

The waitress must have thought we were together because she sprinted out of thin air in a flash. "An extra glass for the gentleman? Or would he prefer a cocktail?"

Tom appeared perfectly at ease. "He'll take the extra glass and, ah, another bottle of what the lady ordered." He plopped into the cushy chair opposite mine as though he belonged there and pulled the bottle from the ice. "Taittinger. You have excellent taste in champagne, Flip." The hawk eyes settled on me. "I wonder where you acquired it."

For once, he didn't ask a question outright, but he may as well have.

"That's a sneaky way to ask the town maid how she knows anything about the finer things in life. What champagne to drink, what nice hotel to stay in, the right kind of clothes to wear." I aimed the point of my new shoe at him accusingly. "I think maybe it's time I get to ask the questions."

The waitress sidled up to him with a flute glass and another ice bucket of champagne. She filled his glass from my bottle, inquired if we wanted the other one opened, and zipped away when Tom said, no, he preferred to pop the cork himself on this occasion. I wondered what sort of occasion he thought it was.

He held up the glass. "Fire away."

"What brings you to Baltimore?"

"I'm a lawyer. They have courtrooms here."

"What brings you to this hotel?"

"A meeting with an out-of-town client."

"Male or female?"

"Male. Unfortunately."

"What brings you to this bar?"

"I wanted to relax with a drink after a long day of jousting with a hostile court and an uncooperative client."

"Come here often?"

"Not often enough."

"Why haven't you ever asked Lee out?" The heart of the case. The Right Question.

He opened his mouth to speak, closed it, stared through the golden liquid in his glass and took a long swallow. "Only recently have I felt this attraction. I'm not sure how real it is or what to do about it."

I didn't know whether to laugh at him or pat his hand. How could a man with Tom's looks and abilities have the slightest struggle of indecision about a woman?

"Tom." I shook my head. "How old are you?"

"Older than you. Certainly older than Lee."

"Then don't be such a schoolboy." Now was my chance to salvage the best for myself. "Ask her to something that doesn't seem like a date."

His eyes rolled skyward. "A county bar meeting, perhaps."

He wasn't getting it. "It is rumored by drunks and thieves that lawyers *are* fun, but I doubt she'd see the humor."

"I'm overwhelmed by the compliment. What then, counselor? We don't even go to the same church."

The image of Tom and Lee sliding next to each other at a pancake prayer breakfast made my throat contract.

I drew the Taittinger out of the ice, finished it off, and stuck the bottle upside down in the bucket.

"My cue." He rubbed fingers together like a safe cracker and expertly pried open the cork in the second bottle.

All the time, my mind raced. What were Tom's hobbies? His interests? His sports? As the cork slipped out with a smooth, enticing hiss, I blurted, "Why don't you take her fishing?"

I expected to hear "Objection, Your Honor," but his face softened. "That may not be such a bad idea."

I worked up some enthusiasm. "It beats a bar meeting. Or a prayer breakfast. And it's not so romantic that she'd get suspicious."

Tom leaned back in the overstuffed chair, deftly loosened his silk tie, and beamed. "Flip. I toast you. You're a genius."

Genius. What a laugh. Devious, mean, backstabbing — yes. And for what? For the minute chance I could get Sam interested in me instead of Lee.

"You still have to ask her out. And she still has to say yes. But I don't mind accepting a toast. I deserve it for other reasons."

With questions in Tom's searing, dark eyes, we both drank to me. Me in my pretty new suit, queen for the day. Me, the maid of Solace Glen, living the high life at the Harbor Court. Me, the caregiver, the peacekeeper, the listener. The good friend. The very good friend.

Chapter 17

Roland was nowhere to be seen when I spied Lee sitting at my table behind the cash register finishing a meal. I took a deep breath and made a beeline for the chair beside her.

"So." I slid behind a menu, one eye on the lookout for Roland, one eye catching Officer Lukzay's grimace. "What's new with you?"

"Not much." She kept her nose in *The Sotweed Factor*. "I'm supposed to meet with Sam and his expert about the letters next Friday."

"Good." I scribbled an order. "You seem pretty matter-of-fact about it. Aren't you excited?"

She lay the book down and thought a moment. "I'm mostly curious, I guess. Curious to know if J.E.B. Stuart really wrote them. Curious who the woman was he wrote to because they're . . . they're so beautiful, aren't they, Flip?"

I nodded, remembering.

"And I'm curious about why the Bell women kept the letters such a closely guarded secret. I don't get it. And why only the women in the family?"

I thought about the Bible on my kitchen cabinet. "Beats me. The names on the family tree can't exactly talk."

We sat there, shaking our heads in puzzlement. Finally, I sighed. "So, what else is new?"

"I decided to get Jeb spayed."

"Always a good idea."

"I accepted Tom's invitation to go fishing Saturday."

"Gooood."

The hazel eyes bore into me. "What do you mean by that? Nice hair."

"What do *you* mean? Thanks."

"That 'good' had a little something extra on it."

"I'm sure I don't understand," I said primly. Then I added under my breath, a very loud breath, "Except Tom is becoming quite the ladies' man." There. I'd opened the door to the lie. Devious. Mean. Backstabbing.

"Whoa, whoa, whoa." Lee flung her book to the side. "Tom Scott, a ladies' man?"

"Uh-huh." I fooled with a pencil.

"Our Tom Scott? The legal eagle who probably wears a suit to bed?"

"Trust me. He has a way of loosening a tie that sends a tingle to your toes." I swallowed hard and fast. "I ran into him when I was having a drink in Baltimore at the Harbor Court."

"Whooo-eeee," she shook her wrist. "The Hawba Coort."

"Yes, it was very nice, thanks for asking. And Tom strolled into the bar with a really tall,

161

good-looking model-type woman clamped on him tight as an oyster and she was laughing like crazy. He must be real funny when he's out of town."

"I can well imagine."

"And this woman, this girl-child, couldn't keep her hands off him. I mean, it was embarrassing."

Lee bought every word. "What was he doing?"

"Tom? Eating it up, of course. Having the *best* time. Bought a bottle of champagne. Was running his finger sloooowly up and down her leg. She had on a real short skirt, up to here. Was nipping at her neck. She had cleavage down to there." I jabbed my diaphragm with the pencil.

Lee's eyes popped wide, "Ohhh myyy Looord! Did he see you?"

"No, I was hiding behind a palm tree." Once I stuck my toe through the door, who was there to stop me? "But when she got up to go to the ladies' room, I followed her."

"You didn't!"

"Oh, yes. I wanted a close-up, you know. So there I was, standing at the mirror, pinching my cheeks, a regular Scarlett O'Hara, and she walks over to reapply her makeup."

"Did you talk to her?"

"Of course. Struck up quite the conversation. I said, 'Why, I used to have a blouse just like that.' "

162

Lee clapped a hand over her mouth, stifling a yelp.

"Said she got it at Neiman Marcus and that's where she met her date."

"Tom?" She slapped her thigh. "At Neiman Marcus?"

"In the lingerie department."

She slapped the other thigh. "Get out! What was he doing?"

"Buying panties for another woman. Asked her opinion, then asked her out."

"What a wolf!"

"That's not all. She said he ended up buying those panties for her and she was wearing them right then and had promised to model for him in their suite later on."

Lee beat the heel of her hand on the table. "NO!NO!NO! This is not our Tom Scott!"

"Keep it down." Tom walked in with Ferrell T. I slid my eyes sideways until Lee saw him, too. "I tell you, Lee," I hissed, "he's one of those Jekyll and Hyde types who goes out of town and turns into a sex maniac. And the women *love* him."

"I'll be damned," she said in a disbelieving voice, but believing every word. "Gaaaa, what should I wear on this fishing trip?"

"Something revealing," I suggested, such a big help. "You'll be out of town."

She peeped at Tom over one shoulder, nose wrinkled up like a bunny's. "I know. I'm excited."

163

I'll show you excited, I thought. Excited is what Tom's going to be if he ever finds out about this. He might even get excited enough to chop my head off.

Hilda swooped by and grabbed my order. While I was planning my funeral, Sam strolled in. Lee was too busy stealing glances at Tom and readjusting her image of him to notice. But I did.

Fingers flew to my hair and started fluffing. I couldn't quit wetting my lips. I pulled at a bra strap under my sweater, tugged my shirt down tighter, straightened my spine, lifted my chin. Smiled like I was running for Miss Maryland. If anyone had shown me a video of myself later, I'd have thrown up.

He didn't even look our way. Nodded politely at the Eggheads, Garland, Hilda, Reverend McKnight and Father Gower, made his way straight to Tom and Ferrell T., shook hands, and flopped into a chair.

"Is that Sam?" Lee twisted full around. "What's he doing here?"

"Must have a luncheon date with Tom." A different spin came to mind and I added suggestively, "Maybe there's something we don't know."

Lee snickered. "I don't know about Tom, but Sam's *definitely* more interested in bra straps than jock straps."

"Oh. Really." I glared at the back of her head. More than anything at that moment, I wished

Lee was ugly. I imagined car wrecks, flying glass and terrible operations. Skin grafts and the immutable tracks of stitches crisscrossing flesh. Then I remembered Henry and Marie, Jake and Leona. That was all it took.

"Why don't you go over and say hello?"

The edges of Lee's lips curled. "Ooo, what a good suggestion." She oozed out of the chair and slithered across the room to where Tom and Sam sat unsuspecting, ankles boyishly crossed over their knees. Spanky and Alfalfa.

I must say, Henry and Marie would have been proud of their girl. I crouched in the chair, mesmerized, while the custodian of the Historical Society played two men against each other like the bookie at a cockfight. Ferrell T., of course, didn't figure into it, a sack of potatoes with a bow tie. His only reaction to Lee was annoyance at the interruption.

Chairs scraped and four eyes lit up. Two mouths tried to speak at once. Four hands grabbed a chair, pulling it tug-of-war for the golden girl to sit on. Four ears waited to hear the magic. Two egos pawed at the gate of the pen.

Lee ate it up, confident of Sam's interest and believing my lie that other women pursued Tom. Both plots intrigued her.

Hilda dropped off my lunch, but I couldn't eat for watching the show. Lee barely glimpsed in Sam's direction, that territory already conquered. Instead, she aimed all weapons at Tom

— the dazzling smile, the starry eyes, the flip of her auburn hair, the cock of her pretty chin. She even reached out at one point and touched his arm. I thought the man would blast out of his chair, toes flapping like propeller blades, steam pouring out of each ear. Frankly, the whole scene made me feel sort of sorry for Tom, even though Lee was delivering what I'd paid for. A jiggly ankle signaled the only give-away of Sam's jealousy.

When Lee stood to go, the Little Rascals popped out of their seats like jack-in-the-boxes, bowing and scraping. Her performance had been perfect and the exit would have been, too, but she backed straight into Roland coming the other way. The laughing face turned bitter.

"Ex*cuse* me, Mr. Bell." She shook him off as she would a nasty horsefly.

Roland possessed none of the basic social skills. He pointed at Sam. "That the man you got living in my family's house, isn't it? Sam Gibbon?"

"It's my house and it's none of your damn business." She started to go, but Roland clamped onto an elbow.

"I'm not finished with you yet. What're you doing about those letters?"

Lee wrestled her arm away from him. "What the hell is it to you, Roland?"

By this time, both Sam and Tom began closing the distance between them and Roland, flashing that protective warning sign men get in their eyes. Roland measured their interest and drew a few inches away from Lee. His tone mellowed instantly.

"Just curious, like everybody else in town. My offer to you still stands. After all, if it weren't for Flip, you wouldn't even have those letters. They'd be mine by right." He shifted his gaze from Lee to me, the brave soul hiding behind her iced tea. "Ain't that right, Flip?" The harsh tone returned.

Lee would have none of it. "Flip was nothing more than Leona's messenger and you know it, Roland, so don't you go attacking her." There I sat, Lee's Judas, intent on going after Sam, and she still came to my aid. I said nothing and let her do all the talking. "Anyway, those letters might amount to zilch. We'll know soon enough."

"What's that supposed to mean?"

I watched as the Eggheads rose from their seats, Roland's Greek chorus on the subject of the letters. "You getting that expert from the Smithsonian to look at 'em, Lee?" one sang. "That friend of Sam's?"

Garland stepped out of the kitchen, wiping her hands on a dishtowel, forehead creased.

"Oh, Sam Gibbon's involved in this thing now, is he?" spat Roland. "A perfect stranger! Get back in the kitchen, woman! This is none of your concern!"

Garland zipped through the swinging door and disappeared.

"Well hell, Lee, why not turn all the Bell property over to him right now?"

"Maybe I will." Lee stepped a foot closer and Roland matched the move.

Finally, somebody with some sense took over.

"Lee, go home." Tom edged between Roland and Lee with the ease of Fred Astaire and whisked her toward the door. To Roland, he smoothly suggested that the service appeared slow today and could he check on their table's orders in the kitchen. Then he escorted Lee through the door and out on the street where I saw him motion her to trot on home as he would a truant caught hanging around the candy store during school.

He walked back to his table, sat down, and calmly resumed his conversation with Sam, who plopped into his chair with a lop-sided grin, and Ferrell T., who had not risen an inch from his spot.

I twisted my watchband between nervous fingers. With Lee gone, I had no idea what tune Roland might play. I gobbled lunch, threw money at the plate and would have made a clean getaway, but for Reverend McKnight asking how I was getting along since the break-in. Roland came barging out of the kitchen. He made straight for me.

The whole of my scalp tingled, and the food I'd gulped so fast rose in my throat.

He hesitated when he recognized McKnight

and stopped in his tracks the moment Sam stepped into his path.

"Flip, I've been meaning to ask you something." Sam picked up the carryall as if he always scooped it up, a boy carrying his girl's schoolbooks. He started walking, motioning me to slide along beside him. Side by side we bustled past Roland with his popping veins and flinty eyes.

I met Sam stride for stride until we were outside where I swallowed a mouthful of fresh air.

"Thank you, Sam." I took the carryall from his hand, eyes on the sidewalk. "That was very kind."

"Don't thank me." He skipped backward into the Café, relishing the game. "Tom thought you could use a friendly face."

My head jerked up. I stared at the closed door a moment, whipped around, and marched to my car, teeth gritted, ears ringing. It wasn't Sam. It wasn't Sam rescuing me at all. He'd only helped out because Tom Scott thought I could *use a friendly face*. Well, thanks a lot, Tom Scott! How very, very kind of you!

As I stepped into my horrible car, Sam's voice called out. I looked up to see him running down the street. "Oh, by the way, I really did have something to ask you!"

He pulled up a few feet from the car. "How about a fishing trip Saturday? You up to showing me the Monocacy?"

He was using me. Using me to spy on Tom

and Lee. Using me to get Lee jealous. Did he think I didn't know?

"Sure!" I called out, bright as a Christmas star, summoning everything I had to cover the catch in my voice. "You got yourself a date!"

Not that Sam Gibbon considered me his date, but that could change. He was, after all, giving Judas her chance.

Chapter 18

Sally Polk, Solace Glen's barber and beautician *extraordinaire,* understood perfectly why I got my hair done once a year in Baltimore and once a year with her.

"I know that hell-out-of-Dodge feeling, honey," she'd drawl through her chewing gum. "I won the Hell-Out-of-Dodge pageant."

A year younger than me, Sally had lived a pretty packed life for a forty-one-year-old woman. Born in North Carolina, a speedway queen at seventeen, married to a NASCAR driver at eighteen, pregnant with twins at nineteen, divorced at twenty-one, remarried three times before thirty-five, now on husband number five and pregnant out to here.

"What are *you* doing here?" She popped her gum in my direction as she worked on Miss Fizzi.

"Don't you remember?" asked Miss Fizzi. "I'm having my hair done."

Sally threw her head back and almost choked on her Wrigley's. "No, Miss Fizzi. Flip just walked in. See?" She swiveled the chair around so Miss Fizzi could eyeball me. "She got her hair done in the big city. Her next appointment here isn't for six months. What's the deal, Flip? That break-in make you go crazy?"

I slipped into a chair next to Margaret who politely put aside her magazine for conversation. Melody waved one freshly polished hand at me while Tina worked on the other one. They all waited for a logical explanation to my bizarre behavior. I could tell they wanted to discuss the break-in, too.

"Maybe I've decided to get my hair done once a week like all of you."

"And maybe the Pope's Jewish," said Melody.

"Or maybe I've decided to pamper myself more often."

They weren't buying it.

"Or?" asked Margaret, skeptically.

"Or," I pretended to search for a magazine, "maybe I have a date."

"A date!" Melody jumped in her chair, eyes large and mouth open, the same reaction as when she thought I was engaged — equally impossible announcements.

Tina yanked her hand down. "Melody, you'll smear." But she could hardly contain herself, either. "Who is he, Flip? Somebody you met in Baltimore? You can't date somebody from Baltimore without makeup. Oh, I hope that's why you came in!"

Poor Tina. We both knew she'd never get me in that makeup chair.

"No," I cut her off. "I had a little time and I

thought maybe Sally could work me in at the end of her day for a touch up."

"Want that freshly made look, do ya?" Sally gleamed as she finished up Miss Fizzi's standard coiffure. "Who is the gentleman, pray tell?"

Miss Fizzi tried her hand at guessing. "Pal? Jesse? Jules?"

I was surprised she didn't say Suggs. With each guess, my nose wrinkled tighter.

"Oh, Miss Fizzi," Margaret sighed, "Flip has some taste. All those boys are too young for her."

As if I could only attract centenarians.

"You'll at least want a manicure," suggested Tina, desperate to do something, anything, to improve the pitiful town maid.

"Noooo," I said between clenched teeth. "Could you give me a wash and blow dry, Sally?"

"Only for you, hon. You're *finito*, Miss Fizzi. Hit the highway."

Both Margaret and Miss Fizzi knit their brows together. Miss Fizzi because she could not understand half of Sally's slang expressions, and Margaret because she thoroughly disapproved of the uncouth tone.

"You're up, Margaret." Sally took a long drink from a Mountain Dew while she waved Miss Fizzi out the door.

"You mean, 'You're next, Miss Henshaw,' or 'It is your turn now, Miss Henshaw.' "

Sally shrugged, a good-humored grin on her face. "Whatever, hon." She had not had the

173

benefit of Margaret's grammar and public speaking class.

The subject turned to concern over my break-in and expressions of doubt whether Officer Lukzay would get off his lazy butt and investigate. None of them could imagine Roland taking the risk of criminal conviction for a Bible, of all things, and assured me the ransacking held all the marks of wild teenagers on a trick-or-treat rampage. I wasn't convinced.

Thankfully, the subject switched back to the topic on everyone's lips before I walked in — C.C. and Leonard. I joined in, hoping I could avoid the dating inquisition and keep my date's identity a secret. If things went as planned, my romance would be a nice surprise for everyone later on. If the whole thing fizzled, no need to embarrass myself further.

"What I don't get," said Tina, apparently picking up where she'd left off, "is why Solace Glen? Why do we have to be the town to get C.C. and Leonard? We usually have such nice people move here." Under her breath she added, "Except for Suggs, of course."

"Tell me about it," Melody took over. "That Leonard, that fox in Brooks Brothers clothing, he comes into the store and orders Michael around like he's a lowly office boy. Lemme see this. Lemme see that. I was thinking, OK, Mr. Tall and Handsome Big Bucks, show us the money, but nothing. Didn't buy a thing after all that ordering. Just questions, all the time questions."

"What sort of questions?" My ears perked up.

"Wanting to know about certain people."

"People with Civil War letters?"

Melody emphasized each syllable. "And others."

"What others?"

"Like you, for instance."

My cheeks burned and my stomach lurched. "Me? Why would Leonard Crosswell want to know about me?"

Everyone wore concerned faces. We all sensed a malevolent air about Leonard.

Melody went on with her story. "At first he made it sound like he simply wanted to check out your references before you came into his house. But then he mentioned your inheritance from Leona, as if old Bibles really knock his silk socks off, and wondered in an oh-so-innocent manner what else you got in the way of old publications. Then he had the nerve to ask, is it certain *all* Leona's old papers are accounted for? Does the man who lives in the house — Sam Gibbon — does he have any control over things or is it all Lee's?"

Margaret could not believe her ears. "Of all the gall! What is that man thinking?"

"He gives me the shivers." Tina's large body shuddered dramatically. "You better watch it, Flip."

A picture of my wrecked house came to mind and I began to wonder.

"If ya want my opinion . . ." Sally stopped

175

combing Margaret's hair and tapped the comb against the sink to knock out the strands. "Lee's the real target. I mean, that Bible's not worth anything, is it, Flip?"

"To me it is."

She raised one shoulder. "Well, sure, but maybe Leonard knows something you don't. At any rate," she tilted the chair back and Margaret's head disappeared into the sink, "Lee's the one with the most goods. He'll go where the money is. That's his type."

I rubbed the back of my neck, suddenly tense and tight. "Yeah, that is his type. I better warn Lee about him."

The topic of conversation changed again, the usual comments about Marlene and how badly she treated Louise. The deteriorating health of Louise. Poor Joey Sykes and what in the world was he thinking driving so fast? Bets on what Larry would finally do to get back at C.C. Whether Charlie Scott would ever return to Solace Glen. Whether Marlene's mysterious ex-husband would ever show up and beg her to come back — that one always left us laughing.

My sense of humor evaporated, though, when I left Sally's and got back behind the wheel. WFIB played "I Get Along Without You Very Well."

One thing was sure. We could all get along very well without Leonard Crosswell.

Chapter 19

Mid-November in central Maryland can catch your breath in the early morning. Frost strikes with predictability and dead leaves, no longer in the crisp and crunchy state, cover the ground, soaking up moisture, wet and black. Snow is a promise in the air, right around the corner of the breeze.

I knew exactly where Tom would take Lee — a boat landing just off Route 15. If they took two cars, they could cover more distance canoeing downstream, but I figured for this first time, he'd want to drive her; he'd have a captive audience.

Sam picked me up in his decrepit jeep. It stank of raw shrimp and vanilla air freshener. I named the boat landing and we took off, the sun peeping over bare hills and stripped cornfields outside of town. I cracked the window to let in sweet, crisp air and stared at the landscape flashing by. If Sam wanted to use me to make Lee jealous, fine. I'd lead him to the object of his desire and make him compare. The slim chance did exist he'd find my company easier to take. To give myself a little head start, I'd packed a picnic that included a jug of red wine.

Sam and I had pulled the same things out of the drawer that morning: jeans, plaid flannel shirt, down vest, hiking boots, and heavy socks, but even with the same outfit, he looked L.L. Bean, I looked Kmart. At least my hair shone, and the gold hoops added a feminine touch to my drab appearance. I tugged at a thread on my sleeve and silently carried on a conversation. *You should have seen me in my silk suit at the Harbor Court. Boy, was I a hot property.*

"You and Tom good friends?"

The question took me by surprise. "Yes and no. It's only been the past ten years or so we've had any real conversation." I fiddled with the thread on my sleeve.

"Ten plus years is a long time for an answer like 'yes and no.' Seems you ought to know by now."

I jerked the thread and ripped a hole in the shirt.

"Well," he wouldn't let go, "is it more yes or more no?"

I rolled the sleeve up over the hole. "Tom makes me nervous. He's real smart and blue-blooded, so I feel like a poor, dumb relation most of the time."

My arms hugged my chest, the air blowing in from the window cold against my face. I didn't know what more to say.

Sam let the silence flow awhile then quietly commented, "Lee told me how much you like to read." I didn't respond so he continued, dropping all pretense of interest in my hobbies. "I've spent a lot of time on the telephone with her. I've asked her to a few things at the college. She doesn't seem interested. Then I run into her and we're on a totally different level, get along great. I get encouraged, call and ask her to something. She declines. I'm spinning in a circle with this woman and I want to break through, you know? I just want a normal *date*. Doesn't she date?"

"Sure." I got a little huffy. "She's out fishing with Tom this morning." My fingernail scratched at a dead leaf stuck in the window. "Same as we're out together."

He remained quiet a minute then said, "To be honest, I was hoping you could help me with Lee. Not that I don't think you're good company. I think you're great. . . ."

I turned and looked him right in the eye. No more shy glances or shuffling feet. He'd laid his cards on the table, so would I. "You asked me out because I'm Lee's best friend."

"Well, yeah." He took his eyes off the road long enough to toss me a helpless look, as if he knew I'm a sucker for that look every time.

"Mmm. I figured you were just trying to make her jealous, because I'm so stunning and everything, but I decided to come, anyway, because . . ." I hoped my voice wouldn't crack, "I think you're a really nice guy."

"Thank you. I mean that, Flip. And if you could give me any advice, I'd really appreciate

179

it." He blew out a breath. "I thought for awhile she was playing hard to get. But she ain't playing."

So there it was. My bubble burst. Sam Gibbon harbored no more interest in me than the road sign we'd just passed. I could give information; I was a means to an end. At least he was nice about it, honest, and I could do with a day on the Monocacy with good company.

In the back of my mind, though, I couldn't help holding onto that thin sliver of hope that he still might pick me at the end of the day.

The scenery passed by quickly. Church steeples on hilltops in the distance, clapboard farm houses with red barns and rusty silos, Canada geese blanketing the chopped brown fields. We took the Creagerstown exit off Route 15, arrived at the landing, unloaded Sam's canoe and all our gear at water's edge, and parked the jeep under some trees.

For a waterman's son, Sam didn't possess much in the way of fancy fishing equipment: one busted up, plastic tackle box crammed with lures, lines, and hooks and two disassembled reel poles that he spliced together before we climbed into the aluminum canoe.

"You sure there aren't any holes in this thing?" The canoe looked like something he'd scavenged at a flea market for fifty cents, the color of a thundercloud, dents and dings pocked each side. "Where are the life preservers?"

He pulled something out of a ragged duffel bag stamped U.S. ARMY.

"What's that?"

"A life preserver, what do you think?"

I punched two thumbs in the rust-colored vest. They sank into the crumbly insides without resistance. "What vintage?" Besides the normal fear of furry spiders, hooded snakes, and long-toothed rodents, I held a healthy respect for the power of running water.

"Not to worry." Sam delivered a tightlipped, reassuring teacher's smile, dealing with yet another pupil, scared how she'll do on an exam. "We'll stay close to shore."

One of the belts fell off in my hand. It couldn't save a Chihuahua. Nevertheless, I popped the moldy preserver over my head, gripped a paddle and climbed into the bow of the canoe. Sam pushed us into the river and jumped toward the stern, steering for the current.

The Monocacy runs slow and easy in mid-November, slightly up from the autumn rains, not fat and hurried as in the spring. The current, a small resolve against the press of a paddle, pulled gently beneath my knees.

"Go upstream," directed Sam, and we lined up our oars parallel to the riverbank, easily pushing the boat northward. "Not too bad, is it?"

The fungus smell of the life preserver was dizzying. I tossed it behind me. "No. Not too bad. So far."

It was barely eight o'clock, and I hadn't eaten breakfast. We slid into a little cove. Slick, black tree branches stuck out of the water where they'd broken off from the trees that encircled the bend of the river. I reached into the picnic basket and grabbed a sandwich.

Sam helped himself to a bag of chips, idly fixing a neon yellow glowworm onto a hook. "Do much fishing?"

"Nope. I like my water in a tub or a glass."

He lightly flicked the rod backward and let go of the line on the downswing. The smooth *zing* of the reel and the plunk of the lure broke the monotonous gurgling of the river. "This is most pleasant," he sighed.

I had to admit, alone in a beautiful place with a handsome man — there were worse things in life. I nibbled the sandwich, content, watching the swirls in the river, the play of morning light, hoping Tom and Lee wouldn't show up.

"What's your favorite era in history?" The reel clicked as Sam wound in the line.

Good God, a test. "I thought men didn't like to talk when they fished."

"Oh, I've always associated fishing with deep, honest conversation. I used to ask my dad a million questions about fishing and life and death and sports and women. He listened. Told me what he knew about each painful subject."

I examined the pole at my feet. "Sounds like the two of you were close."

"Your mom and dad died when you were in high school, right?"

Lee must have told him my life story. "Yeah, young enough to be completely devastated. Old enough to fight to live on my own."

"You won the battle and lost the war?"

"I thought living alone at age eighteen would be a kind of paradise. Every teenager's dream. I craved independence, but what I ended up with was isolation. When I finally discovered the difference . . . well." I flicked the rod backward and forward. The pole flew out of my fist into the water.

"We'll continue this deep, honest conversation after we retrieve my fishing gear."

He plucked the pole out of the river. The tangled line shook in his hand. "Jeez. You might try sticking some bait on it next time."

He baited the hook with an ugly piece of plastic goop, picked up his own pole, and demonstrated the correct way to cast. With both our lines in the water, we settled down to the sluggish repetitions of fishing out of a drifting canoe: cast out, reel in, eat something, paddle upstream, cast out, reel in, on and on.

"The American Revolution," I said.

Sam pitched a crust of bread into the Monocacy. "That's what I thought you'd say."

An hour later, we'd progressed beyond the American Revolution to history of a more personal nature. I dipped a finger in the river, the

water cold as February. "So you arrived in Solace Glen and you're happy. Ever married?"

"No. I was too much of a cad and a bounder."

"But you've seen the error of your ways?"

He tilted his face into the sun, smiled like
there was no place on earth he'd rather be.
"I've seen the error of my ways. I've seen that
my parents were right all along, horrible
thought. And I'm at a place in my life where
I'm ready."

"For what?"

"To share." He reeled the lure in and tossed it
out again in the same smooth, lazy manner I'd
watched for over an hour. "I cast selfishness
away. Sharing is the watchword of this man
from now on."

"And you've got your eye on Lee."

"Speaking of . . ." He pointed through the
leafless trees on the opposite bank. Tom's car
crept down the road to the boat landing. "You
were right. Here they come."

We watched, camouflaged in the cove, as Tom
parked the car and the two of them unloaded
the canoe. They didn't notice Sam's jeep in the
trees. The two of them climbed into the red
canoe, spotless, dingless, and toting the proper
form of life preserver, I noticed. A big picnic
basket along with a cooler served as ballast in
the middle of the boat.

Our sandwiches had disappeared, as had the
chips and cookies, leaving only the jug of red
wine. "Wonder what they brought to eat," I

thought out loud, hungry again though it wasn't ten o'clock.

"Probably goose liver pâté, a fine round of French Brie, whole grain bread, assorted fruits, and champagne." He wiggled his pinkie finger.

My face went cross. Champagne. Probably Taittinger.

The red canoe hit the current and stroked upstream. I squirmed on the hard aluminum, knees stiff, and glared at the approaching boat, disappointed they'd shown up in the first place, but also brazenly curious.

"Sam?" Lee squinted as the canoe neared. "Flip?"

"Why, hello there." Sam blinked at her, creasing his forehead. "Are you following us?"

Tom drew the red canoe along side ours. "Why, no." He zeroed in on me. "But you might have told *us* of *your* plans."

"Yeah, Flip," Lee smiled with a question in her eyes, "I didn't realize you and Sam had plans. The two of you. Together."

Before I could open my mouth, Sam blurted, "Well, you know us. Spur of the moment. Wild and wacky." Eyes trained on Lee, he flung a hand out to pat my back and whacked my head. "Sorry, baby doll."

Tom laid his paddle across the canoe, sneered and mouthed the words *baby doll?*

"Catch anything?" Lee peered into our dingy canoe. "Where's your cooler for the fish?"

185

"We forgot it," I said. Catching fish wasn't the point of this game.

"But we remembered the vino, didn't we, hon?"

I screwed my head around to get a good view of Sam. He'd gone crazy and beamed like an Irish setter out for his first romp in the cow pies.

"Oh, yeah. We wouldn't forget the vino."

"Tom brought champagne," Lee twittered. She'd left the top three buttons of her chamois shirt undone, revealing a camisole's lace and a hint of cleavage.

Tom pulled a bottle out of the cooler and held it like a trophy over his head for me to admire. Taittinger.

"Tom has such good taste in champagne," I snipped.

Sam sat mesmerized by Lee, practically drooling. "You really look pretty today, Lee." All pretense crumbled into the water.

She smiled ear to ear, biting the tip of her tongue, hazel eyes sparkling.

"Time to fish!" Tom pushed away from us and dug a paddle into the current. "Paddle, Lee. I said paddle, Lee!"

They disappeared behind the bend.

"They'll be back." Sam shook a finger wisely in the air. "The river flows this way."

I slapped both hands on my knees. "*Ooooo, Miss Lee, you really look pretty today.* That was cool, I must say."

He leaned back on one elbow and clucked his

tongue at me. "What about you? *Tom tastes so good in champagne.*"

"Has good taste in champagne!"

"Whatever." He yawned and whizzed a line into the river. We sat in silence a few minutes. Finally he said, "Lee did look pretty."

"I'm sure Tom thinks so, too."

"Yeah, but he probably hasn't said so. Too uptight, our old Tom."

"He's not that old."

"He's what, ten years older than we are? Good God, the man should be on oxygen."

I poked a lip out and zinged a line into the same spot I'd been splashing down in for what seemed like days. "There aren't any fish in this river and there's no food on this boat. I suggest inebriation."

"That's the frontier spirit." Sam popped the cork on the jug and filled two plastic cups. "It's women like you who made this country great."

We toasted. To women like me.

By noon the jug lay empty. I hooked my fishing line on it and tossed it overboard. The jug bobbed cheerily down the current.

About that time, we heard laughter. Tom and Lee drifted toward us, but pulled into a basin of still water before rounding the curve. We could just make out the tops of their heads through the underbrush.

"What are they talking about, do you think

— Medicare or Social Security?" Sam strained an ear. "Naw. That'd be too personal for old Tom."

I slumped into the bow and dangled my legs over the gunwale. "Ha! That man could beat you in the hundred yard dash, argue you into the ground, and deliver a heart-stirring eulogy at your funeral while sipping the perfect Merlot."

Sam snickered. "Probably regaling her with quotes from Nasdaq."

"Yeah, that'll get her so worked up he won't have any trouble making his move."

"What move?"

"You know. A move. A pass. A kiss."

Sam's face collapsed. "He is not going to try to kiss her!"

"Oh, yes, indeedy he is. Tom is quite the wolf. Quite the ladies' man."

At this point, Lee's laughter acquired a riotous edge to it.

"She's screaming!" Sam yelled. "Old Tom's attacking her!"

He plowed through the water, splashing me with freezing river water. I lay crunched in the bow, feet in the air, trying to reel in the jug. As we slid around the bend, Sam mumbled curses. I crooked my neck over the gunnel. First Lee, then Tom came into view. They faced each other in the red canoe, sitting Indian style with the picnic basket set up as a table between them. Flute glasses, a red and white checkered cloth, linen napkins, dessert plates with apples and pears, cheese and bread. Sam had pegged it.

I called out, "You two gonna eat all that?"

Lee turned around, eyes glassy, lips covering half her face. "I never knew I liked champagne." She let out a squeak and drained her glass.

"I might try one of those apples," I pointed at the largest one just as our canoe slammed into theirs. "With cheese, if you don't mind."

Lee whooped and broke into a giggle fit as Sam maneuvered the boat so she practically sat in his lap and Tom and I could arm wrestle if we wanted.

"Isn't this cozy now?" Sam glowed from the wine. "We ran out of food. Didn't we, sweetie pie?"

I reached into Tom's plate and plucked off half an apple and a hunk of Stilton.

Lee cradled her empty glass and turned flickering eyelashes on Sam. "You want some of my champagne?"

"I would love some of your champagne." He leaned into her.

Tom and I caught each other's eye; they weren't talking about the wine.

"Well, you can't have any," Tom snatched Lee's glass away. "It's mine."

"We can share," pouted Lee.

"No, we can't."

"That's not very adult of you."

"Call me an old-fashioned fool." Tom crammed a stopper in the bottle.

"Party pooper." She leaned back and propped two elbows across the canoe. Her shirt pulled open where the buttons were undone. "Where's that red wine you guys brought?"

I stopped eating and reeled in the empty jug.

"So what now?" asked Sam, staring intently at Lee's exposed cleavage.

"What do you mean 'what now'?" Tom growled. "We all came here to fish, didn't we?"

"We came, we saw, we fished," I munched at the apple. "Pass the Brie, please."

Tom slapped a slice of goo into the palm of my hand. "Then I suggest we all go home."

Lee put on a Mae West act. "Oooo. And sleep it off?"

"It wouldn't hurt you any."

"I have a better idea," chirped Sam. "Tom, you go home and sleep it off. I'll chauffeur the ladies around the river having deep, honest conversation for a couple of hours."

"I'm all for that!" Lee shot up and clambered into our canoe.

"I've had enough fun for one morning." I licked the last of the cheese off my fingers. "I'll go with Tom."

"Wait a minute!" Tom clutched the gunwale as Lee and I fell into each other's spots. "Lee!"

Sam pushed away the moment Lee landed safely in and I thudded safely out. She peeked a sheepish eye over the edge of the canoe, saluting us as Sam whisked into the current paddling hard. He called over his shoulder, "Thanks for the picnic, Flip! Catch ya later!"

In an instant, they were gone. Tom shut his open jaw with a loud bite then turned on me. "You!" he roared. "You did this!"

"Did what? Pushed Lee out of your boat into Sam's arms?"

"You brought him here! You did it on purpose!" He jerked the stopper out of the champagne and searched for a glass. "Oh, hell." The bottle went into his mouth.

"You could at least be a gentleman and offer me some."

He glared sideways as he slurped, popped the bottle out of his mouth, and offered it to me, wiping tight lips with the back of his hand.

"No, thank you," I said primly. "I've had enough."

"I have, too." He took another swig. "I've had enough of this Lee and Sam thing."

"Then do something."

"I was trying to do something when you screwed it up!"

"My, aren't we touchy. When were you going to do something, when you took her home? A peck on the cheek?"

"No." He grew quiet. "I had it all planned. I was going to ply her with wit and champagne, fruit, bread and cheese, a box of Godiva," he drew out a small golden box for me to inspect, "then I was going to recite one of my favorite poems, Walt Whitman, 'Are You the New Person Drawn Toward Me?' "

The dark eyes looked right through me, focused on something far away.

"Are you the new person drawn toward me?
To begin with take warning, I am surely far
    different from what you suppose;
Do you suppose you will find in me your
    ideal?
Do you think it so easy to have me become
    your lover?
Do you think the friendship of me would be
    unalloy'd satisfaction?
Do you think I am trusty and faithful?
Do you see no further than this facade, this
    smooth and tolerant manner of me?
Do you suppose yourself advancing on real
    ground toward a real heroic man?
Have you no thought O dreamer that it may
    be all maya, illusion?"

I felt my face flush and go red. "Oh."
Only the river spoke for awhile, sweetly, sadly.
Tom smirked at his reflection in the bottle. "Then I was going to slowly lean forward and gently kiss her. Lightly, but insistently, holding her face between my hands."
He kissed the reflection, sighed heavily, then wrapped one fist around the neck of the bottle and scraped it against the floor of the boat. "BUT. You . . . screwed . . . it . . . up." He tore

192

open the Godiva and bit into a chocolate square.

"I think I will have a drink," I whispered.

We sat in the drifting red canoe, me sucking on the heavy green bottle, Tom stewing over his box of sweets. Both of us scheming how to get what we wanted, though I was no longer sure what that was.

Chapter 20

A week after I'd last touched it, I reached for the Bell family Bible and again let my imagination supply the missing pieces.

Ferrell Bell, who'd married Gretal, the sturdy German girl, had two first cousins, both bearing the same middle name: John Bell Paca, who died during the war in 1861, and Lucy Bell Paca, his little sister, born in 1829. Their mother, Lucinda, must have been awfully proud of her maiden name, a pride of name that extended well into the twenty-first century.

Nine years stretched between Lucy and her brother. She must have looked up to him, that big brother who played games with her during the early 1830s. Then came the day he went away to school and she missed him. When he returned home, he was all grown up, tall and handsome. Lucy probably didn't know what to make of John Bell, but I bet he doted on her.

In the mid-1840s, she suddenly sprouted and became a magnet for all the county boys. I could just imagine her — medium height, reddish hair, green eyes like Leona's, lots of freckles, and an infectious laugh. Her brother must have advised her: *This boy's an arrogant son-of-a-gun, Lucy. This boy's from a trashy family, Lucy, for all his good looks and charm. This one's suitable, Lucy. Good family and a solid career in business.*

She quickly settled on one, and at age eighteen married a man named Jason Tanner, twenty-nine years her senior. What could she have had in common with a man forty-seven years old? Did she have affection for him, or was it purely a business deal, promoted by her brother now that her father was dead?

From father to brother to husband, Lucy had little chance to try her wings at an age when most modern girls already know all there is to know. So Lucy moved in with her older husband, and three years later, mid-century, her life took another turn. She had a baby girl and her husband died.

Maybe the shock of fatherhood at age fifty caused him to keel over. Maybe once she got pregnant she thought, *I've got what I want,* and she poisoned him. Maybe her brother shot him in a duel over a business venture gone bad. Or maybe he just took ill and passed away in a fever. However it happened, Lucy found herself a single mother with a sort of freedom she'd never known before.

At about this time, John Bell Paca started building the big house that Leona's parents left to her and Leona passed to Lee. John's name and the date 1855 are inscribed in a cornerstone. Even though her husband probably left behind a nice house and a good income, family ties would have prompted Lucy to move in with her bachelor brother. She never married again, but raised her daughter, Lucinda Ann Tanner, in her own way.

In 1861, the country went to war, with Lucy thirty-two years old raising an eleven-year-old child. She and Lucinda Ann might have helped sew uniforms or make bandages. They might have visited soldiers in the hospital. They were proud when John Bell Paca rode off to war and wept when he was lost to them so soon.

Lucy and Gretal must have commiserated together, two women alone with their two children during the long four years. Gretal, at least, had a husband coming back to her while Lucy had no one but her little daughter.

I contemplated the war in Maryland, how it reached out and touched even Solace Glen, especially in 1862. That was the year of South Mountain and Antietam. The year J.E.B. Stuart rode with his troops through our little region of Maryland. I thought of Leona's story and the letters Lee still held out of Roland's reach, safe now in the hands of Sam's Smithsonian expert. We would know something soon, Lee had told me, after a couple of tests.

How a woman like Lucy made it through the war, I could only guess, nor did I know how in 1912 she died, having outlived her parents, her only brother, her husband, her cousin and his wife, and her only child, Lucinda Ann.

Beneath Jason Tanner and Lucy's name was written, "Lucinda Ann Tanner (1850–1890)." But underneath Lucinda's name was something else — empty parentheses. As if somebody was missing, and they didn't even know who.

Ferrell T. jeered when I walked into Tom's office to clean.

I smiled sweet as cinnamon sugar. "Ferrell T., you're so much like your daddy. Except for the lack of brains." I set the carryall down. "Why are you still here, anyway? You always manage to be gone when I show up."

"Mr. Scott has a motion that must be filed in Baltimore tomorrow. As if I owe you any explanation." His bad skin looked like he'd gone bobbing for apples in a mosquito pit.

"You don't owe me a thing, thank God, and I can't think of anything worse than being obligated to you. Where's Tom?"

He looked down his nose. "*Mr. Scott* is in the conference room with someone."

"Look here, Ferrell T." I didn't care if he was Roland's son; Tom's office felt more my territory than his. "You are Tom's young secretary/paralegal and are supposed to call him Mr. Scott. I am his independent contractor and only ten years younger than he is. Plus, I've known him all my life, as if I owe you any explanation. I can call him Tom, Tommy, Tom-Tom, or anything else I want and I don't need your permission. You got that?"

A familiar voice answered, "Got it." Sam swept in and pinched my waist.

You could have knocked me over with a pencil point. "What are you doing here?" I searched his face for bruises.

"Had a little business with Tom."

He looked fine enough. Very fine, in fact. "Is Tom still in the conference room?" Decked out on the floor, maybe?

"Yeah, I'm showing myself out. Just dropped by to apologize so I may as well ask your forgiveness, too. I was rude. I'm sorry."

"No harm done. I enjoyed myself. You and Lee have a nice evening?"

He actually blushed, leaned over, and kissed my cheek. "Thank you," he whispered. Then he was gone.

"Guess so," I said to the door as he walked out.

I lifted the carryall and crept down the hall to the conference room. The door stood ajar. Tom hovered at the window, hands in his pockets slowly jiggling loose change.

"I see you had a visitor," I said to announce myself.

He remained silent, dipping his head slightly.

"Oh." I entered the room and got to work. "You're still in a mood."

His eyelids shut tight and popped open again. "And what mood is that, pray tell?"

"A childish one." I dusted around his books and papers on the table. "A little-boy-who-

198

didn't-get-his-way-having-a-long-pout kind of mood."

He whirled around, a broad grin on his face. "That is the first time you ever dressed me down. Please," he sat, swinging side to side in the swivel chair, "don't stop. I'm sure I deserve it."

"I haven't yet decided what you deserve." Nor could I decide what to make of this new Tom Scott.

"Whoa. She's on a roll now, boys. She draws back for the pass, she's looking, looking . . ."

"Isn't it strange when men don't know what to say, they fall back on sports analogies."

"Ho! She's sighted Tom Scott, she lets one loose and it hits him — POW! — in the chest!" He clutched his heart, doubled over and sprawled across the conference table. Eli showed some concern.

"Are you done?" He didn't move. "Are you?"

"Asked you first."

"Asked you second." My teeth chomped my bottom lip to keep from smiling.

Tom slid into the swivel chair while Eli shoved a cold nose under his hand to check the pulse. "Sam came to apologize for absconding with my date."

"I hope you were gracious."

"Yes, Mother, I was. Told him it worked out fine. More champagne for me."

"Quite the cavalier attitude we've adopted. If I recall, you were a bit upset at the time. With all three of us."

"You at least got in the canoe with me. That's more than I can say for Lady Lee. Apparently, she couldn't wait to get out."

"Tom." Cards were laid on the table all around. "Lee is falling in love with Sam. And I know he is in love with her." My hand slapped the dust rag against a chair. "Don't think it gives me any pleasure to say so."

The dark eyes narrowed. "Why wouldn't it give you pleasure to say so? You have something against Sam? Or don't you want Lee to be happy?"

I sat down in the chair I'd slapped and faced him across the table, a client telling her side of the story. "I think Sam Gibbon is a very attractive man. He's someone any woman would find agreeable."

"Agreeable? What a nineteenth-century word."

"So I read a lot of Jane Austen, what of it?" He clamped his mouth and waved a hand for me to continue. "OK. Not just agreeable. Sexy. Smart. Funny. Handsome. A good companion. Easygoing."

"Fine, fine, fine." He started swiveling again. "I get the drift. He's perfect."

"No, not quite. I did have my doubts about him in the beginning, especially about his interest in Lee's letters. But I found myself attracted to him, anyway, knowing he was attracted to somebody else. One of my best friends. And I realized pretty quickly that Lee had feelings for him, too." While I spoke, my toe tapped against the base of the table.

"How quickly?"

"Ohhhh, the first five minutes they met."

Tom's eyes soared into his forehead. "Thanks for telling me."

"I didn't know you were interested until too late. Then I tried to help you and I was trying to help myself, then Sam, and I had Lee to deal with. Well, I did what everybody wanted, brought everybody together hoping the chips would fall," I exhaled, "and they did. Not where I wanted them to, but they did fall."

Tom stared into space a moment. "At least I never kissed her. I would have felt compelled to propose."

"Yeah," I mimicked the serious tone. "She would have been ruined for Sam."

"I bear a clear conscience on that score."

Tom displayed a ton of bravado for a man who'd been dumped before he even got started.

"I am sorry, Tom."

"Aw, that's all right. I'll survive." He ran ten fingers through his thick hair. "How about you?"

"Sam didn't ruin me for anybody else, if that's what you mean." I pouted.

"No surreptitious kisses on his yacht? A stolen embrace in the shadow of the trees?"

I shook my head sadly.

He returned a grim smile. "Then we're both saved."

"Yep. Pure as mud."

He propped an elbow on the table and tapped a fist lightly against his mouth, black eyes boring into me until my skin prickled.

"What?"

"I was just thinking." Long pause, all the while staring at me.

"What?" My patience snapped. "What are you thinking?"

"I was thinking of that lingerie model you saw me with in Baltimore." He leaned toward me. "What was her number?"

As a result of my big wipeout in the romance field, I hadn't had the chance to warn Lee about Leonard Crosswell's intentions — too busy licking my wounds. I still wanted to expose his character and relay other people's impressions of this snake in the grass. Sam's preference for Lee may have hurt my pride, but that didn't mean I'd stop looking out for her.

After I finished up at Tom's office, I drove over to the Historical Society, but waiting five days to expose the fox proved too late. Leonard's black BMW sat parked out front, a dark omen. I pulled up behind it and hurried to the front door.

The door stood slightly ajar and I paused to eavesdrop, more to confirm my suspicions than to arrive at any revelations. I knew the sort of man Leonard Crosswell was. If Lee needed backup, I could always burst in to the rescue.

Lee's laugh rang clear and sweet. Sure enough, the fox intended to charm the pants off the hen.

"That's a great story, Mr. Crosswell. I hadn't heard that one about General Longstreet."

"Call me Leonard," the fox said in a voice dripping with honey. "You and I shouldn't stand on formality."

"Oh? What should we stand on?" Lee's low purr had that Jenner edge to it. She remained friendly, but wary.

"Informality, of course. Generosity? Friendship?"

"Generosity." Lee jumped on it. "That's an interesting choice of words."

You tell him, Lee, I rooted.

"Yes, it is." Leonard obviously wanted to get right to the point along a sly, if charming route. "I think we could mutually benefit each other."

"How so, Mr. Crosswell?" She fell back on formality.

"*Please* — Leonard. I do want us to be good friends."

"What else do you want?"

"Hoho. Good looks and smart to boot. An enticing combination."

Compliments will get you nowhere with this woman, fox face, I sneered to myself. The wind picked up, and I wrapped my coat close but stayed put. Lee could obviously hold her own ground. She didn't need me charging in, a one horse cavalry.

Leonard wormed his way along. "I hear we have a mutual interest."

"What might that be?" But I could tell she'd guessed.

"I collect Civil War memorabilia, quite a substantial collection, if I say so myself. Books, military documents, *letters*." He let that settle in, as if she needed time for the light bulb to click on. "Do you see where I'm going with this, Lee?"

"Gee, Mr. Crosswell," I heard her pour two cups of coffee and the warm aroma drifted through the cracked door. "I'm only guessing, but I'd say you're about to make a monumental offer for the letters my Aunt Leona left me."

"Well," the fox chortled, "I don't know about 'monumental.' I don't even know if the letters have been authenticated yet."

Lee kept those cards close to her vest. "It doesn't matter one way or another. They're not for sale. Not now. Not ever."

The fox sat silent, cataloguing his options. At last he spoke. "You appear to have made up your mind. I won't try to change it."

Oh, no? I rubbed my freezing hands together, dying to ambush the coffee.

"But, Lee, take it from an old courtroom warrior, it's never wise to rule out something that could prove so helpful down the road."

"What do you mean?" Her spoon clanked impatiently against the coffee mug.

"If the letters are authentic, I'd like to see them. Once I see them, I know I'll want them.

When I want something, I'll do anything and pay any price to obtain the object of my desire."

I didn't like the way he said those last five words.

Neither did Lee. "Sorry. They're not for sale. You wouldn't understand."

"Perhaps I'd understand better than you think. I can be a very understanding man. Your Aunt Leona would want the best for you, wouldn't she? The best house. The best car. The best life has to offer. I can help you."

I smirked. If only Margaret stood outside listening with me. She'd be appalled at Leonard spouting off about what Leona would want.

"Thanks." Lee dismissed him, employing a tone of voice Leonard was accustomed to using, not hearing. "I don't need your 'help.' And you have no idea what my Aunt Leona would want for me. So unless you have any other business, Mr. Crosswell, the Historical Society is closed."

The hen kicked the fox out.

I ran like wildfire to my car and started ambling toward the front door as if I'd just arrived.

"Why, good evening, Mr. Crosswell," I greeted him formally as he swooped by, buttoning his coat.

His head reared up momentarily and I almost fell backward from the look in his eyes. The charm had drained away; what remained sent a cold chill through my chest. He didn't return the greeting, only growled and hurried to his BMW.

I watched him drive away, the ominous black car an unshakable image. Even when Lee spotted me and announced she had an untouched cup of coffee, I couldn't shake the bad feeling Leonard left behind.

Tina's words popped into my head and I tossed them around. Why Solace Glen? Why us? Why did we all know in our hearts that Leonard Crosswell brought nothing but trouble?

Chapter 21

"Lately, it seems I have more bad days than good."

I helped Louise out of bed and into her rocking chair so I could change the sheets. "Have you had somebody over to help? You been eating right?"

"Haven't felt like eating. But yes, the Circle Ladies have been most helpful, and I've had more than enough attention. My refrigerator is packed full enough for a football team. Those Episcopal women tend to go overboard, you know, trying to outshine the rest."

I covered her legs with a throw blanket and got to work. Such a big bed for such a small body.

"How was your weekend?" Louise never stopped wanting to know about everybody else.

"Enlightening."

"Oh?" She let it pass. "And did you go into Baltimore last week for a good time?"

"Yes. That was enlightening, too."

"I'm happy to hear you're so well lit."

"I'm happy you're happy. That's all you'll get out of me." I stripped the mattress bare and threw on the fresh linen. "What have you been up to?" I expected to hear about her latest book.

"I went to see Marlene," she said.

My head whipped around. "Why would you do such a thing, feeling the way you do?"

"That's exactly right, Flip. Feeling the way I do." She swallowed, a simple reflex, but it seemed such an effort for her. "I know it won't be long, and I had to see my only child."

For some reason, I thought of Lucy and Lucinda Ann when she said that. The faceless names from the past were starting to people my present.

"Whatever you had to say to her, I'm sure it went straight over her head."

"Doesn't matter. I said what I had to say."

"What did you say?"

"That I would be dead before the year was out. That I was sorry for any mistakes I made with her, but I really couldn't think of many. That our relationship, or lack of one, was largely due to her own self-centeredness and cold heart. That I had tried my best, like any parent, but my attempts to love her were thwarted at every turn because she revels in bitterness, takes delight in it, wants me to grovel and pay homage to her, a mother to her child. I let her know that's not how God intended us to act. We owe our parents something, even bad parents, but I've been a good mother. I know I have in my heart. I've only wanted the best for her, and she has hurt me whenever the opportunity arose. Getting married and not even bothering to call. What kind of daughter treats her mother like that? She's lived half a mile from me for twenty-five years and has never asked me to dinner. Won't even cook a meal for me. Won't pick up a telephone to say hello, how are you feeling, what can I do for you? Because all she cares about is what the world can do for her. If you have nothing to offer — no money, no social position, no material gain — she cuts you off like a dead limb. I told her I felt sorry for her. That I prayed for her and always would. With my last breath, I will still be praying for her."

She buried her face in one hand, fingers spread temple to temple.

I dropped what I was doing and knelt beside her chair, hoping the right words would come. "Louise. Louise, look at me. I can't explain why a child ends up the way she does. I can't explain why some are born giving and some are born taking. God gave you a loving, giving spirit. You have not wasted that gift, ask anybody in this town. There's not a soul in this community who has not been touched by your generosity. It is a mystery to me, and a tragedy, that the one person you want so much to reach will not be reached. Don't fret about it, Louise. Don't let Marlene distort the truth of your whole life. She's been your cross to bear for many years. It's time to hand it over. It's time to let go. You took the first step when you confronted her and got all those feelings off your chest. Now let it go. Drop the burden and be free of it."

Her hand dropped from her face to her lap. Tears spilled across the pale cheeks, but she smiled. "Flip," she whispered hoarsely, and took my hand, "your friendship has meant the world to me. You know that, don't you? If I lost a daughter in Marlene, I gained a child in you. You don't give yourself enough credit. No self-confidence. But you possess the heart and the stamina to sustain us all. You," she squeezed my hand so slightly, "are a giver, too. A treasure, that's what Leona called you. Take a lesson from my life, sweetheart. Give the most to those worth giving to. Don't do what I did and throw all your seed on hard, unforgiving ground. Nothing grows, try as you will, nothing takes root. You deserve better than I got. Please. Promise me. Give to those worth giving to."

I nodded, again and again, as if I understood her meaning, but all the while I grappled with the problem — who? Who were the ones worth giving to? Nobody? Everybody? A select list that never changed or a list that changed daily? She'd handed me my own cross to bear, but I nodded because it gave her peace of mind, and if I could give Louise peace of mind, then I had fulfilled my promise to her at least once. A gift to one worth giving to. A mustard seed thrown on rich and fertile ground, soft, forgiving soil.

She fell asleep almost instantly. I finished my work, cleaned the room, changed the sheets. It was almost five o'clock. I half-lifted, half-sleepwalked her back to her bed and laid her gently down, wrapped between clean, white sheets.

I did not turn the light out when I left. I wanted it on so when she awoke, she could see all the familiar things in her room that had always given her comfort. The books and china doodads, the mohair throws and needlepoint pillows. The pictures of Marlene, the first-born, the only born, from birth to age eighteen.

Before going home for the day, I made a last stop at Marlene's Gift and Flower Shoppe. Not a soul browsed in the Shoppe among Marlene's tacky "country" gifts — homemade pot holders with badly quilted images of dogs and cats, tiny glass animals with plastic black eyes, cardboard picture frames glued with hideous, cheap fabric, glopped with ribbons and fake lace.

Marlene busied herself sticking outrageous price tags on the new collection of Christmas ornaments. I'd never seen so many rubber figures on skis.

"Hello, Marlene." I picked up one of the rubber ornaments and scowled at it.

She struggled to conceal her natural aversion to me with polite shoptalk. "You looking for some tree ornaments, Flip?"

"If I were, I wouldn't buy any of these gross things."

She snatched the cow on skis out of my palm. "Then what do you want? Spit it out and quit wasting my time."

"Time is a valuable commodity, isn't it, Marlene?" Her eyes held no reflection, completely blank. "How much time do you suppose your mother has left?"

"That's up to God, not you," she sniffed. "It's none of your business."

"Why, Scrooge, don't you remember what season it is? 'Mankind was my business. The common welfare was my business. . . .' Your mother's health is this whole town's business, except for you. Her own daughter."

She tried to run off and hide in the storeroom, but I grabbed hold of her arm and wouldn't let go. The image of Louise, my mother and father for nearly twenty-five years, cleared everything else from my mind until all I could see was her worn out, cancer-ravaged body lying solitary and alone in a bed that swallowed her whole.

"Whoa now. You're going to listen to me. Everybody talks about you behind your back, but nobody has ever said to your face what a cold-hearted bitch you are. Please. Let me be the first. You cast souls into hell for the tiniest slight against you. Somebody doesn't do things your way, you act like that person no longer exists. There isn't one iota of compassion or forgiveness inside you. You care only about you, yourself, and the almighty dollar. How a woman such as Louise, so warm and full of goodness, mothered a robot like you, I cannot fathom. Ever since she disapproved of your terrible taste in boyfriends, you've done whatever you could to spite and hurt her. She's gone out of her way to put things right between you, but you love your hatred, don't you, Marlene? You've nurtured it so long, it's a part of you. So sad. Such a waste. All those years you could have enjoyed the sweet friendship of your mother, who would have done anything for you. Now she's dying and you haven't made peace with her. It would make all the difference in the world if you did. If you went over there and made her comfortable in her last days. Can you do that, Marlene? Do you have it in you to do such a small thing that would mean so very much?"

She jerked her arm away and leaped behind the counter. "Get out. If you're not buying anything, get out."

A face without remorse, no twinge of guilt. Just meanness and spite and flat, dull eyes.

"I am buying something," I said quietly. "I'd like to order a bouquet of Thanksgiving flowers. On the card write, 'Hope you are feeling better. We all love you.' Sign it, 'The Town of Solace Glen.' You know where to send it, don't you, Marlene? Don't you?"

Chapter 22

Wednesday found me working furiously on several houses — my usual ones, plus a couple of emergency treatments. Women with visiting in-laws. Husbands whose wives had gone out of town for a week and now whimpered like puppies, scared to death the little woman might notice the barbeque chips and cigar ash ground into the bedroom carpet.

I looked forward to the weekend and two whole days of time. Here it was, almost the end of the year, and I hadn't bought one Christmas present or picked out cards or figured what to bring to the Thanksgiving Day Picnic.

Solace Glen partied together as a community twice a year: Thanksgiving and the Fourth of July, two nondenominational holidays. The four town churches could commingle, sing the same songs, and pray the same Lord's Prayer without too much politicking, except our congregation always said "Forgive us our *debts*" instead of "Forgive us our *trespasses*" during the prayer. A minor point, maybe, but we relished the difference and put aside our usual Presbyterian dignity, shouting out "debts" and "debtors." I don't think God minded. I'd spent some time in the early morning before work poring over cookbooks, searching for a nice casserole recipe to whip up for the picnic. I chose something called Carolina oysters, a stewy mix of oysters, butter, cheese, and cracker crumbs sprinkled on top with parsley and more cheese. Anything with seafood the Thanksgiving crowd demolished in ten seconds. Anything with spinach or cauliflower found its way back into the refrigerator.

By the time I left the house, the morning hung heavy with gray clouds; autumn seemed gone already. Any moment now the first snow would fall and we would gasp and say, how beautiful, knowing in another month or two we'd be sick to death of it, longing for robins and baseball. By noon, the air blew frigid as I finished cleaning the third house. I gave in to a craving for Roland's oyster stew, the one thing in the world he did right.

I slipped into the Café. Rarely did I discover anybody sitting in my seat since the table melted into the back wall, out of the way, unsavory to most tourists, and the regulars knew my schedule. I glanced over the specials and wrote down oyster stew, hot tea, biscuits, and apple crumble.

Hilda showed up to take my order. She'd been experimenting with pink and green eye shadow. Her eyes looked like frogs draped in flamingo feathers.

"Hey," she said.

"Hey," I replied, prepared to pull out the atlas if she went on a gab streak.

"Somebody was asking about you."

"Who?"

"That lady with the BMW." She took the order and headed into the kitchen.

I made a face like I'd caught a whiff of something foul and cussed under my breath. In seconds the object herself appeared, dressed in a tight black jumpsuit that showed off the expensive gym work.

"Flip Paxton," she singsonged, "I've been looking for you." She invited herself to sit down. "I have good news."

"Oh?" *Leaving town?*

"I have been driving those stupid workmen to distraction, but it has paid off." She paused, waiting for the drum roll. "We can move in the weekend after Thanksgiving! A whole month ahead of schedule!"

I pictured C.C. wearing a lime green, monogrammed hard hat, standing on the necks of those poor construction men, screeching over the sound of electric drills and hammering. No wonder they finished the job early.

She babbled on about painters and cabinet people, the work on yellow pine walls and how gorgeous they'd turned out, the window people and how she designed those touches herself because the right lighting was crucial and she was a child of the light. Hilda dumped my lunch on the table and shoved off, probably wondering why I didn't flip open the atlas in C.C.'s face.

"Anyway," she finally sucked in a breath, "you can start Monday after Thanksgiving. How's that?"

"I'm full up Mondays."

"I'm sure you can work it in. It's the best day for me. I'll be home so the time isn't important. Seven o'clock at night for all I care. Leonard's home then and can show you his silly Civil War collection."

That *would* make my day, spending hours with him.

"Or seven in the morning." She bit a lip, worried. "But I'm not a morning person."

I couldn't imagine she was. Probably slept till noon then took two hours to apply her eyelashes. I opened my mouth to reemphasize a packed schedule when the door swung open and Screamin' Larry strolled in, larger than life in a fur-lined, red hooded parka and boots the size of Detroit.

"G'day all!" He glowed as bright as Santa Claus.

C.C. slit her eyes. The powdered face turned into a prune. "That man is a monumental nuisance. How does anybody put up with him?" She glared self-righteously at me until I answered the question.

"He's a damn good disc jockey. And a credit to the high school cheerleading department. Also," I leaned forward, "if your husband goes out of town a lot, Larry's available for . . . whatever." I wiggled my eyebrows and slapped an evil leer on my face, as though I'd enjoyed the fruits of Larry's labor myself. C.C. brought out the worst in me.

She turned up the self-righteousness full force, twisting her mouth in disgust. "I should have expected this from you. Nevertheless . . ." She scrambled to her feet, afraid to sit with me any longer as if something wicked might rub off. "I will look for you on Monday."

She hustled away. Unfortunately, the floor plan forced C.C. to pass by Larry's table. She reined up, studying the options. Finally, she jutted her chin as high as a thoroughbred and pranced ahead in long strides. Larry sat perusing the specials, apparently oblivious to C.C.'s moral dilemma, but when she swished by his table he reached out fast as a cobra and clamped onto her hand. He yanked it to his lips and planted a loud, wet smack across her knuckles.

"S'damn great to see you again, Mrs. Crosswell! How's the hubby?"

C.C. stared at him, horrified, and threw me a glance that said, "My Gawd, you're right!" She snatched her hand back, rubbing the spit off diamond and emerald rings.

"You are a sick man," she muttered between gritted teeth. "And I told you to stop playing those songs for me on the radio."

Larry clapped his hands and bounced in the

chair. "Oh, goodie! You're a listening fan! Would you like me to autograph something? A thigh, perhaps?" He scooped up a pencil and aimed it at her hip with a polite bat of the eye.

"Stay the hell away from me, you pervert." She stalked away, retrieved her purse, and stormed out of the premises. Several customers applauded the slammed door.

Larry yelped, amused as hell, and returned to the all-consuming task of writing down his lunch choices.

"You ain't through with her yet, are you, Larry?" One of the Eggheads chuckled.

"Far from it," answered Larry, not bothering to glance up and engage in conversation with one of the town idiots.

"You gonna sit with her at the picnic?" The other Egghead snorted into a paper napkin. "Serve her up a plate of arsenic crab balls?"

Larry smiled down at his lunch order, clearly delighted by the picture of that scene, and started humming, then broke into song. His voice, a truly beautiful gift, could charm the beak off a canary, but he refused to donate time to any church choir (against his personal religion, he said), so we rarely got the chance to enjoy his talent.

Don't sit under the apple tree with anyone
　　else but me,
Anyone else but me, anyone else but me. No,
　　no, no!

He rose to have more room to swing his hips and interrupted himself once to boom, "This goes out to everybody's favorite red-lipped babe in the brand-new BMW!"

As he sang, the Eggheads beat time against tea glasses and even Roland's kitchen staff crept out from their slave quarters to clap along. When the song ended, Larry leaped around the table taking bows in all directions, never shy in the limelight.

I could have departed the Café in a good humor after that, but I had to pass by Roland at the cash register. He didn't speak and neither did I, but I read something in the depth of his cold eyes that sent a shiver down my spine. A promise of winter, sure to come. A promise of ice, the purest form of treachery. A promise that he would have what he wanted.

That night, exhausted, anxious, pushing down a troubling premonition that had haunted me all afternoon, I opened the Bible.

Ferrell Bell/Gretal Stubing Bell. Lucy Bell Paca Tanner/Jason Tanner.

Lucy and Ferrell, first cousins, represented the second generation of Americans in the Bell family. I set out to study the third generation on Ferrell's side.

Roland Bell was Ferrell and Gretal's only child, born 1851, died 1908. In 1878, he married a girl named Florence Openheim, herself only nineteen.

Both Roland and Florence walked and breathed in two centuries. Both played, ate, and slept as children during the Civil War. Both witnessed incredible changes in their country and the world. Florence lived through a World War in her middle age and died at the height of economic prosperity in 1929. She saw skirts go from the floor to the knee. Florence could count herself fortunate to have a husband around while her two children, a boy and girl, entered young adulthood. Still, she outlived her husband by twenty-one years and rejoiced in the birth of a grandson who fathered, unfortunately, Roland and, fortunately, Leona Bell Jenner.

Roland died the same year as his German-blood mother, Gretal. I wondered at the coincidence of the two reaching heaven the same year and puzzled over who went first. Was he so dependent on Mother that her death drove him to suicide? Or was it the other way around?

With nothing but names and dates in front of me, I cast dullness to the wind and turned my speculation into a Hollywood production. Occasionally, a dried leaf or flower petal floated out from between the pages of the Bell Bible, and I carefully picked it up by a fragile edge and placed it safe in Psalms or Luke or wherever it fell from. I noticed scraps of paper and little envelopes stuck in the Bible, too, but decided to familiarize myself with the family tree before sorting through the poems or notes jammed helter-skelter among the pages.

So the first Roland and his wife, Florence, were born, grew up, lived, gave birth, and died here in Solace Glen. Florence helped found the Solace Glen Presbyterian Church in the late 1890s, joining forces with dissatisfied Methodists and Episcopalians. Both Roland and Florence's names were etched in a window shining down on the Bell aisle, shining down on Roland and Garland, Ferrell T. and Hilda.

I had worshipped beneath that window every Sunday of my life, and now I had a part of them, Roland and Florence, sitting on top of my kitchen cabinet, hidden in a basket under a mound of Spanish moss. The sad thing was, I was hiding that part of them from their own flesh and blood, their own great-grandson.

The thought occurred to me that maybe I should give the Bible to Roland. When I was through reading all the names and dates, all the poems and notes on yellowed scraps of paper, maybe I should hand it to Roland for his children and his children's children. Then he would leave me alone.

I closed the Bible and moved the tips of my fingers up and down the spine. Maybe that's what I'd do. But something nagged at me and wouldn't let go.

Why didn't Leona want Roland to have it? Why leave the Bell family Bible to me?

Chapter 23

Thursday afternoon, I worked on two small homes, then drove to Miss Fizzi's house sometime after four o'clock. I climbed the front steps and rang the doorbell, gave her a minute, then walked inside, yelling, "Hey, Miss Fizzi! It's Flip!"

The house smelled of freshly baked lemon chess pie.

Maybe she was in the powder room. "I'll start downstairs today!" I called. Downstairs didn't include the basement apartment. I wouldn't touch Suggs' lair with a ten-foot pole and Miss Fizzi knew it. No telling what crawled around down there. "That pie sure smells good!"

I hadn't spent fifteen minutes vacuuming and dusting the parlor when Lee burst through the front door.

She drew up, surprised. "What are you doing?"

"Earning a living. What's it look like?"

"Why aren't you at the clinic?" Solace Glen wasn't big enough for a full-fledged hospital, but we supported a pretty good health clinic where a parade of residents cut their teeth delivering babies, listening to bad hearts, and sewing up victims of farm equipment.

"The clinic? I just walked through the door a few minutes ago."

"Miss Fizzi had a bad fall."

My veins went cold. "What kind of fall? Where?"

"Tom called on his way to the clinic. He said a neighbor was in his backyard and heard a crash. He looked over the fence and saw Miss Fizzi lying on the ground. One of the back steps off the kitchen must have rotted out."

"How is she?"

"Conscious enough to ask for Tom when the Eggheads got her to the clinic."

I remembered how the Eggheads tossed her around like a football recently. "I hope they didn't hurt her."

"Give them a little credit. At least they got her to a doctor."

We stood shaking our heads and grinding our teeth a minute. Finally, Lee said, "Are you thinking what I'm thinking?"

We hustled through the hall to the kitchen. The open door creaked in the breeze. Two curious squirrels, we crept out on the landing and peered over the edge. The top step lay broken in two, straight down the middle. Miss Fizzi must have tumbled headfirst down the next six steps.

We bent to examine the broken wood. It was not an old piece, none of the edges were jagged or soft.

"Somebody sawed this step underneath," said Lee.

I put my hand over my mouth, eyes big as doorknobs.

"We have to tell Tom about this." She straightened her back. "Roland's lost his mind. He's out of control."

"How do you know it was Roland? Suggs could've done it." Spite and envy know no boundaries.

"He could have, but he's lived here for three years. Why would he do it now?"

"I don't know. Property. Money. He's her only blood relative and stands to inherit this house if nothing else."

"Let's talk to Tom about it. Then we need to report this to the police."

"Lukzay?" My heart sank at the thought, but Lee gripped my hand.

"We'll go over his head if we have to. This is attempted murder. Come on. Let's get to the clinic and talk to Tom."

We crept back into the kitchen and closed and locked the door. Lee hurried out, saying she'd meet me at the clinic. I glanced around, making sure the oven was off and the stove cold. The lemon chess pie Miss Fizzi baked sat on a rack, cooled to room temperature. Almost in tears, I wrapped the pie pan in plastic and stuck it in the refrigerator.

On the drive to the clinic, I kept seeing Roland's icy eyes and the promise they held.

Only now, he'd made good on the promise. But other eyes swirled into my mind, too — Suggs' envious eyes and Leonard's awful, black eyes, glowering from Lee's stinging rejection. Was this his way of getting back at Lee? Scaring her, using Roland's open greed to hide his own tracks?

One thing I was sure of, the Bell family Bible was mine for keeps. No matter how badly Roland Bell needed to read it or how desperately Leonard Crosswell wanted to collect it.

When I arrived, minutes behind Lee, Tom greeted us with encouraging news.

"She's banged up all right. Two badly sprained ankles, a gash on her temple, and a broken wrist, but it's a miracle she didn't crack her head open, break a hip, or worse."

Lee and I shuddered. Then we told him about the step.

"Tom," I spoke in a low voice, "we're afraid Roland's gone crazy. He could have tampered with Joey's brakes. I know he's responsible for my break-in. But to try and kill a sweet old lady for inheriting a little money . . ."

A dark cloud passed over Tom's face. The ebony eyes narrowed and focused hard on the floor. His chest heaved. "There's something I have to do," he said quietly. "Tell Miss Fizzi not to worry about a thing. Don't say a word to her about what you suspect. And don't breathe a word of this to Officer Lukzay."

"Where do you think he's going?" Lee was already moving toward Miss Fizzi's room.

"I don't know." I watched Tom fling a black wool topcoat over his back and quickly stalk out of the building. A red cashmere scarf floated out of a pocket to the floor where I bent to retrieve it. I placed the scarf around my shoulders and kept it there the rest of the evening.

There wasn't much Lee and I could do for Miss Fizzi short of giving in to her demand for a shot of sherry with the pain pills. We simply made sure she was comfortable in mind and spirit before leaving, assuring her the oven was off and the house locked up.

I'd finished reading a couple of books from the Historical Society, so I followed Lee home to pick out two or three more. The sun had set, and a brisk wind blew through the leafless trees. Smoke poured from almost every chimney, and the streets lay empty and forlorn, no holiday decorations yet, nothing to draw people away from their warm fireplaces on a night like this. A cup of coffee at Lee's would taste awfully good.

We pulled off the street and into the cramped parking space behind the house. We walked up to the back door together. Lee fiddled in her purse for the right key, but as a course of habit I reached for the doorknob and tried it. The door slipped open.

"I could have sworn I locked it," she murmured. "Oh, well."

She started to go in, but I pulled her back. "Wait a minute." The premonition that had nagged at me earlier in the week returned in almost palpable form.

Lee didn't wait for explanations. "Damnit to hell." She bulldozed past and banged the door wide open with the heel of her hand. A light flicked on in the narrow hallway, the kitchen, the dining room.

I stood on the outside looking in, feet nailed to the ground, picturing the shambled mess of my own home only weeks before. I could hear Lee stomping from room to room, cawing damnittohelldamnittohell, a bird returning to her damaged nest.

Curiosity at last overcame fear and I inched inside, stepping lightly into the hallway. Overhead, Lee trudged through the four small rooms on the second floor, cussing. From my place in the hallway, I could see into the kitchen and dining room where Plain Jane sat undisturbed at the farmhouse table, a stoic, unperturbed expression on the Pandora face, cotton fingers dipping into the butter bean bowl as if all bad things had just now escaped into the world and she searched the wooden bottom for what was left.

I started toward her just as the broom closet door at my left creaked. Mid-step, I froze, breath cut off, eyes adjusting to the half-light of the shadowed, narrow space while the door slowly inched open toward my face. A shoe emerged from inside the shallow closet, paused, then a hand edged along the side of the door, another shoe appeared, a body in a large black overcoat and a black rain hat stepped into the hall and backed silently out.

In total quiet, the body in the black overcoat and I stood in the same tiny square footage. A banging from Lee upstairs sent the overcoat stumbling backward into me. I whooped and the body grunted, then bounded past me into the dark night.

Within seconds, Lee came storming down the stairs. "Roland Bell! Is that you, you sonofabitch! You are going to pay for what you did to my house!"

I pointed into the night from the floor where I'd fallen flat. Lee stood in the frame of her open door, shouting after Roland, "You think you're so smart! But you didn't find them, did you, Roland? You couldn't find them! Miss Fizzi still has her trust and Flip still has the Bell family Bible! And if you had anything to do with Joey's car crash and Miss Fizzi's fall — you'll get yours, Roland, don't you worry! You'll get what you deserve!"

She slammed the door, boiling mad, immediately jerked me up by the shoulders and led me to the farmhouse table. I sat down next to Plain Jane, shaking, willing my breath back while Lee made coffee, violently clanging and banging spoons, mugs, pots. While the coffee brewed, she marched over to Jane and with a tight face unbuttoned the doll's blouse. The letters lay safe in the bosom buddy. She drew them out, gingerly lifting the three letters as if she held a poker hand that no man at her table could beat.

"Just got them back today," she said, "special delivery. They're authentic. And you know what's funny?"

"No," I rubbed the tender, bruised small of my back, shoulders, and neck. "What's funny?"

She shuffled the letters, one, two, three, three, two, one. "Even if Roland had found these letters and read them, he wouldn't get it. He wouldn't understand."

That's what she'd said to Leonard. She spread the envelopes on the table and together we stared at them.

"But that's not really the point, is it?" My finger tapped one envelope. "It doesn't matter if he gets it or doesn't get it. The important thing is he *wants* the letters, he *wants* the Bell Bible, he thought he had a right to the house, the car, the property, the money."

Lee picked up the yellowed envelopes and returned them to Plain Jane's safe keeping. "That *was* Roland, right? You saw his face? Because I'm about to call the Frederick police."

For the first time, a coldness gripped my stomach, a hard doubt. "No, I didn't see his face. I couldn't even tell if it was a man or a woman. Maybe because of the coat and hat, but whoever it was sure *seemed* bigger than Roland, now that I think about it."

Lee twisted her mouth. "Oh, come on. Who else could it be? Who else would go after you, me, and Miss Fizzi? Miss Fizzi, for God's sake! You heard Roland after Pal's car was wrecked — 'One down.' It's got to be him."

I looked around at the godawful mess in Lee's house and my blood boiled. I stood, both hands holding onto either end of Tom's cashmere scarf. "You're right. It has to be Roland. It would be so easy to just let him have what he wants or hide everything away in a bank vault. But Leona wanted you to have those letters and keep them here in the Historical Society. She wanted you to figure out their importance. And she wanted me to use that Bible, keep it in my home, not stick it in a bank. I may be a Paxton, but I won't give up the Bell family history. No matter what. Call the police."

Part Three

Chapter 24

Louise lay like a doll baby in her big, king bed, supported on every side by soft, white pillows. She spoke little as I dusted around the room, barely tapping a rag over Marlene's many faces. She'd ask a question and I'd run on and on, saving her the trouble of speech.

"I wanted to call you about Miss Fizzi, but Lee said she hadn't talked to you in a while and wanted a nice visit. Did you enjoy your time with her yesterday? Don't bother talking, just nod and smile like a good girl."

Louise barely moved her lips. It broke my heart to watch her struggle so hard to smile.

"I tell you, Louise, when I got to the clinic, I was scared, really scared for Miss Fizzi. I kept picturing her frail, little old lady body slamming down those wood steps, lying there on the ground in her flimsy housedress until the Eggheads arrived to gawk at her. Don't you know how mortified she was, half-conscious. Fortunately, she passed out soon after the sight of them and stayed unconscious until they got her to the clinic, into *expert* hands."

Louise's eyebrows twitched. She knew my opinion of the Eggheads.

"She asked for Tom as soon as she came to. I believe she thought she'd die. He got there right away, he's so good, and called Lee. She ran into me at Miss Fizzi's house. You know the rest."

"Tom thinks Roland did it all, doesn't he?" The words, barely audible, disappeared into the mound of pillows. I couldn't lie to Louise; she'd know it.

"He's trying to keep an open, lawyerly mind, but he was so disgusted. I've never seen him so mad. He even checked the steps himself right away and immediately called an investigator friend of his from another county to look into it. Somebody independent, you know, with higher connections and morals than dear Officer Look-away."

"You called Lukzay?" asked the small voice in a tone of incredulity.

"No. Tom said don't bother. We called the Frederick County station, though. First they referred us to Lukzay, but Lee flat out told them she'd found his investigative abilities lacking. A tactful way of saying nonexistent. They sent a couple of bodies over to have a look-see and we unloaded our whole theory on them — the car brakes, the two break-ins, Miss Fizzi's step. We pointed our fingers at Roland, but the questions they asked did make me wonder. I had to admit my doubts about the figure in the black over-coat. Anyway, they dusted around and said they'd start questioning people. So we'll see. Their professionalism satisfied me and Lee.

That's what she told Sam. Her boyfriend." I shot her a coy grin and poked a finger in my cheek like a schoolgirl.

"Lee is very happy," she said. The effort drained her and she closed her eyes.

"Yes, she is. I think we can all rest comfortably in the hopes of a spring wedding."

Of course, no such word had been spoken by either Lee or Sam, but I knew the thought of a beautiful, flower-packed church event would bring Louise a measure of joy she badly needed. It would give her something to plan and imagine as she drifted in and out of sleep, picturing satin gowns, sculpted cakes, and baby showers to come.

"How is Miss Fizzi today?" she asked softly behind closed eyelids.

"Better than yesterday. She's bandaged and bruised but that little woman must have bones of steel. She'll be at the clinic another week, in high spirits and making impossible requests of the nurses."

"Sherry, of course. What about Suggs? Has he been to see her or done anything for her?" Again, the effort it took to speak drained Louise.

"You know better than to ask that. Save your strength." The comparison between Marlene and Suggs was an easy one to draw. "He doesn't think about anybody but himself. Personally, I believe she's better off if he stays completely out of it."

I dared not confide my niggling suspicions about Suggs to Louise. It would drive her crazy to imagine Miss Fizzi living under the same roof with a man who possibly tried to kill her. So I rambled on about the Thanksgiving picnic in two days, the fabulous oyster casserole I'd chosen, about Screamin' Larry grabbing C.C.'s hand and C.C. expecting me to come work for her next Monday. I told Louise I'd go at least once, if only to see what she'd done to that ramshackle old barn. It would give us something to laugh about.

She didn't answer, and when I bent to inspect her breathing, I saw she'd fallen asleep. I tiptoed out and climbed in the car. As I pulled out of Louise's driveway, I flicked on the radio. Larry announced the next song, "It Might as Well Be Spring."

Cherry, peach, and pear trees bloomed by the first of April in Solace Glen. Louise Lamm would not live to see them. The best any of us could do was give her a little springtime now.

Chapter 25

I never worked the Wednesday before Thanksgiving or the Friday after. That way, I had a nice little break, same as a high school student. As a result, my adrenaline rose to the freakish level of a teenager's and I zipped around, Christmas shopping nonstop over the long weekend. I zeroed in on the little towns surrounding Solace Glen in a thirty-mile radius, and the city of Frederick's downtown shopping district. Forget the big malls; I'd discovered many a Christmas knickknack in the antique stores of New Market and the odd shop here and there in Buckeystown and Urbana. I'd travel as far north as Emmitsburg, as far east as Ellicott City, as far south as Germantown, as far west as Hagerstown. Baltimore represented a whole other solar system and Washington a distant universe, if not a black hole.

After the escalating acts of violence in my own little world, getting out of town to do something as normal as Christmas shopping offered sweet relief. All day Wednesday I combed the eastern part of my shopping world, trudging up and down Ellicott City's Main Street, sifting through shelf after shelf in the town's oak-planked boutiques. You could have lifted the town itself out of a Beatrix Potter picture book. I half-expected a porcupine dressed in a cotton skirt and wool shawl to pop up from behind a counter and ask, "May I help you?" Beatrix Potter's version of Melody. When I sat down to lunch at a café overlooking a trickling Tiber River, the waitress bore a peculiar likeness to one of Tom Kitten's sisters.

I bought the oysters required for my casserole at a seafood take-out place and drove the thirty minutes back to Solace Glen, the back seat of my car loaded with shopping bags. I liked to pick theme gifts at Christmas, and this year everybody on my list could expect a present connected to gardening. Very chic, C.C. might say, always an elegant choice, not that she made my list. Plus, a mountain of cheap gardening stuff filled the stores: gloves, pots, tools, books, calendars, seeds, plants, diaries, knee pads, soap. I gave myself a hefty pat on the back for dreaming up this one.

At home by dusk, I lined the ingredients for Carolina oysters across the kitchen counter and got busy. I covered the finished casserole with plastic wrap and shuffled off to bed, confident that once again my offering at the picnic would glean some attention.

Every Thanksgiving morning started out the same way — agonizing over what to wear to the picnic and dancing around the house to the music from Macy's Thanksgiving Day Parade, the one day of the year lip-synching on live television achieves cultural status. I finally decided on black jeans, hiking boots and an over-sized sweater with a striking design of bright pink embroidery across the chest, a gift from Louise after a trip to South America.

While the casserole heated up in the oven, I laced the hiking boots and wrapped a couple of presents. A miniature herb garden for Lee's inside windowsill. A colorful plant pot for Louise to look at lying in bed. A pie plate painted with dogwood and lilies for Miss Fizzi. A gardening diary for Margaret's meticulous approach to planting.

I crammed the casserole into a carrier and drove to the fire pond where the Thanksgiving and Fourth of July picnics had been held for more than fifty years. A small, man-made body of water built by the town behind the old brick fire department in the late nineteenth century, the fire pond proved a perfect spot for big events, bordered by acres of open, grassy meadows for kids to run wild, shade trees where the adults spread their blankets and snoozed after a big lunch, and the pond itself, which served as a miniature boat race arena on the Fourth of July. The rules were you had to make the boat yourself and could only race in one category: sail, motor driven, or animal driven. Lee won one year by harnessing a water snake that zoomed ahead like Secretariat and scared the bejesus out of all the hamsters rigged to paddle-wheels.

I pulled into the grassy parking area a little after noon. People poured in toting huge round platters and bowls the size of laundry baskets. Little boys lugged lacrosse sticks and footballs; little girls did the same, although I did see two Barbie dolls — Beauty Pageant Barbie and the large head Make-Me-Up-Fix-My-Hair Barbie, no doubt birthday gifts from Sally and Tina who favored that sort of thing.

All four churches in town donated long picnic tables and paper tablecloths that flapped in the wind. Each table sagged under the weight of a different course — vegetables, meat and sea-food, breads, desserts, drinks, and salads. I set my casserole on the seafood table and checked out the other dishes, a smattering of the usual fare: the turkey, the chicken, the venison, the roast beef, and the Smithfield ham. At the sea-food end, a tremendous bowl of iced shrimp reigned as centerpiece to crab balls, breaded catfish fingers, fried scallops, and steamed crab legs. Nobody had done a thing with oysters. I proudly arranged a serving spoon by the casse-role and stood there a minute or two.

A lady from the Methodist Church passed by and cooed, "Oh, is that oyster dish yours?"

"Why, yes." I practically shouted her ear off. "*I'm* the one who brought the oysters."

Two times a year I acted like such a showoff.

She lingered, pressing me for details about

any connection between my break-in and Lee's, Miss Fizzy's fall, and what the police had come up with. Apparently, this was all anybody could talk about and I got bombarded with questions by each passerby.

"So you think the two break-ins are connected, Flip?"

"I do."

"Who do you think is responsible?"

"I have my opinion." Thanks to the beauty parlor crowd, the whole town already knew what that opinion was, but I wasn't about to give Roland ammo for a slander suit. I kept answers short and information tight to the vest.

"I heard Miss Fizzi's fall was no accident."

"True enough."

"The woman has no enemies! Who'd want to hurt her, for God's sake?"

"That's a question for the police."

I was patting myself on the back for exercising such wise discretion when Marlene appeared with her usual nasty plate of hot dogs. She said she brought hot dogs so the poor little children would have at least one thing they liked, but I knew she did it because it only required her to boil water and slap a weenie on a bun.

I expected the same questions from her as everyone else, but she simply asked, "What did you bring, Flip?" The round fish eyes scanned the table. "Those bologna sandwiches?"

"Of course not," I said down my nose. I swung her plate of weenies around, scowling, as if a different position might make them look worth eating. "I baked an oyster casserole, m'dear."

She spouted like a whale and moved away, fumes of Vicks VapoRub trailing behind. I watched her go and found myself wondering, just for an instant, if Marlene really would do anything for money.

Several other women floated by, friends from church, clients. Everybody had something nice to say before launching into the topic of the day. When I felt pumped full enough of compliments, I scouted out Lee. She was standing by the dessert table with Sam behind her, his long arms wrapped around her waist, both of them feigning interest in cakes and pies. No keeping those two a secret any longer. A steady stream of old ladies trotted by, gathering a bit of information from one, a new fact from the other, their questions on the none-too-subtle side. So you're planning on settling in Solace Glen, Sam? How long's it been since we had a wedding around here, Lee?

I stood to one side, arms crossed, watching the show. After a good ten or fifteen minutes, I made a discovery. It didn't hurt. As a matter of fact, seeing the two of them together, so openly agog with one another, gave me a pleasant sense of satisfaction. Somehow, Henry and Marie, Jake and Leona — the four of them must have had a hand in it.

"Gold Medal is best."

"How can you say that? Pillsbury's always made a better flour."

The Eggheads faced off at the bread table, one on each side. Pal dumped a tin of crusty corn muffins in the middle. "What's wrong with Wash'ton flour milled right down the road in Ell'cott City? That's what I use. Done good by us all these years."

"Gold Medal."

"Pillsbury."

Before they could give me a headache, I hurried off in the opposite direction.

"Hey, where you going?" Lee caught up with me, leaving poor Sam with two particularly persistent ladies.

"Back to the car for a blanket. You think that was a nice thing to do to your intended?"

She tried to act mad. "My intended? Come on, it's not that serious. Everybody's getting so worked up." She couldn't look me in the eye.

"I'd say the two of you were pretty worked up back there at the dessert table, having a little rub fest. Why not knock a few cakes off the table and have at it? Be more fun than listening to the Eggheads fight about what type flour to buy."

"Gold Medal," she said.

"Pillsbury."

She pushed my arm. "Why don't you come sit with us? We've already got a bedspread set out over there." She pointed to a chestnut tree and a massive red cloth.

"Ooo, a bedspread. How subtle. OK, meet you there after the prayer."

She skipped away to rescue Sam and I headed to the edge of the pond where a group of children threw pebbles in the water, making circles. One child silently handed me a couple of stones and I imitated his aim, falling into a contest.

"Don't try to out-throw Flip Paxton, Jeremy. Her aim is sure."

Tom picked up a handful of pebbles and joined us. "Yes, siree. She's been known to bring down a moving lawyer at fifty paces."

"Ha, ha."

"Happy Thanksgiving. Heard you brung ersters."

"You hear that while you were drooling over Marlene's weenie dogs?"

"How'd you know?"

"You've always been a dog man."

"Only of the Labrador variety." Eli took this as his cue to appear and plunged into the pond, snapping his massive jaws at pebbles skimming by.

Tom tossed in a pebble and I threw one in after his. We watched our expanding circles loop into one another like magician's rings.

"So," he kicked at a small rock, dislodging it, "where are you sitting?"

"Where else? With Sam and Lee."

I expected to hear the name of the important family or client he'd been invited to sit with, but he said, "Oh, good. Mind if I join you?"

"What? No bigwig clients to entertain? No senior citizens itching to get a little free advice about their estate planning?"

His head wagged forlornly. He reached for the rock at his foot and chucked it into the water, kerplunk. "Not even a lingerie model from Baltimore."

I feigned embarrassment and watched the circles on the surface of the pond expand. "Naw. You have to settle for the domestic help."

That's when I felt his arm link through mine. "I'd say that's a step up, wouldn't you?"

For a second, I froze. I wanted to jerk my arm away and lecture him. *What do you think you're doing? You can't fool around like that! People will think we're together! Every dowager in Solace Glen will have us married, same as Sam and Lee!*

That's what I wanted to say. But Tom grinned at me with his magazine smile and started walking off, no hesitation, me on his arm. My boots dragged, weighted down with worry, but he pulled me along and my frozen smile melted into a shocked daze. Faces in the crowd blended together as we drew into the heart of the Thanksgiving gathering. He stopped, waiting with the rest of the community for Reverend Grayson from the Methodist Church to call for quiet and recite the Lord's Prayer.

Our Father which art in heaven, Hallowed be thy name.

The palm of my right hand practically gurgled with perspiration. Any moment it would squirt him in the face like the buttonhole flower of a circus clown.

Thy Kingdom come, Thy will be done in earth, as it is in heaven.

I panicked over what to do once the prayer stopped. Would he let go of my arm? Would I need a crowbar?

Give us this day our daily bread. And forgive us our trespasses/DEBTS, as we forgive those who trespass against us/OUR DEBTORS.

I opened my mouth to whoop it up with the other Presbyterians, but nothing came out. I'd lost feeling in my arm.

And lead us not into temptation, but deliver us from evil: For thine is the kingdom, and the power, and the glory, forever. Amen.

Tom shouted a hardy Amen and gracefully let my arm slip away.

"After you," he said, placing the tips of his fingers on my spine. He steered my lobster face through the crowd to a table with paper plates and utensils, sliding a place setting into my hand. "Now let's grab some of your oyster casserole before it's completely demolished."

Sam, in top form, played class cutup all during the meal, reeling out story after story. Lee rolled off the bedspread more than once, holding her ribcage, laughing so hard she choked and sputtered. An unladylike exhibition, Louise would say.

Like indulgent parents, Tom and I sat gazing

on the two of them, making a comment here and there, sipping coffee, the fringe grownups. I had no idea what I'd spooned onto my paper plate. The colors of the food mixed and ran together.

I avoided eye contact with Tom except to acknowledge cooking compliments, scared of what I might or might not read in his look. Lucky for me, Sam's Thanksgiving goal seemed geared to impress his lady love, and he and Lee, giddy as spring colts, provided the comic relief. In the middle of all this revelry, Ferrell T. and Hilda stumbled by, stuffing chocolate eclairs down their windpipes, whipped cream and streaks of dark goo melting down their matched faces.

There walked the seventh generation of Bells in Maryland. What a letdown.

I excused myself to pick out a dessert, but when I reached the dessert table, my eyes ricocheted from plate to bowl to tin container. Too many choices and nothing made sense. Around the table spun bodies with faces and voices.

"Canola beats all."

"How can you say that? The only way to go is olive oil."

"Olive oil? Pompeian makes a good olive oil."

"Not as good as Goya."

"Crisco. That's what everybody on TV uses. I wouldn't use anything but Crisco. Makes the best crust."

I wheeled around, dizzy, and bumped into Roland.

Our eyes locked. Almost at once, I could see in that icy stare a frail old lady toppling down hard wooden steps, a boy in a coma, two ransacked homes, a basket of Spanish moss covering a secret. In that moment, I felt absolute certainty that Roland committed each crime.

"How could you?" I hissed, pulling up resolve. "How do you live with yourself?"

"What the hell are you talking about?"

"You know what I'm talking about." The doubts seeped back in; the doubts held me in check. Hadn't the body in the overcoat been bigger, taller?

A flicker of anger sparked the ice, but he curled his lip and cast me away, almost laughing, "You're a stupid, crazy broad and everybody knows it. That's what I told those two cops you and Lee tried to sic on me. I referred them to my good friend, Officer Lukzay. He set them straight."

He strutted away and I yelled after him, "You think this is over? I might be stupid and crazy but at least I'm not guilty of —"

Two hands grabbed my elbows, whirled me around, shoved me several yards down the dessert table. "Would you like some devil's food cake?"

I wrestled free of Tom. "What'd you do that for? And stop grabbing hold of my arms every time I turn around. You want people to think we're engaged?"

"I want you," he said, grabbing hold of my

hands with surprising strength, "to keep your distance from Roland because somehow you've lost control of your tongue and temper. Both will be your undoing."

I let steam blow out my ears for a minute. "You think we should let him get away with trying to kill a woman? Or tampering with brakes and getting a boy almost killed?"

Tom, cool as ever, didn't appear the least ruffled. "Do you know for a fact he did any of these thing? Would you be willing to testify under oath?"

"Or breaking into two houses and tearing through like a hurricane?"

"You and Lee reported those crimes to the police. Now let them do their job. Are you so convinced the criminal is Roland? Out-of-control, crazy Roland?"

I studied my feet.

"You *are* convinced Roland did all of this, aren't you, Flip?"

I had to confess. "I'm not sure. Sometimes I think I'm sure, then I get doubtful. The person in the coat at Lee's house seemed bigger and taller than Roland. So I guess I'm not sure."

He pressed his lips together tightly and slowly nodded, as if letting something sink in. "Fair enough. We're dealing with criminal offenses, but this is a tight community. Nobody wants to see Garland or Hilda hurt. We all want to do the right thing. Do you agree with me?"

I pouted. "I guess so."

"And you will back off and let the police and my investigator do their jobs? Let experts handle this situation with Miss Fizzi, which is by far the most serious unless it is *proven* the car's brakes were tampered with?"

I chewed the inside of my mouth and mumbled, "OK."

He leaned into my ear. "And if you don't want me touching your arms, is there some other body part you suggest I hold that will attract less attention?"

My face went crimson and my mouth dropped. "I can't believe . . . you are . . . who do you . . . this is just . . ." I pulled away from him and meandered off, weaving through the crowd, the sound of his building laughter ringing in my ears.

Somewhere in the throng, C.C.'s commandant voice bugled, "Flip Paxton, don't forget! Monday! Not in the morning, I decided! Definitely not in the morning!"

Monday morning it would be, then. I careened back to my car and drove home, completely forgetting my nice casserole dish and serving spoon laid out on the table, right by Tom Scott and his awful laughter.

Even before the break-in at Lee's house, the Bell family Bible had taken on mysterious qualities and become a mission of mine. And a comfort in times of stress and doubt. I pulled the basket down from the top of the kitchen cabinet that night and lovingly took out the Bible determined to learn what facts I could and imagine the rest.

I scanned one branch of the family tree: Roland Bell (1851–1908) and Florence Openheim Bell (1859–1929). Across the way hung the other branch, Roland's contemporary, Lucinda Ann Tanner (1850–1890), his second cousin and the daughter of Lucy and Jason. Below Lucinda's name, the empty parentheses, no explanation.

Lucinda was eleven — not quite a child, not quite a young lady — when the Civil War broke out, fifteen when it ended, never married, and died at age forty, twenty-two years before her mother. She never knew a father; Jason died the year she was born, her mother, Lucy, never remarried.

Lucinda Ann marked the end of the female branch of the Bell family, going all the way back to Lucy Hanover Bell, her great-grandmother. For some reason, that saddened me, especially when I realized only one branch of the family still walked the planet and how degenerate that bloodline flowed.

Poor Lucinda Ann. Her generation of choice husbands got fairly swallowed by guns and cannon fire. Nobody much left but old men and little boys. Maybe she wasn't a looker or clung too tightly to Lucy's skirt. Maybe she suffered a disability like a clubfoot or harelip that put off men. That's how I imagined her — a pitiful sort of woman, sheltered by an independent mother, her only friend a leather-tooled diary where she poured out her heart. Perhaps there had been men she admired from afar: a widowed preacher with a bad lisp, a one-legged soldier who refused comfort, a local recluse people talked ugly about. All misfits like herself, sad and sorrowful, leading miserable lives. At least poor Lucinda Ann died before her mother. Alone, she would have drifted on a perilous sea, taken advantage of by con artists and ne'er-do-wells.

Roland and his wife, Florence, gave Lucinda two little cousins to spoil, a boy and a girl. Lucinda, no doubt, doted on the children. No matter what her impairment, they would have loved her unconditionally, as children do. When they reached a certain age, they might have asked, "Cousin Lucinda, why is your mouth so different from ours?" Or your leg, your eyes, your skin, your hands.

She might have replied, "God made me this way for a purpose. To help others develop a blind and accepting heart, and help me develop a humble and meek spirit."

Roland and Florence might have chided the children for their blunt questions, but little Roland, Jr. and Florie would have remembered Lucinda's answer all their lives, and learned from it.

When Lucinda died in 1890, it was a small funeral, only the immediate family: her mother Lucy, cousin Roland, wife Florence, ten-year-old Roland, Jr., and Florie, six. Nothing spectacular — a simple, dignified affair with a couple of hymns, a psalm read, a favorite poem. No husband looking lost and bewildered, holding a weeping toddler. No siblings, shaking their heads and commiserating with each other, asking what if.

Just Lucy, wondering if things could have turned out differently for her child, reflecting on a short, secluded life with comfort enough, but little joy. No father, no husband, no child. Not even a secret lover. Forty years, only forty years.

I pictured Lucy telling the others to go on home, back to the house her brother John Bell Paca left her, that she needed a minute alone to say goodbye. What did she say? Thank you? I'm sorry? Forgive me?

Or something else? Something so hidden and secret, the words could not be spoken out loud for ears to hear, or written down for eyes to see.

I stared at the empty parentheses beneath Lucinda's name, and I knew what was not written there was engraved like granite on Lucy's heart.

Chapter 26

Early Monday morning, I stopped by Miss Fizzi's house and got everything in order before she arrived home from the hospital later that day. The Episcopal Ladies Circle rallied to handle her food and care for the next week or two when she'd require extra attention. I knew if she had to depend on Suggs to help her, she'd be dead within forty-eight hours. Fortunately, in Solace Glen, the four church ladies circles didn't serve as mere excuses to get together and socialize. They served. The community would have been in a sorry state without those energetic bands of women, like Melody and Tina, roaming the countryside with plates of home-cooked meals, visiting the sick and disabled, assisting with births, deaths, and weddings.

The Presbyterian Circle extended a yearly invitation to me to join, but I always declined. I told them they were wonderful, but unlike most of the members, I carried a full workload. Besides, I ended up doing a lot of what they did, anyway, in an unofficial capacity.

I left Miss Fizzi a note saying get well soon, this cleaning's on the house, compliments of Flip Paxton's Circle of One.

It was almost nine o'clock when I rang C.C.'s doorbell. The landscaping still needed work, but she was probably driving the local nursery insane, calling to squawk about why this and that hadn't been done and what the hell happened to her shrub delivery.

The improvement to the exterior of the house couldn't be denied. Three stories of barn now looked like three stories of *House Beautiful*, the eighteenth-century lumber rejuvenated, a new roof, a covered front porch that ran the length of the house. A line of rocking chairs creaked in the stiff breeze, waiting for summer. A gleaming oak door graced the entrance with shiny brass lamps on either side. The welcome mat held a flock of Canada geese in V-formation.

I rang the doorbell again and noticed the windows still had manufacturer's stickers glued to the glass. C.C. would no doubt want me to kill myself scrubbing them off. I stepped back and counted windows. She'd gone crazy installing them on all three floors, being such a child of the light.

After the third ring, the oak door swung open and C.C., a vision of loveliness in her leopard print bathrobe, hair net, and face cream, glared at me and lit a cigarette.

"Good God, what time is it?"

"Good morning to you, too." I walked into her hallway, set the carryall and vacuum down and closed the door. Then I took a look around.

"Whooooeee. I don't know what you paid your decorator, but he was worth every penny."

C.C. inhaled her first hit of nicotine for the day and picked a speck of tobacco off her tongue. "He did what I told him to do." Her left arm draped across her waist and propped the opposite arm up, right hand waving the cigarette. "I have a way with color. Even Leonard was impressed and, God knows, little in life excites him except the stupid Civil War. But he loves the entrance way, just adores it."

"I can understand why." The floors, a buttery pine, refinished, buffed, and polyurethaned to a mirrorlike gloss, laid the foundation to a soaring, three-story-high atrium. On the yellow pine walls hung huge gilt-framed oil paintings that probably belonged in a modern art museum in San Francisco or New York. An open stairway led to the second and third stories, the banister sleek and simple. C.C.'s taste in furniture ran on the Shaker side. Nothing overdone, nothing ornate. Tables, chairs, sofas — all basic lines, cool, teak woods, no carved seat backs, no clawed feet, no feeling (as at Miss Fizzi's house) that you'd eaten too much dinner and needed a nap. I had to admit, C.C. nailed it. She was a damn child of the light. The sun poured in from every direction on the simple, bare furnishings, setting the bold colors of the paintings on fire.

"Well!" I'd drunk my fill. "I expect the workmen left an inch of dust top to bottom. I'll start on the third floor and work my way down. I dust, vacuum, scrub bathrooms, empty trash, and change beds. I leave no germ untouched in the kitchen. If you want others things done — refrigerator, oven, *windows*, that's extra." I took a breath. "I haven't decided whether to take you on as a permanent client or not. I'll give us a month, once a week."

Given the fact I represented the only game in town and C.C. knew it, she bit her forked tongue and nodded, slouching off to the kitchen for espresso, the folds in her leopard-print bathrobe hanging like loose skin.

The top two floors of the house gave the same impression as the ground floor. Basic, stark furnishings, expensive-looking artwork, well-placed windows, and warm, wonderful smelling pine floors and walls. Except for the workmen's dust, an easy house to clean. The top floor contained two libraries, his and hers. I took a slow tour of Leonard's half as I dusted. His shelves bulged with thick law books and thicker Civil War histories, many volumes behind glass. Perfectly framed historical documents covered the walls, ceiling to floor at points. A letter written and signed by General Longstreet drew my interest.

"What are you doing?" A voice barked behind me. I jumped in my skin, but quickly recovered my composure.

"I was admiring your collection, Mr. Crosswell." I faced him head on. "You haven't exactly kept it a secret. In fact, you're really proud of it, aren't you?" I plastered a sweet, innocuous tourist expression across my face as my eyes swept the room. "You must have spent years putting this together."

He said nothing for a few seconds, the steel eyes reading me as if perusing the contents of a business journal. Finally, he responded gruffly, "Of course I've spent years assembling this collection. Look around you. Every major Civil War general is represented."

I didn't take my eyes off him. "Where's J.E.B. Stuart?"

The black, fox eyes gave nothing away. "He's in storage. I'm having a short note of his reframed."

"Only a short note? Don't you have any letters?"

He smiled charmingly and said, "You never know." He started to leave, but hesitated a moment to add, "Is the publication date of your Bible pre or post Civil War?"

"To tell you the truth," I lied, "I hadn't even noticed."

He blessed me with another glimpse of white teeth and headed downstairs. When I heard the BMW start, I breathed easier.

C.C.'s library contained steamy romance novels and decorating references with an exercise bike in the center. Stacks of *Architectural Digest* formed three towers against one wall. I moved down to the next floor. The master bedroom and huge bathroom took up most of the second floor, with two small guestrooms and a connecting bath on the opposite end of a hall. Nowhere did I see photographs of children, pets, or family. She kept a 4×6 picture of Leonard in a silver frame by her side of the bed; he kept an 8×10 of C.C. on his side. They were an evenly divided couple it seemed to me. I worked down to the ground floor, lugging the bed linen and a bag of trash. C.C. sat at the dining room table, sipping espresso, puffing on a cigarette, and reading the *Washington Post*. She didn't glance up.

I found the laundry room off the kitchen. The appliances in those two rooms could have come off a space ship — modern, glossy black finish with tons of computer options, no avocado greens or Acapulco golds, no unsightly buttons and knobs to twist, like my own thirty-year-old kitchen equipment. The dishwasher looked like something in which you could blast off to the moon.

I cleaned the downstairs, working hard as a beaver, then wrote out a bill to cover the two-hour job. I handed the bill to C.C. "All done."

She glimpsed the amount and pulled a blank check out of her thin robe, writing in a number that covered a whole month's cleaning. "This should take us through your little trial period," she said, shoving the check into my stomach.

"Fine by me." It was a good amount of money, just in time for Christmas. I'd charged extra for the third floor.

As I started to go, C.C. decided to strike up a conversation. "Marlene tells me the whole town turns out for a big Christmas tree lighting at the fire station. A sort of Williamsburg."

"Yes, that's right. Just like they do in Williamsburg." I wondered if she aimed to involve herself in the community now that she and Leonard were settled in.

"When is that exactly?"

"On the twelfth. At six o'clock."

"Eleven days. Doesn't leave me a lot of time."

"You need to prepare for lights to switch on?"

She looked completely bored with me. "I need time to give a party. I suggested to Marlene that after the big tree event, a select group be invited to a small cocktail party here."

"Oh." So Marlene lurked behind it. "Marlene's writing out the 'select' list?"

"She did volunteer to be in charge of the invitations. They should go out in a couple of days."

"Why are you telling me all this?" I knew I wouldn't be receiving any pretty printed invitation urging my appearance for cocktails.

"Marlene thought perhaps you could help serve."

Tom always said a good trial lawyer takes a spear to the heart without flinching so the jury never suspects he's in trouble. I struggled to do just that, to hide the humiliation she'd so blithely doled out.

"She did, did she?" Marlene would love to see me dressed in a plain black maid's uniform with

262

a crisp, starched apron, offering her stuffed mushrooms on a silver tray and running to fetch another glass of chardonnay.

"She thought you'd jump at the chance to earn a few extra dollars."

"You can tell her there's no need to concern herself. I'm declining your offer."

C.C.'s forehead wrinkled under the coat of face cream. "Well, who else is there? Who can help me?"

"Ask Marlene," I bolted for the door, vision blurred. "She's been such a big help so far."

C.C. shrugged and mumbled something about a D.C. catering service and she'd see me next Monday, but in the afternoon, for God's sake.

I threw my stuff in the car and climbed behind the steering wheel, tears spilling over.

They wanted me at their party, all right. As the maid. As the hired help. Waiting hand and foot on the socially acceptable citizens of Solace Glen. Like C.C. and Leonard. Like Marlene. Like the Bells and Lee and Sam. Like Tom.

I imagined Tom showing up at the party and spying me in an ugly black-and-white uniform, kowtowing to the gentry.

No way! I might be the town domestic. I might clean people's houses for a living. But I was also a businesswoman, owning and controlling my own firm, doing well enough to own a home, support myself, and even indulge in luxuries now and again. My clients counted as

263

friends and family, and I was proud of what I had accomplished all alone from the time I turned eighteen.

I drove home, skipping lunch at the Café, avoiding contact with Marlene until I'd calmed down. Wait until Louise heard about this tomorrow. She'd roll her eyes and wrinkle her nose over C.C.'s fine house and poor manners and how Marlene wanted to humiliate me.

Just wait until Louise heard about this.

C.C. had gotten me so rattled, that night I took the Bell family Bible down for a therapy session. It occurred to me, glimpsing the entire tree, that the women in the Bell family had a tough time staying alive, getting married, or having children. The one female line died out with Lucinda Ann. The one remaining male line produced one or two offspring per generation, and only the male produced children.

Roland and his wife, Florence Openheim Bell, gave the world the first generation of Bells born after the Civil War, Roland Bell, Jr. and Florie O. Bell.

Florie appeared in 1884, the year Mark Twain wrote *The Adventures of Huckleberry Finn* and Chester A. Arthur was president. She probably lived a pretty fine childhood, spoiled by her parents and a big brother, her early years untouched by war and deprivation. Imagine the excitement she felt, at age fifteen, when the clock struck twelve and a whole new century dawned. She must have had the world by a string, so full of promise. Eight years later, her father died; Florie was twenty-four, old enough to be a wife and mother, but no man had attached his name to hers. She no doubt lived with her mother, Florence, and kept living with her until Florence passed away in 1929. She found herself alone, except for her brother and his family. Had she, I wondered, turned down suitors early on, a woman who rejected this man because he whistled too much, that one because she hated the way he parted his hair? By the time she started to feel desperate, in her early thirties, her luck would have run out. World War I swallowed a lot of good men beneath foreign ground. Years later, when Roland and Leona came along, she was just the old maid aunt, like her cousin before her, Lucinda Ann.

Florie O. Bell was born, she died. She left nothing behind but her name and the dates, 1884–1939. She led a spinster life — a barren, solitary moon orbiting the lush lives of others. She died at age fifty-five, probably from something like breast cancer or ovarian cancer, too embarrassed to go to a doctor.

I had at last reached fruit of the family tree that those living might remember. Unfortunately, Roland could best answer most questions. Miss Fizzi, however, might know enough to satisfy my curiosity, and I decided to ask her at our next visit.

Though studying and admiring the Bell

family tree normally calmed me, doubt clouded the usual effect. I felt only depression as I pondered the lives of Lucinda Ann and Florie, the two spinster women, dead at forty and fifty-five, living their entire existences celebrating other people's weddings and births, sewing other women's trousseaux, knitting booties for babies they could only baby-sit, worrying if their time would ever come, if they'd be stuck serving the party punch, never offered a taste from the cup themselves. I knew how they felt, and I hated that I knew.

I slapped shut the Bible. How I hated that I knew.

Chapter 27

By Tuesday morning, I'd finally calmed down from my excursion to C.C.'s house, but it took a full twenty-four hours to work the thorn out.

I drove by Miss Fizzi's house on the way to Louise's. Miss Fizzi lay propped up in bed, surrounded by flower bouquets, with Melody and Tina talking at once, filling her in on the doings at church and in town, the latest on Joey's condition, and the two break-ins.

She beamed bright when I swooped into the room with my own token of good will, a can of orange spice tea. Melody and Tina drew to the side so I could visit, holding back their insatiable curiosity about the police investigation. (Everybody had seen the flashing lights at Lee's house that night, and a few people had already been questioned.)

"You look pretty spry for a beat up old lady." I kissed Miss Fizzi on the cheek.

"I am spry," she tooted. "You could enter me in the Preakness." Both feet rested on elevated pillows along with the right wrist, which sported a splint. She'd taken three stitches over the right eye. Whoever did this should not be walking the streets a free man.

"By Preakness time, you'll be right as rain. Here's some tea."

"Thank you, dear." She whispered, "I'm sorry I have no pie to offer," and shot a meaningful glance at Tina who appeared to be licking her fingers.

"Think nothing of it. You just get better."

We talked a little more. With Melody and Tina hovering, both of whom loved to gossip, I thought it best to save the Bell family questions for another time. Instead, I filled her in on the Thanksgiving Day picnic and delivered an abbreviated version of my visit to C.C.'s house. Tina and Melody uttered "oh's" and "no's" at all the appropriate moments.

"Wait'll I tell Michael!" I knew Melody couldn't wait. She'd be out the door as soon as I left.

"Can you imagine what Margaret will say?" Tina already wrestled with the best way she'd divulge this information to her good friend.

"I'm on my way over to Louise's now to tell her about it."

Nobody spoke. I threw Melody a question in my eyes.

"She's not doing well," she answered.

"Not well at all," echoed Tina.

"She's slipping fast," sighed Miss Fizzi. "I called a couple of times this week and she couldn't speak. You run on over there and send her my love. It'll do her good to see you."

I said my good-byes before anyone could

break into a long discussion of police investigations and hurried to Louise's, afraid of what I'd find. A car pulled out of the driveway as I drove in. To my surprise, I spied Garland at the wheel. She lowered her head as she drove by, as if she didn't want me to know she'd been helping Louise with the morning routine. I entered the house and went straight to the bedroom.

Louise's face, once so vibrant and expressive, showed no movement, the white skin translucent as still water. Scared, I crept closer until I recognized the tiny rise and fall of her chest. She must have heard me gulp.

Eyelids, thin as cobwebs, fluttered open. "Fli . . ."

"Don't talk. You probably wore yourself out, talking up a blue streak with that lady who just left."

"Gar-land."

So I was not mistaken. "Garland? Since when is Garland a member of a Circle? Roland keeps her chained to the kitchen. But then, I don't pretend to know everything around here."

I started dusting as I babbled. "I'll start with your bureau here, then do the bathroom. Guess I could vacuum after that and finish dusting. Those sheets look fresh. Don't tell me Garland took care of that for you."

Louise struggled to communicate with a bat of the eye, a twitch of the lip. I knocked the dust off Marlene's baby pictures and went in to clean the bathroom, shouting my one-sided conversation through the open door.

"Louise, you won't believe what happened at the picnic." I needed to tell her about Tom. Maybe she could advise me with a squeeze of the hand. So I told her everything. About the great casserole I baked, and Sam and Lee making things public. About my aborted little spat with Roland.

I finished scrubbing tile and porcelain and stepped back into the bedroom. Louise's face was turned toward the bathroom, so I knew she'd been listening. "There's something else, too, but I'll tell you after I vacuum."

The machine whirred to business and I zipped around the carpeted room. When I'd run over every strand of fiber twice, I shut the vacuum down and wrapped the cord in a neat oval. Louise turned her face to the center of the room.

"Would you like something to drink? Some water or juice?"

Her brows joined, which I took to mean no, thank you. I walked to her desk and started dusting Marlene in elementary school, an exceptionally unattractive child.

"I need to tell you about Tom," I said slowly, knowing I was about to sort through feelings out loud, very confusing feelings. "He . . . surprised me at the picnic. Maybe it didn't even start there. Maybe it started in Baltimore, at the Harbor Court. Or maybe that day on the

Monocacy. Maybe it was in his office afterward. I don't know. I don't know when it happened, Louise, but he's been treating me like I was somebody special. Like I was somebody special to *him*. At the picnic, he actually took my arm and linked it with his, as if we were a courting couple in an old movie. And he looked at me differently than he ever has before, as though he really does see a different Flip Paxton. And I don't know why. I'm not different. I'm not."

When I glanced over at Louise, the pale face wore a strange smile, one tinged with mystery.

"So, the thing is, I don't know how to play this out. I'm not sure I'm reading him right. And if I am . . . if I am, God help me."

"He will," said Louise in a voice so faded, I half-expected the bed to be empty when I looked up. But there she lay, still wearing the mystery smile.

"He better because I have little else to go on. Anyway, Tom's on my schedule tomorrow. Maybe I'll get a better fix on him, who knows?" I moved to the bookshelf and to Marlene in her teen years, no improvement. "Now let me tell you about C.C. and her gorgeous home and terrible manners." I'd decided to leave out Marlene's role in the party snub. No sense adding to Louise's misery.

"I'll give C.C. the month. She did pay in full, but after that, it's *adios, amigo*. She'd do well to buy herself a live-in slave."

I slapped the last dot of dust off Marlene,

crossed over to the bed and sat on the end. "Louise," I addressed the strange smile, "I know you don't have the strength to talk and barely the strength to listen, but I want to thank you for letting me ramble on about my big questions in life. Not just today. I mean for all the times you've listened. You sort of took up where my mother left off. I hope I did the same for you, as a daughter. We've been lucky — no — *blessed* to have had each other."

I reached for her open hand and my heart lurched. The place where my fingers touched her skin — the lifeline, etched in the center of her palm — felt cold as winter. She was gone. She had left me.

All my mothers had left me.

Chapter 28

I didn't expect to come away from Louise's funeral uplifted, but I did. The Episcopal minister, Reverend Farlow, a fairly young man, conducted the service as Louise requested. She'd had a good amount of time to plan and had given a written copy of her wishes to both Reverend Farlow and Tom.

She did not want her coffin in the church during the service. Instead, she'd picked out a nice photograph of herself taken ten years earlier to prop up on the altar table, the Caribbean sun beaming bright across her face, arms draped over a white fence with the sparkling, aqua blue sea in the background. She wore an orange sundress, white sneakers and red Marilyn Monroe lips. Her skin glowed pink and healthy, and the wind whipped the gray hair off her face. A picture to wipe away the cold image of her deathbed.

Sam, Lee, Tom, and I sat together in the second row on the left. Marlene took the pew opposite with C.C., her new best friend, and Leonard, whose cellular phone went off during the opening prayer. I noticed him staring at Lee before he disappeared down the aisle, nobody upset to see him go. The small church over-flowed with people touched by Louise Lamm. Young children, teenagers, families starting out, middle-aged parents with kids in college, the el-derly — every age and generation, male and fe-male, all colors, all sizes, all beliefs represented in the gathering.

And almost everybody was smiling.

"What a good life she had!" I heard a lot of people say.

"What an example that woman set!"

"I remember the time Sally got sick with the scarlet fever and Louise organized everything from taking care of the twins to meals to car pools to cleaning house. She was a whirlwind when she had her health."

I also heard a lot of comments that ran in an-other vein. "Too bad about Marlene."

"I can't believe she even had the nerve to show up at her mother's funeral."

"Probably hoping for an inheritance. Her type never changes."

We sang the first hymn, "My Faith Looks Up to Thee."

While life's dark maze I tread, And griefs
    around me spread, Be thou my Guide;
Bid darkness turn to day, Wipe sorrow's tears
    away, Nor let me ever stray
From Thee aside
When ends life's transient dream, When
    death's cold, sullen stream

274

Shall o'er me roll, Blest Saviour, then, in love,
   Fear and distrust remove;
O bear me safe above, A ransomed soul!

Then a couple of lay readers delivered the scripture passages Louise had chosen from the King James version. She liked it best, she said, because the old English sounded soothing to the ear.

I thought her choice from the Old Testament strange and foreboding. Deuteronomy 11: 26-28.

Behold, I set before you this day a blessing and a curse;
A blessing, if ye obey the commandments of the Lord your God, which I command you this day;
And a curse, if ye will not obey the commandments of the Lord your God, but turn aside out of the way which I command you this day, to go after other gods, which ye have not known.

The New Testament passage that followed consisted of only one verse, John 13:34. "A new commandment I give unto you, That ye love one another; as I have loved you, that ye also love one another."

Then we sang "Here, O My Lord, I See Thee Face to Face" after which Reverend Farlow took the podium and preached a few words. He hadn't known Louise half as long as most of us, he said, and thought the loveliest form of tribute would be our own stories of how she'd touched our lives.

One by one, people stood and briefly recounted some tiny incident that had meant the world to them. How she'd come in the middle of the night to help their mother or child. How she secretly sent money to this person or another, only to be found out later. Her sense of humor, her love of life, her warmth. Several who stood were brave enough to say she'd been a wonderful mother, then shot Marlene a poisonous eye before taking their seats again.

None of it fazed Marlene Lamm Worthington, who sat stiff-necked the entire hour, jiggling her crossed ankle like she couldn't wait for the bell to ring and school to be over. C.C. put on a sweet show, reaching across periodically to pat Marlene's greedy hand, a strained, courageous smile on her face.

Tom stood and said a few words, hand resting comfortably on my shoulder, telling the story of how Louise got a recipe mixed-up so bad one Thanksgiving, dumping in pepper for flour and flour for pepper, that folks were on their knees slurping water out of the fire pond. Louise compensated everyone in town by hiring a catering service to bake a cake the size of a Buick and we all feasted on it during the Christmas tree lighting ceremony. The icing on top spelled out, "I'M SORRY, SOLACE GLEN!", which, Tom reflected, told you everything you needed to know about Louise Lamm. If she wronged you, she righted the wrong, but those wrongs consisted of such inconsequential things as too little flour, too much pepper. Nobody, he concluded, could accuse Louise of any real sin. Nobody could throw stones at that great lady.

I flashed a glance at Marlene, expecting her to jump up and heave a few rocks of her own, but she only coughed and unwrapped a peppermint, making as much rattle as she could. C.C. cooed and patted her hand for the hundredth time.

With stories told and everybody smiling at the happy memories, Screamin' Larry blessed us with the most beautiful, devout, reverent rendition of "Dear Lord and Father of Mankind" I had ever heard. Even C.C.'s mouth dropped at the dignity and emotion he put into that song, especially the last two verses:

Drop Thy still dews of quietness, Till all our
    strivings cease;
Take from our souls the strain and stress, And
    let our ordered lives confess
The beauty of Thy peace.
Breathe through the heats of our desire Thy
    coolness and Thy balm;
Let sense be dumb, let flesh retire; Speak
    through the earthquake, wind, and fire,
O still, small voice of calm!

"Well, I never," I heard C.C. mutter.
Then Larry ruined the mood by leering at her

and making his tongue flick like a lizard's. She jammed on her sunglasses, high heels clicking as she left the church with Marlene.

The four of us walked out together and thanked Reverend Farlow for a service we were sure Louise would have been proud of. Sam and Lee drove off for a quiet Friday night outing in Frederick; Tom patted me on the back and said he had business to wrap up.

I watched him drive away, wondering if I'd read him wrong, after all. A linked arm at the picnic, a brief hug at his office the day after Louise's death. Nothing more.

At once, I missed Louise.

"Flip." It was Margaret. She slipped a hand under my elbow and guided me a little ways beyond the lingering crowd. She obviously wanted to say something important and private, but seemed to be struggling.

"What is it, Margaret?" I really had no idea.

She drew herself up as if preparing to deliver a long speech. But this was all she said: "You're not alone, Flip."

In her eyes, I saw loss — terrible, devastating loss. I also saw compassion and warmth and strength. Dressed in black, her smile lit the lamp of comfort, and I was transported back in time, twenty-four years before, to a grave site where my whole world lay silent and still until I raised my eyes and discovered how many mothers called me daughter.

In that instant, Margaret took all their places,

those women who'd come before, those women who'd saved my life — my saviors of Solace Glen.

We hugged each other, knowing without words what had passed between us. She squeezed my hand, a brief kiss on the temple, and walked on.

Gratitude overwhelmed me. Louise had left me, but not all my mothers had gone. Not all.

Margaret's tall, straight form disappeared around a corner just as Pal came racing up from out of nowhere, shouting, "He's awake! Joey woke up outta the coma! Everybody! He's woke up!"

Plenty of people still milled around after the funeral, sharing a story or a remembrance of Louise. The occasion quickly turned into a rally for Joey Sykes and words of thanks to the Lord were not forgotten given the ground where we stood.

"Oh, mercy, mercy, Praise the Lord!" Miss Fizzi, determined to attend the funeral in a wheelchair driven by Sally and her strapping twin boys, could hardly sit still. "Is he *himself*, Pal?"

"She means is his brain working normal or is it cracked," explained one Egghead to Pal, using his best technical jargon.

"Oh, yeah!" Pal practically rose from the sidewalk in his ecstasy. "He's himself, all right. Already ordered a pizza and a number four from the Burger Hut."

"Does he remember the accident?" Melody and Michael asked in near perfect unison.

"Yeah, pretty much. At least what led up to it. A couple of cops from the county showed up and asked about it. Joey admitted he'd been speeding, but said he tried to stop and there were no brakes."

A little gasp escaped my mouth and I searched out Roland, standing between Garland and Lukzay, all three interested in Pal's announcement.

Pal's face crumpled as if in deep pain and he whimpered, "It's my own fault. I'm the one who worked on the brakes. I musta screwed up."

"That's highly unlikely, Pal," I said in a strong voice. "You're an expert mechanic. There has to be some other explanation."

Lukzay and Roland huffed at the dirty look I sent their way and Lukzay said roughly, "Boy admitted speeding. Pal admitted being the last to touch the brakes. End of investigation."

"But was he really the last one to touch the brakes?" I asked, hoping to fan a tiny flame. The crowd began to rumble. "I hope *somebody* examined that wrecked car top to bottom."

"Did they, Pal?" An Egghead pressed. "Is the car still at that garage?"

"I-I don't know," Pal replied, blinking in confusion. "I haven't seen it since the accident, I've been so upset and busy."

I saw Roland and Lukzay slide eyes at each other and skulk away from the crowd.

Everyone refocused on Pal and congratulated him on Joey's return to consciousness, assuring him that he was not to blame.

"Maybe those other policemen will get to the bottom of this," Tina offered, and Tom's warning to let the experts do their job came back to me.

I headed for home and slowly my thoughts switched from Joey's "accident" to more reflective thoughts of Tom. Louise could have told me which end was up. Yet she did say God would help, her last words, "He will."

But were those her last words? The scripture Louise planned for her funeral she chose carefully, purposefully. A blessing and a curse. Other gods. Love one another.

A blessing and a curse.

I smiled to myself as I walked. Knowing Louise, they were one and the same. We take the bitter with the sweet, she often said whenever I got whiny, the vinegar with the honey. We take the blessing with the curse, she was saying now.

I wrapped my coat tighter against the December cold and set out to make a mental list of blessings and curses in my life. The blessings mounted — eighteen good years with two loving parents; my "mothers": Marie, Leona, Louise, and now Margaret; my deep friendship with Lee; a business that gave me independence; a network of love and support in a tight community; the precious inheritance of a family tree.

Before I realized it, I was home, safe and warm, no curses yet on the list.

On my answering machine, the voice of Marlene, snippy and authoritative, instructed me to call her. I brewed a cup of tea and erased her with the press of a button.

I knew the curse in Louise's life; I dreaded discovering my own.

Chapter 29

Saturday, the day after Louise's funeral, I slid into my regular seat behind the register feeling a little sad for myself and everybody in town. Hilda slouched over and picked up my order. She looked similarly down in the mouth, although I knew it couldn't be because of Louise.

"What's got you so depressed, Hilda? Maybelline go out of business?"

"Naw." She'd used a heavy hand on the eyeliner and cheek blush that day, a cross between Cleopatra and Ronald McDonald. "I flunked a geometry test."

"Why don't you get a tutor?"

"I guess Ferrell T. could help me if I asked."

Guess again. "Ferrell T. wasn't so hot at math when he was in high school."

"No," she agreed, "but he did pass it at last."

"Why don't you ask the teacher to suggest somebody?" Why was I even trying to help? She had two parents, even if one of them was Roland.

"That's what Momma said to do."

"There you go." At last. "Listen to your mother."

"I guess I could."

She guessed she could. I gave up and scrambled for my pocket atlas. Hilda shrugged and slouched back toward the kitchen. I caught a glimpse of Garland staring at me through the window of the swinging door. I smiled, but she ducked away.

Just then, C.C. and Marlene whirled in out of the wind. C.C. wore what all us ladies in Solace Glen donned on our day off: knee-length fox fur, slinky cashmere wrap dress, black suede boots, and a fur-lined hat. She spotted me and waved. Marlene did more than that. She stormed over.

"You didn't return my call."

I put on a Queen Mother accent. "Oh, did you rrrring me?"

"You know I did." Her eyes looked ready to pop out, lotto Ping-Pong balls complete with dollar signs stamped on the corneas. "You have the keys to my mother's house, don't you?"

"And Tom has the other set." Her mouth dropped. I knew she'd demanded the keys from Tom seconds after hearing of Louise's death so she could go into her mother's house and "get some things that belonged to her." Tom wouldn't hand them over, saying the estate would have to be settled first.

"You know," I admired my hideous fingernails, "I didn't get my invitation to C.C.'s party next Friday."

"DO you have the keys?"

I clapped the pocket atlas shut. "If she left the

284

house to you, I will give you the keys. Otherwise, don't hold your breath."

"You impudent bitch."

"Gee, Marlene, that's not very Christian."

"How dare you. . . ."

She was winding up to run all day, but Tom, thank God, appeared out of nowhere. He took her arm, pulling her away from the table. "Marlene. Can you come by my office Monday afternoon, about three? We need to go over some things."

Her nostrils flared, but she nodded, throwing me a snitty look before tramping back to have a lovely lunch with C.C.

"Mind if I join you?" He pulled out the other chair and sat down hard. "What a day. What a week."

Hilda brought me a tuna sandwich and hurried off again with Tom's order.

"It's been a week, all right," I said. "Want my pickle?"

He screwed up his nose. "By the way, you need to be there, too. You're in Louise's will."

My hands fell to my lap. "Good Lord, I hope she didn't leave me a family Bible. I can't sleep at night as it is with this Bell and that one floating through my dreams."

He grinned. "I hope that's not all who floats through your dreams."

There he went again. I wanted to cuss. Instead, I bit into the sandwich and changed the subject. "Wonder who'll flip the switch this year."

Each year, the Tree Lighting Committee chose someone to light the tree and the town Christmas lights, usually someone who'd given an obscene amount of volunteer service to the community. Usually a Circle Lady.

"No idea. Who do you think?"

"Oh, probably C.C. Although she is new to our little community, she has shown extraordinary care and concern for the pitiful outcasts of society who appear to thrive in Solace Glen like termites. After all, she employed me."

"You going to her party next Friday?"

I almost choked. "No. No, I'm not going to the big shindig."

"Would you like to go with me?"

"You?" I quickly lifted a glass of iced tea to my mouth and hid behind it.

"Should be mildly entertaining. Screamin' Larry has vowed to crash it. If we're lucky, he'll arrive drunk as a skunk and sing Broadway hits all night."

Before I could respond, Ferrell T. came galloping through the door like a bloodhound on the trail, caught sight of Tom, and whisked him away, babbling something about a judge on the phone. Tom grabbed the remainder of my sandwich, told me to take home his lunch when it came, and he'd talk to me Monday.

While I waited for Hilda, someone else slipped into the chair opposite mine. I looked up to see Roland glowering at me, claws methodically tapping the top of the table.

"I was about to leave." I pulled bills out of my wallet — one's, five's, anything.

"Not just yet." He reached across the table and latched snaky fingers around my wrist. "We need to have a little talk."

I tried to pull my wrist away, but he only tightened the grip. "What do you want, Roland?"

"I want what I've always wanted, Flip Paxton." His mouth curled at the corners, not quite a smile, not quite a grimace. His eyes gleamed like the eyes of a stove slowly heating. "You see, I finally figured out the big picture and my focus has been out of whack. I've been concentrating on the money end of things, like Leona's house. I shouldn't feel angry about Lee getting that old ramshackle money pit. Mine's better, anyway. The stuff in the house — I got most of what I wanted long before Leona left this earth. Miss Fizzi's trust — she's gonna keel over dead any day at her age. Those things aren't as important, though, as the good name you leave your kids. That's where my focus has been out of whack, you see. I've come to what you call a *realization*."

I noticed he left out any mention of Pal's car. "What are you saying?"

His nails dug into my flesh and he took a sip from my water glass. "If those letters turn out to be historic, you know, elevating the Bell name in the history books, then as head of the Bell family, I'll take Lee to court to get the originals for my kids' inheritance. I'll go through the proper channels."

Somehow I doubted that, recalling Joey's coma, my torn up house, Lee's break-in, and Miss Fizzi's so-called accident. "And?"

"And you ought to think about what you want to give me for Christmas. Soon." He released his grip and flung my wrist down. "Remember, you're only the hired help. No relation. Don't fancy yourself keeper of the flame."

With that, he stalked away, disappearing through the swinging doors of the kitchen. I heard Lukzay chuckling hoarsely over his meal.

I rubbed my wrist as Hilda dropped off the wrapped plate of food.

"Can I get you anything else?" she asked.

"No," I snapped, "nobody can get me anything. I don't want any*thing*." Not a drink, not a sandwich, not a car, or a house, or a painting, or china. Not a book. Not a Bible.

Nothing that held names and dates, dreams and secrets. Nothing that began with the tree of life and ended with an apocalypse.

For the rest of Saturday and most of Sunday, I moped around the house, glaring at the basket on top of the kitchen cabinet, wishing Leona had given me a bracelet or a picture frame, anything but that Bible. The irony was, if Roland had inherited the letters and the Bible, he never would have cracked open a page, but because a Jenner and a Paxton held possession, he'd gone off the deep end. What part Leonard or anybody else played in this soap opera was anyone's guess.

By Sunday night, I'd worked myself from a frenzy back into a state of resolve. I couldn't give in to Roland. For whatever reason, Leona wanted me to have the history of the Bell family — not her brother and certainly not a man like Leonard Crosswell — and I would honor her intentions, no matter what. *Let the experts do their job.*

I climbed up on the counter and pulled down the basket. Born in 1880, four years ahead of his sister Florie, Roland Bell, Jr. could have joined the navy for the Spanish–American War in 1898, but he didn't. At age 37, he wouldn't have joined up to fight in Europe, either.

No, my picture of old Roland, Jr. rang clear. I saw him as an overweight, spoiled young man who rolled contentedly into middle-age and beyond, taken care of by women, given to practical jokes, admired for his knowledge of trivia, and baffled and frustrated by the demands and responsibilities of husbandhood and fatherhood. A momma's boy who never left Momma, grateful as hell she left him her fine, big house that he poured his wife's money into collecting art, carpets, furnishings, and china.

His parents guided him in the choice of a helpmate, picking from the field a passive, plain, unremarkable woman seven years his senior with tons more money than looks. Roland, Jr., a

bare eighteen years under his wide belt, con-
sented to the union, delighted he'd have so
much wealth to squander at such an early age.
He could show his friends a high time at the
races.

So in 1898, Roland, Jr., wed Katrina T.
Chapelle. It was she, so grateful at age twenty-
five to have landed a husband, who received the
Bell family Bible as a wedding present and
began the process of recording the generations
of her young husband's family. From 1898 until
1940, Katrina Chapelle Bell penned the births,
the marriages, and the deaths of the clan. It was
she, not a blood member of the family, who felt
the importance of family history and tradition,
who wanted her son to know his heritage and
take pride in his birthright.

Young, spoiled Roland, Jr., at least gave Katrina the two things she wanted most — a Mrs.
in front of her name and, in 1899, a son, Roland
Bell, III. After those two unselfish acts, which
required nothing more than to say "I do" and
consummate the union, Roland, Jr., drifted on
his merry way through life, adored by mother
and sister, occasionally patted on the head by
father, taken advantage of by friends ever short
on cash, and tolerated by a wife who gradually
ignored him and lavished all her time and attention on the son.

Poor, unwitting Katrina. She only added to
the pattern of raising and nurturing the sins of
the father. Men spoiled by their mothers, over-

protected, handed no responsibility in life, nothing required of them. Teaching her boy early on that he equaled the sun and whatever he touched turned to gold. Materialistic, greedy, and ruthless. Like grandfather, like father, like son.

Katrina died in 1940 at age sixty-seven. Roland, Jr. lived through the Second World War, going to his reward in 1945 at age sixty-five. They left behind a son, a daughter-in-law, and two grandchildren: a girl, Leona, and a boy, Roland, IV.

They left behind a legacy of self-absorption, self-importance, and greed, greed, greed.

How Leona became the person she did remained a mystery to me. The answer probably lay with her mother, but I could wait to wrestle with that generation next time.

I closed the Bible and sipped a glass of wine. I hoped Miss Fizzi's long-term memory outshone her short-term memory. At any rate, it would be intriguing to see if my imagination hit the target or completely missed the mark.

The Bible went back to its honored place under the Spanish moss on top of the cabinet. A lamp under a bushel. I went back to my honored place, a single body in a double bed, curled tight beneath the sheets and quilt, still counting the blessings on my list, leaving the curses in darkness.

Chapter 30

Marlene, dressed in black to resemble a sainted nun sporting a fish face, licked her lips when Tom entered the conference room and closed the door behind him.

"Is that the will?" The saucer eyes fixated on the papers in his hand.

"Yes. I have the original and two copies. One for each of you." He placed an envelope in front of both of us and sat down. "Rather than read Louise's Last Will and Testament word for word, I'll simply give you the gist of it. Then you can read through it at home, consult other counsel if you wish," he aimed this last part at Marlene, "and get back to me with any questions."

Marlene fingered the envelope suspiciously. "Well? What is the gist of it?"

Tom sucked in a gallon of air, blew it out again. "Your mother left you one thousand dollars a month for life."

The pop eyes stared at him. "A thousand a month."

"Yes."

"That's it?"

"That's it."

I squirmed in the chair; really, it was Roland all over again.

Marlene sputtered, "I've got debts to pay! What about the rest of it? What about the house?" The only reason she cared anything about the house, a modest rancher, was because the house she'd rented for nearly twenty-five years was falling in on itself and neither she nor her cheap landlord wanted to pour any money into it. "Don't tell me she left it to *her*. Haven't you inherited enough of other people's property, Flip?"

Tom and I ignored the insult. "The house," he continued, "which is unencumbered, is to be sold or rented and the proceeds placed in trust with the remainder of the estate. The personal property in the house goes to Flip, who is named Personal Representative of the estate, to do with as she chooses."

Her breathing came hard and fast. She leaned forward. "You said the estate, the bulk of the estate is to be put in a trust?"

"That's right."

"Who's the beneficiary?"

"Several named charities, plus, the trustees are given wide latitude in distributing income to entities or individuals who fall under certain specified categories."

Marlene stopped breathing altogether. "Who are the trustees?"

"I am one. Flip is the other."

I felt an electric shock and Marlene toppled backward in her chair.

"Me?" Now it was my turn to sputter. "What do I know about being a trustee?"

"You might be surprised," said Tom. "All it takes is good judgment."

"A thousand dollars a month." Marlene spat the words. "From a three-million-dollar-plus estate?"

I stared at Tom, eyes wide as Marlene's.

Marlene turned on Tom and spoke in a superior tone. "I *know* that's what the sale of my father's business brought her. She told me when I was eighteen. Plus, she inherited tons from her own family. Old money." She sneered at me like I was a caterpillar she had a mind to squish. "Very old money."

Tom listened patiently to the ranting tinged with accusation. "You're right. It is more than three million. Your mother invested wisely. I put it more in the neighborhood of nine or ten million."

"And I get the grand sum of A THOUSAND DOLLARS A MONTH!" She went so scarlet in the face, I thought we'd have to call the Eggheads.

I was fool enough to say, "A thousand bucks is nothing to sneeze at, Marlene. You can save up and buy a condo."

"Shut up! Shut up! You did this! Both of you did this! You influenced her to write me out! I was her only kin!"

I bolted up and crossed to the window, needing a whiff of cold air. "Now you really do sound like Roland."

She turned on Tom. "You wrote this will, didn't you?"

"As a matter of fact, Louise used a Baltimore law firm, then advised them when the time came that I was to handle the trust. If you fight this, Marlene, you will be fighting a losing battle. Don't believe me, though, take the will to another attorney. Please."

"You better believe I will! I bet Leonard Crosswell would *love* to take you on. Ten million — you *know* I'll fight this!" She sat in the chair, one hand tugging at her black sweater, glaring at the envelope in front of her. "Why should I let you and Flip have a high time blowing ten million on cancer patients who are going to die, anyway. Just like my mother." She reared up, snatched the envelope off the table, and stomped to the door. "In the meantime, you can mail me my first check. I wouldn't be caught dead stopping by here once a month to grovel from the likes of you. As for you, Flip Paxton, you'll get what's coming to you soon enough."

She blew out, slamming the door.

"Nice doing business with you, too," murmured Tom. He tossed an ink pen on the table.

I turned away from the window and faced him. "So," I said.

"So," he said, stretching his legs out, causing Eli to switch positions. He remained quiet for a time, then said, "Your hair has a blondish halo to it in the sun."

"That's called gray." My finger wrapped

around a piece of hair and made a curl. "Anyway, you're only flattering me because I'm almost a hot-shot trustee. Subject to legal wrangling, of course."

"You're right. The very word *trustee* has a certain sex appeal, don't you think?"

I started to laugh, but there was something in his eyes that caused me to hold my breath. He parted his lips to speak, but Ferrell T., such an efficient little secretary, burst through the door.

"Tom, circuit court just called."

"Thank you." Tom didn't move or take his eyes off mine. "You may go now."

Ferrell T. stood rigid as the king's guard. Tom turned to dismiss him again, but I cut them both off.

"What should we do about Louise's house while Marlene drags this thing out?"

The moment vanished. Ferrell T. picked up a pile of books from the conference table and busied himself shelving.

Tom rubbed the back of his neck a long minute, eyes downcast. "OK. The house. We'll need a professional appraisal of the real and personal property. You can still go over there and make your own inventory of what you would want to eventually keep, give to charity, sell, hand over to friends. We can discuss whether to sell or rent later on, as soon as Marlene discovers she doesn't have a leg to stand on."

"OK." I nodded and swallowed hard. "Thanks." I scooped up my coat.

"I'll walk you out."

"No, no, you're busy, and I've got a lot to think about now with this house and getting ready for Christmas. I got behind this past week."

He stood up, took the coat from me and wrapped it around my shoulders. I stuck a hand in the pocket, searching for the car keys. The red cashmere scarf felt soft and warm. "Oh, this is yours. You dropped it at the clinic."

"There it is." He unfurled the scarf and gently placed it around my neck, the touch of his fingertips against my throat. "It looks better on you. Keep it."

I didn't know what to say, so I said, "Yes, I'll go with you."

"Good," he whispered, and smiled. "Let's hope Larry shows up."

I flew down the street to my car, talking to Louise as if she was hurrying along right beside me. "Did you know, Louise? Is that why you bound us together as equals in your will? You planned this. You planned this as a blessing."

Marlene would never understand that the curse in her life at her mother's death had nothing to do with the inheritance, or that the blessings she could have had during her mother's life had nothing to do with riches.

I drove straight home, the copy of Louise's will tight in my hand. Whether I ever got around to reading it or not, I knew what Louise would have wanted.

Two days later, I walked through the empty house into the bedroom. A little more than a week before, Louise had lain in that bed and quietly slipped away from me, nothing more than a mysterious smile as her good-bye. Now I had a job to do, and I didn't want to attend to it. I carried a clipboard and started jotting notes.

The books could be divided between Lee's Historical Society and the school system. The clothes, which filled two closets and two chests, everything good quality, could go to friends or charity. Melody certainly matched Louise's size and Sally would eventually, after the baby arrived. The furniture, too, stood as a testament to Louise's good taste, most of it fine antiques. I hoped to keep a Martha Washington chair I'd always admired and picked out a couple of things for Lee and Margaret, but most of the furnishings should go to auction and the money used for one of Louise's worthy causes.

I continued through the house. Linen, silver, china, a couple of oil paintings, kitchenware, rugs, an old upright piano I knew the Methodists could use. Nothing lavish, nothing ostentatious. Louise lived a simple life for a woman with nine or ten million reasons to go berserk. Outside I listed garden tools, hoses, a new lawn mower, a Blue Martin birdhouse, stone figures of St. Francis and three rabbits, a birdbath, and a fountain. A car.

The idea hit me like thunder — Pal's new car.

Not a Cadillac, but a perfectly decent Chevrolet. I skipped inside, toothy as a game show host giving away the big prize behind door number three. My eyes skimmed around the rancher. I'd covered everything but one small concern and for that I'd brought along a box.

In Louise's bedroom, I walked methodically from corner to corner, clearing shelves and tables and bureaus of a baby, a toddler, a girl, a teenager, a young woman. With the room stripped bare of pictures and the box filled to the top, I taped the cardboard tight and wrote in black ink, TO MARLENE FROM MARLENE.

The Gift and Flower Shoppe was closed when I left the box on the front door steps with all the other UPS shipments of tacky, hollow trinkets and cheap merchandise.

I hoped she'd be very happy with herself.

Chapter 31

Friday morning, Solace Glen woke to the first snowfall of the season. I opened my bedroom window and leaned out, face to heaven, mouth open to catch the fat flakes. Workmen clambered up and down the linen white streets, stringing lights, preparing for the big tree lighting ceremony that night. People smiled and opened shops. Children's voices grew louder by the hour, tuning up for Christmas morning. Peace on Earth seemed real enough to wrap your hands around and bring inside by the fire.

I closed the window and got dressed, humming, coaxing last winter's thermal underwear onto my body. When I caught a glimpse of myself in the mirror, the woman in the glass fairly shimmered.

Sam's house was a mess, and I scolded him up and down as he sat at Leona's huge dining table wrestling with scotch tape and Christmas wrapping.

"Two weeks! You made all this mess in two weeks?" I kicked at a plastic mixing bowl, leftover popcorn kernels, yellow and gloppy, stuck inside. "Has Lee seen this place? No, I know she hasn't or she'd have torn up the lease and kicked your butt out in the street."

He jerked a rectangle of tape off his finger and stuck it on a present. "I'd sue. Right after I told her how much I adore the ground she walks on." He reached up and unzipped another inch of tape off one of his eyebrows. "Owww. And it's been four weeks. You didn't come the day after Thanksgiving. Then last Friday we buried Louise."

I counted in my head. "You're right. Now I feel bad. Good God, you're a victim."

"I am. But," he brightened, the boy who caught the prettiest salamander, "Lee loves me even though she agrees I'm a slob."

I started picking up dirty plates and T-shirts with my fingertips. "You and Lee going to the tree lighting?"

"Wouldn't miss it."

"How about C.C.'s party afterward?"

"Yeah, that, too. Lee's making me go. She wants to see the house. Speaking of the Crosswells . . ."

He paused dramatically, forcing me to stop cleaning and look him in the eye. "Yeeesss?"

"I had an interesting visit from Leonard yesterday."

My forehead wrinkled. "Leonard? What in the world would he want to talk to you about? Oh, wait. Let me guess. Letters."

Sam lifted one brow. "Letters. And lawsuits."

301

The pit of my stomach fluttered and I sat down hard in a chair, giving Sam my full attention. "Tell me."

"He came on the pretext of seeking advice about adding to his Civil War document collection."

I pictured the Longstreet letter on the wall of Leonard's study, so perfectly framed. "What kind of advice?"

"Whether Lee's letters are authentic and written by J.E.B. Stuart. What the contents of the letters are. If I think they're worth anything. If I've stumbled across any other historical documents while living here in Leona's house. If I might like to make a few bucks."

My skin blazed. "What did you tell him?"

Sam shrugged. "I told him what Lee already told everybody who asked at the Thanksgiving picnic — the letters are authentic and Stuart wrote them. I couldn't tell him the exact contents because Lee hasn't let me read them. She feels protective because of the way Leona and the Bell women kept the letters secret all these years. I know they're love letters, but I don't know who they're written to or what they're worth. No, I haven't seen any other valuable Civil War memorabilia floating around this house because I don't snoop. And thanks, but no thanks, I'm happy with my salary at the college."

"Anything else?"

"Only one thing. I assured him Lee would

never sell, not to him, not to anybody. Those letters are part of her heritage and a part of the history of Solace Glen."

I glowed at Sam. I had a feeling he was going to make himself a part of Lee's heritage and history before too long. But Leonard's snooping bothered me, especially after Roland's threat of a lawsuit to take the letters away from Lee. Two fireballs building in opposite corners. "You said, 'Letters and *lawsuits*.' "

"Oh, that." Sam stacked a couple of gifts he'd wrapped. "He asked me what I could tell him about you and Tom."

My eyes popped. "Me and Tom?"

Sam's own eyes narrowed and he grinned slyly. "You and Tom. You *know*. The cotrustees of Louise's estate. Seems he's been retained by Marlene. He was just fishing. Didn't catch anything. Probably thought I'd be more receptive to questions as a relative newcomer."

"He didn't say anything about Roland? Roland and the letters?"

Sam shook his head, apparently growing bored with the subject. "Nope. No Roland. No more letter talk. How's Miss Fizzi doing? I hear Tom has hired a private investigator."

I confirmed as much, and we rambled on about Miss Fizzi's health, Joey's awakening, and our own conclusions about who caused her fall and the failed brakes. I stuck to the notion Roland did it, but admitted room for doubt because of the figure in the black overcoat. Sam

303

couldn't decide between Suggs and Leonard based solely on the fact he didn't like either one. We moved on to the weather, Marlene, and Louise. Like any secret in Solace Glen, Sam said word of the cotrusteeship had leaked out, except that the Eggheads, who probably heard it from Marlene or Roland, buttered the truth with a coat of acid.

"The Eggheads told me, along with about fifty other intimates, that you and Tom plugged Louise with a bottle of Johnnie Walker Red one night and she changed her will to exclude Marlene. Said Tom slid one thin dime across the table and told Marlene, 'Meet your inheritance.' Did you know you and he are running off to live in Mexico?"

"To escape winter or our criminal past?"

Sam chewed on it a minute. "I'd do it for both. Cover the bases, that's my motto."

"Sounds good to me." I set him straight with the unvarnished story. "Marlene got more than she deserved. Frankly, I wouldn't have been as charitable as Louise."

"She'll still have to work for a living."

"Yeah, too bad. Like the rest of us."

Sam finished a gift he'd been struggling with and held it up proudly.

"A four year old could do better," I commented. "What are you getting Lee for Christmas?"

"I'm getting her a surprise. What are you getting Tom?"

The question caught me off guard. "Tom? I don't usually get him anything."

"But isn't this year . . ." Sam danced a little tap dance, throwing his arms out. *"Special?"*

"Not. Really."

"Oh?" He stood there grinning like an idiot then kissed my cheek. "I hear Tom likes jazz and owns a herd of boring ties."

Late that afternoon, I gift-wrapped a Ramsey Lewis CD and a tie featuring Hogarth barristers in curly white wigs. I placed both wrapped presents in the basket under the Bell Bible, certain I'd never have occasion to take them out again.

The doorbell rang at exactly five thirty, and my skin flushed hot and cold. I opened the door, and for the first time since I'd known him, Tom Scott stepped into my home.

"Hello. How are you? This is lovely." The ebony eyes scanned the living room. "Really lovely. Reminds me of an English country cottage."

"Thank you." I closed the door behind him. "That's what I was aiming for. I used to ride up to York to shop at the outlets, and I'd always grab a few yards of material." Why in the world would he care about that?

He turned to me in wonder. "You sewed all this upholstery yourself?"

"God, no. I'm worthless with a needle. Louise did most of it, and Leona helped." Shoot. I should have lied.

"Well," he rocked back on his heels, snow drifting off his shoulders and bare head, "I am still impressed."

We stood silent for a minute. "Would you like a cup of coffee or something?" I croaked.

"No, thank you. There's still a light snow falling. It's beautiful, the first snow. Let's get out there and enjoy it. Have a walk around before the ceremony."

"Fine." I couldn't resist. I reached up and brushed a patch of snow off his hair. "Do you want a hat?"

"And miss another opportunity to have you run your fingers through my youthful locks? I don't think so."

I flung on my old down coat, wrapped his red scarf around my neck and we waded out into the first snow.

A lot of people had the same idea. The town streamed with unrecognizable children, bundled toe to crown in snowsuits, screaming with excitement, adults shivering behind, calling out not to run too far ahead, almost time for the tree lighting. We plunged into the center of the street, taking advantage of the scarcity of cars, and swam up and down the white-capped roads of our town, winding closer and closer to the fire station. Homes twinkled with Christmas lights. Trees, loaded with silver, red, gold, and green balls, framed window after window. A few front yards staged manger scenes, often side by side with Santa and the reindeer, as though he'd skidded in on his sleigh to lay a skateboard or an action figure by the Christ child.

"No tree yet, Flip?" He caught me as I stumbled over a mound of snow.

"I never get one before the fifteenth and out it goes January first."

"No fire hazards for you, eh? Smart lady."

I looked at him quick, to see if his face wore a touch of sarcasm, but no. He'd called me smart.

We walked on and it occurred to me something was missing — a wagging tail. "Where's Eli?"

"Arthritic hip. He hates the cold. I hope I'm in better shape in my dotage."

You're certainly in good shape now, I thought, admiring his profile on the sly.

The fire station loomed ahead, surrounded by a large crowd of mittened and scarfed citizens. Our mayor rubbed his mitts together and cheerfully introduced the master of ceremonies for the year, Reverend McKnight.

The Presbyterians managed a *whoop,* and the rest of the crowd applauded politely. Reverend McKnight, nose and cheeks as fiery as his hair, took the podium and adjusted the microphone to match his significant height. In the old days, he'd have made a fine champion log hurler.

"Mayor Cummings, fellow clergy, citizens, and visitors of Solace Glen." His voice matched his height. "Welcome, one and all, to the annual tree lighting ceremony! We will open with the youth choirs of our four town churches — Presbyterian, Methodist, Episcopalian, and Catholic — joining together to lead us in song. Please sing along. Sing!" He commanded, lifting both hands, wrists flapping upward.

A drove of preteens invaded the platform erected for the occasion. They banded as one unit and, under the direction of the high school music teacher, launched into a familiar round of seasonal tunes. We all sang and made sure Reverend McKnight saw our lips moving.

God Rest Ye Merry, Gentlemen. The Eggheads, with Pal, lolled against the ambulance, front end sticking out of the station garage, a wreath roped to the shiny grill.

Frosty the Snowman. Roland glared around at the crowd and snarled whenever somebody bumped into him. Garland, enjoying the kids on stage, sang every other word, often tripping up and twittering at herself. Ferrell T. and Hilda stood beside their parents, the son silent and sour, a replica of the old man, the daughter singing without the vaguest idea of the words.

You're All I Want for Christmas. Sam and Lee huddled together, giggling, knocking into each other's hips like thirteen year olds. Melody and Michael watched them, laughing.

Little Jack Frost Get Lost. Marlene stomped her big feet in the snow, impatient for the ceremony to end so she could run play cohostess with C.C.

Deck the Halls. C.C. and Leonard flanked Marlene, the two of them draped in dueling minks. C.C. kept glancing at her diamond watch while Leonard must have made three calls on his cell phone in the span of two minutes.

I Love the Winter Weather. "I love the win-ter wea-ther, so the two of us can get to-ge-ther." Screamin' Larry, a deadly glint in the eye, boomed the words at the top of his inebriated lungs, trying to catch C.C.'s attention, waving a bottle of Peppermint Schnapps in her direction.

Angels We Have Heard on High. I glanced over the crowd at the little house down the block. Through the treetops, I spied Miss Fizzi at her bedroom window, singing along with Tina and Margaret. Sally's pregnant silhouette swayed in the background as she pinned a finishing touch to Miss Fizzi's hair — a pink rose. Suggs probably brooded in his dank basement apartment, occasionally sticking a pin in a Santa voodoo doll.

And finally, *Winter Wonderland.* I sang, tapping my foot, getting into the bop of the rhythm, swinging my shoulders. "A beautiful sight, we're happy tonight, walking in a winter wonderland."

Tom sang, too, louder and louder, snapping his fingers like Frank Sinatra, "In the meadow, we can build a snowman . . ." A wide grin on his face melted into laughter at the sound of his own terrible, off-key voice. "And pretend that he is Parson Brown."

We belted it out. "He'll say, 'Are you married?' We'll say, 'No, man. But you can do the job when you're in town.' Later on . . ." A beautiful sight. We're happy tonight.

Reverend McKnight took the podium again. "Splendid! Splendid! I heard some . . . marvelous voices in the crowd. And now, the moment we've been waiting for, the name of the person who has the honor this year of turning on the lights of Christmas for the town of Solace Glen." He opened a small, folded piece of paper. "This year's honor goes to a woman in my own congregation. A quiet, thoughtful, behind-the-scenes kind of person who uses her kitchen to fill the mouths of those in need, unbeknownst to many, including, I believe, her own family. Our hats off to Mrs. Garland Bell."

I zoomed in on Garland. She'd gone white as the snow at her feet, hunching her shoulders to shrink smaller. Hands and arms around her pushed and shoved the poor woman onto the platform. Hilda and Ferrell T. gaped. And Roland. Her supportive spouse. His face went crimson, lips curved into a scythe.

Tom whispered, "That was the best kept secret in town, now shot to blazes. It should have stayed secret — for a very good reason."

At once, I understood why Tom hired Ferrell T. as his secretary. He'd done it as a favor to Garland. I stared at her, a shaking leaf in front of the crowd, in front of her husband. I remembered her kindness to Louise and my heart went out to her.

Garland tried to put on a brave face, but it

310

was obvious she was scared to death. She'd been discovered. Now Roland could rant, "I'd be a rich man but for you flushing away the profit. You. You. You." Always somebody else hindering him from Greatness.

Garland reached the center podium, propelled by the gratitude of neighbors and strangers into the spotlight. Reverend McKnight heartily shook her hand and placed a mobile light switch in her palm.

"As Christ was the Light of the World, may you, kind lady, light the night and officially begin our holiday season in Solace Glen."

The crowd shouted huzzah, huzzah, with Screamin' Larry's huzzah's loudest of all, piercing the cold air. Garland lost sight of her horrible, depressing family and only heard the cheers of the audience, the encouragement of the Circle Ladies, felt the pats on her back from Mayor Cummings and her strong-willed pastor. She held high the 3×5 card Reverend McKnight pressed into her hand and read, haltingly, the words printed out for her. " 'With mortal hand, I light these symbols of Life, Spirit, Happiness, and Redemption. May we hold in our hearts the true fires that warm the human condition: love, joy, peace, gentleness, goodness, faith, meekness, and temperance.' "

With a nervous hand, Garland lifted the switch and clicked on the lever.

White, twinkling lights starred the streets of Solace Glen, the stores, the businesses, the courthouse, the fire station, the landscaping, the town council building, the telephone poles, and, of course, the official town tree, a newly cut blue spruce. It was beautiful, spectacular, wondrous — the snow providing the perfect postcard effect.

Not three seconds later, as we all *oooo*'ed and *ahhhh*'ed at the change in scenery, the fireworks went off. Only we never set off fireworks at Christmas.

We turned, faces east, drawn to the roar and boom, the flash and fire of a huge explosion in the distance, on the far hill, in the center of the O'Connell property. The Leonard and C.C. property.

Between sonic booms and fiery blasts, C.C. moaned, "No, no, no, no, no, no."

"My God! Is that your house?" Marlene saw her big role as party cohostess explode into thin air.

Leonard started punching numbers into the cell phone and struck out toward his car.

"Damn," Lee hissed in my ear. "I never got to see inside the house."

"Look at Larry." Sam gawked at the platform, the only one of the four of us who didn't know Screamin' Larry's special history of insanity and shady criminal inclinations.

Larry, inspired, leaped to the stage beside poor, pitiful Garland who still held the light switch clamped tight in her palm. She stared off in the distance, convinced, no doubt, that her innocent flick of a plastic lever caused the greatest fireball in Maryland since Antietam.

Larry pranced and danced around her. "This goes out to you-know-who!" he shouted, and started belting out "Smoke Gets in Your Eyes." He threw off his coat and earmuffs, boots and socks. He stripped off his shirt and tossed it into the crowd, and he would have given them his pants, squirming on his back to rip them off, but Reverend McKnight summoned the aid of the Eggheads and Pal. The four of them dragged Larry, kicking and screaming, off the stage and into the back of the ambulance for safe-keeping.

"If I didn't know better," reasoned Sam, shaking a raised index finger, "I'd say Larry had something to do with this explosion business."

We moved away from the fire station, firefighters jumping into action, half the crowd jumping into cars to go watch the action. The four of us drifted toward Lee's Historical Society, the little munchkin house crammed attic to cellar with books, a large, stuffed doll, and a good coffee machine. From that inviting vantage point, we could attempt to solve the puzzle of how Larry managed to pull this one off — a pinpoint of destruction, the cherished home of the town's least favorite new residents, and Larry's hated obsession.

"Yes." Sam bobbed his head, serious, and veered into Lee, who snorted, hysterical, tugging at his coat. "I'm certain that brilliant disc jockey is behind all this fire in the sky."

With the two of them cavorting ahead of us, Tom and I fell into their parade. He linked his arm with mine and as we stumbled in the snow past hundreds of white lights, the serious, incisive, aristocratic attorney of Solace Glen sang and sang and sang.

Chapter 32

The Saturday lunch crowd buzzed with talk of last night's tree lighting explosion. A couple of new customers thought Garland really did set it off, but they didn't know Garland. The silent majority, protective of one of their own (no matter how criminally insane), agreed she had nothing to do with it. Then they turned away and whispered knowingly that our very own Screamin' Larry had finally rigged it so C.C. got her just deserts for denting the Big Orange Volkswagen Beetle. After all, years before when Larry fell under suspicion for blowing up a gas line, the town gratefully watched the disappearing tailpipe of an unsavory slumlord. Pending Officer Lukzay's energetic investigation, Larry walked free.

I smirked when I heard that. If Larry could blow up a gas line and get away with it, one exploding house wasn't going to put an end to his shenanigans, either, especially if "investigated" by Officer Look-away. Fortunately, no one had been inside the Crosswell's house since the caterers mysteriously received two phone calls with conflicting timetables. So, no lives lost, only the presence of two unwanted new residents, C.C. and Leonard.

The Eggheads blabbed that Larry had confessed everything to them, but Pal, stopping by the Café for a rare store-bought sandwich, refuted their account saying Larry passed out once they got him in the back of the ambulance. His last words before oblivion were, " 'Something deep inside, cannot be denied.' "

Word was, C.C. and Leonard suffered well, mourning at the Willard in Washington, this particular dream of a country home smoldering in the melting snow of Frederick County. Rumors ran that they would sell the O'Connell property and start anew, farther out of town.

Hilda came around to take my order and proudly informed me she had a tutor lined up to help her pass geometry. She stood there, waiting, until I realized she expected a word of approval from me. So I gave her one.

"Good," I said. Approval probably counted as a rare commodity in her life with a father like Roland and a brother like Ferrell T. "How's your mother?" I slipped the pocket atlas back in my pocket.

"OK," she said slowly, eyes flashing in her father's direction. "She's OK."

Roland's gray eyes fixed on us, monitoring every movement. I lowered my voice. "Is she here today?"

"No. She didn't feel well this morning."

"You just told me she was OK."

"OK but for that." She turned on her heel and

scampered into the kitchen, as much the scared rabbit as her mother. It was the first time Hilda had ever shied away from conversation and I knew why. Roland watched his daughter hurry away, his expression set firm and hard as an executioner's.

From the time I left Roland's Café on Saturday afternoon until Thursday night, I barely had a moment's rest. Everybody needed a house cleaning before the holidays, there were still people to cover on my Christmas list, and the church needed an extra pair of hands with the baking.

All the while, I didn't see or hear from Tom. Though impressed with my living room decor, the admiration apparently didn't cross over to me as a date. Immediately after coffee at Lee's, he'd walked me home and acted so much the gentleman, I was insulted.

Since I'd promised Miss Fizzi a Friday visit, I put aside some time Thursday night to study the Bell family tree. The basket came down from the top of the cabinet, hardly an ounce heavier with Tom's CD and tie wrapped up in the bottom. The CD could always fit in my stereo, but the tie wouldn't match anything I had to wear.

I opened the Bible and out sprang another generation.

Roland's daddy, Roland Bell, III, was born in 1899, ignored by his father and spoiled to death

317

by his mother, Katrina. In 1930, at the start of the Great Depression, Roland, III, married Penelope Higgins. He was thirty-one, she a mere twenty. The following year, Leona was born. Ten years later, Penelope gave birth to a son, Roland Bell, IV.

A history of sweet women marrying spoiled, awful Bell men. What is it in a woman's background or character, I wondered, that leads her to make such a poor choice?

I thought of Garland who fit the family pattern perfectly — a sweet, passive, giving soul who made a terrible choice in a life mate. She actually had to sneak food to the needy because her husband wouldn't approve. For the first time, I didn't question that Roland beat her.

I remembered Roland's mother, Penelope. She was much like Garland, physically, spiritually, mentally. A woman who tried to emulate her husband against her nature. A mouse. A scared, cornered mouse who simply did the best she could, pouring herself into family.

Both Roland, III, and Penelope died in a plane crash in 1971 when I was a teenager. People whispered he'd been drinking, showing off and flying low down a country road, treating the expensive new Cessna like a toy. He lost control and the plane sailed into a huge oak tree. They were killed instantly. I attended the funeral with my parents who would die three years later, only my father wasn't drunk in an airplane. The other driver was drunk in an eighteen wheeler.

Nobody mourned her husband, but Penelope's name appeared later, etched in a special stained glass window with the words, IT IS MORE BLESSED TO GIVE THAN TO RECEIVE, a tribute paid for by her circle of friends, the Presbyterian Circle Ladies.

Beside Penelope's window was the window dedicated to my parents, Garrett Joseph and Julia Reed Paxton, with the words, HE MAKETH HIS SUN TO RISE ON THE EVIL AND THE GOOD, AND SENDETH RAIN ON THE JUST AND UNJUST.

I closed the Bell Bible. It had taken me a long time to comprehend the meaning of those words and why they were chosen. My parents were the kind of people who would have forgiven the driver who ended their lives and his, but I had always struggled with forgiving anyone I didn't know or love. I struggled with it every day, and it galled me yet that God allowed the sun to rise on a man like Roland Bell, and comforted me none that He sent rain to fall on both my parents' graves and the grave of the man who made me an orphan.

Chapter 33

"Just look," whined Miss Fizzi. "I need a hair job so bad even the Circle Ladies are talking ugly about me."

"Can't you get Sally to come here again?" I fluffed the pillows behind her back. She'd moved from the bed to the Victorian love seat by the bedroom window, sprained ankles propped high on a stack of soft blankets. "If she can't do it, I will."

"No, you won't, either." The bottom lip poked out. "You'd make a mess of it. Sally's the only one can fix my hair right, the way I like it. But would you call her for me? It keeps slipping my mind."

"Sure I will." I hoped remembrance of things past hadn't slipped her mind as well. "Miss Fizzi, I've been reading the Bell family Bible Leona left me."

"I'm so glad to hear it." She laid her good hand on my arm. "Are you a New Testament person or an Old Testament person?"

"No, I don't mean the book. I mean the family part. The Bell family tree that's written out in the first couple of pages."

"Oh." She let that sink in.

"You're almost eighty-five, aren't you, Miss Fizzi?"

"Is it May already?" Her glance skimmed over my shoulder to the trees outside.

"No, you're still eighty-four." I pulled a carved chair from under a dressing table and sat down beside the love seat. "I want to ask you about some of the Bells. Are you up to a little trip down memory lane?"

"My favorite vacation spot." The blue eyes twinkled. She set her shoulders square, ready for the journey.

"OK, do you remember Florence Openheim Bell?"

"Florie?"

"No, not Florie." At least we were on the same track. "Her mother. She died in 1929."

Miss Fizzi's nose wrinkled. "Vaguely. I was just a child. I know she was real big on getting the Presbyterian Church started. The Bells were staunch Episcopalians. But Florence always hated her husband's church and as soon as old Mr. Bell died she banded with her mother-in-law, what was her name?"

"Gretal Stubing Bell."

"Yes! You see, another German Lutheran. Those two hated being Church of Englanders. Anyway, they got together with some others who wanted to go Presbyterian. Florence couldn't persuade them to go Lutheran, but she was satisfied with the end product and spent the last twenty-five years of her life the most devout member of that congregation. Quite a pillar of the community, upright and stern as a telephone pole, except where her son was concerned, Roland, Jr."

I brightened at testing a theory. "Did she spoil him?"

"Lord! You've never seen the like. Except Katrina, his wife. She was worse with her child."

"What about Florie?"

"Florie I remember better. My mother said Florie had all the promise of a beauty as a girl, but once she hit her early twenties, two or three years before her father died, something happened to her. Changed her. She got old overnight. It was rumored some man had forced himself on her and the experience left her scarred."

"Wouldn't her parents have had the man arrested?" Poor Florie. My theory that she'd been too picky flew out the door.

"Well, dear. Under certain circumstances, the family might have wanted to keep it hush-hush. People had more secrets in those days. He might have been a family friend or a relative. To make Florie's tragedy public would have ruined her chances for a husband, and she did have suitors."

"For all the good it did. She never married."

"No, she withdrew from the world, became a recluse, never left Florence's side. When Florence died, Florie depended wholly on her brother. She shot herself."

"Shot herself!"

Miss Fizzi brought her small hand to a cheek and shook her head sadly. "The family couldn't cover up that truth, even if they tried. She did it in front of the Presbyterian Church, ten years to the day after her mother died, as people came filing in for services."

"No!"

"It was in the papers." As if that made it true as the turning of the tide.

"What happened?"

"Well, they buried her, of course. What was left. Katrina had to handle everything because Florie's brother was so 'upset,' she said. But everybody knew he'd gone on a drinking binge in some bar. You know, that's how the family acquired half their lovely things. Roland, Jr., was a big rumrunner during prohibition. Heavy drinker, heavy gambler, heavy womanizer, and just plain heavy. He liked making money the easy way, the way of the devil."

So I'd pretty much nailed him, too. "Did Katrina have money of her own?"

"Oh, I'm sure she brought Roland, Jr., a handsome dowry when they married and, of course, she inherited her father's estate, a right well-off gentleman as I recall."

My guesses proved so on target that we could have been playing bingo, with Miss Fizzi calling out all the right numbers. "What about Roland's parents, Roland, III, and Penelope?"

She closed her eyes and smiled as if conjuring

them up. "Penelope was a dear woman. Can't say the same for her husband."

I recounted what little I could of the two of them.

"You remember correctly, dear," Miss Fizzi agreed. "Penelope gave her heart out to all who knew her, and she was married to the cheapest, lowest backstabber in Maryland. Nothing she did suited him. He treated her like a dirty doormat. What little money he gave her, she sent to people in need or bought toys to spoil Roland. Even the clothes on Penelope's back were given to her by friends who couldn't stand to see the poor thing traipse around in rags. Roland, III, didn't care. He spent money only on himself and his precious namesake. And look how Roland turned out!"

Yes, I thought, *look how Roland turned out.*

"What I can't understand, Miss Fizzi, is why some perfectly normal, respectable women end up with such jerks. Why is that?"

"I don't know. *C'est l'amour.*" She knitted her brow.

"Garland. Penelope. Katrina. And for all we know, Florence, Gretal, Sara, back to Lucy Hanover Bell. Maybe all the Bell wives were sweet little doormats."

"Was she the first one? Lucy? Lucy Hanover Bell," she repeated thoughtfully. "I remember some story about a Lucy."

I ran through the female side of the Bells for Miss Fizzi: Lucy Hanover begat Lucinda who begat Lucy Bell who begat Lucinda Ann. And there it ended.

"What was that story Leona told me?" she asked herself. "It was definitely about a Lucy. Well!" She threw up her hands, the bad wrist mending nicely. "If I think of it, I'll let you know."

"You do that. You've already told me so much. Can I get you anything before I go?"

"No, thank you. Just don't forget to call Sally."

With a work day crammed full with cleanings, I kissed Miss Fizzi's cheek and hurried off, leaving her on the love seat, a book of religious poetry in her lap and the question on her lips, "What was that story? What was that story?"

That night, exhausted, but my mind teeming with Miss Fizzi's recollections, I opened the Bell family Bible and stared at the final two generations squeezed on the page: Leona Bell Jenner, born 1931, and her younger brother, Roland Bell, IV, born 1941; Ferrell T. Bell, born 1977, and his younger sister, Hilda Higgins Bell, born 1986.

A chill prickled my skin. No one had filled in Leona's date of death. Then it hit me — it was up to me. That was my job.

I took a fine point black ink pen and wrote in the month, day, and year of Leona's death, a complete life in the space of two inches. Jake Jenner's name rested beside hers, the life dates filled in, as if two tombstones from the Epis-copal graveyard had chiseled their way into the pages of the Bell family Bible.

Leona and Jake married in 1952, and though no children blessed the union, they were an ex-tremely happy couple, devoted to each other and their families. Leona tried her best to dote on Ferrell T. and Hilda, but as they grew up and their personalities emerged, the doting switched to Lee, the daughter of her husband's brother. When Lee lost Henry and Marie, Leona and Jake stepped right in, and no child could have wanted more for parents.

Leona was a blessing to everyone she met. Like her mother, Penelope, Leona Bell Jenner was a giver. She inherited none of the traits so rampant among the Bell males — selfishness, greed, immorality, cruelty — and spared herself the misery of marrying a copy of her father.

On the other hand, Roland fit the Bell mold exactly. He even found an exact replica of Penelope in Garland Day. They married in 1968; I remembered the wedding. Garland's parents blew the wad, hiring a big band and set-ting up tents with tables of fabulous foods. I heard more than one guest speculate on how long it would last, given Roland's stingy ways and his need to control the tiniest details in life.

"She'll be sorry," clucked one old lady. "And she's pretty enough to snag almost any man in the state."

"She's pretty, but she's got jelly for a backbone," replied another lady. "That's the attraction, you know. He needs to be in charge. She needs somebody to tell her what color checkbook to pick out."

Those two ladies knew their stuff. Garland must have had regrets, but no strength to act on them until she'd been beaten so low, she'd almost disappeared. Like the line of Bell brides before her, she doted on her two children, spoiling Ferrell T. beyond repair. Though, maybe hope hadn't run dry for Hilda.

As for Ferrell T., I knew the path he would take. Like his daddy before him and his daddy's daddy and on and on, he would zero in on some wealthy girl with a low opinion of herself, some passive, sweet, yielding creature who would not understand, until too late, that when you boil it down, our choices are life-giving or life-threatening. And she would have made a terrible choice.

I covered the pages of the tree with my ten fingers, the tips touching every generation. So many lives, so many years, so many choices. They were all gone now, but for the last four names on the tree. No doubt Ferrell T. and Hilda would marry in the not-too-distant future, and I would be the one to pen new names onto the spreading branches.

I would be the one because Leona chose me.

I closed the Bible, looking forward to reading each little envelope, poem and scrap of paper scattered throughout its pages, happy at the thought of new discoveries. I hugged the precious treasure to my chest and knew I could never give it up to Roland. One day, though, one day I would hand it over to some other woman, maybe even Hilda, a woman who would appreciate these faceless scratches of ink that took shape, lived and breathed, loved, gave birth, suffered, and died, not only in my imagination, but here in this real place of ground and sky and seasons where she and I would someday rest, a stone above our heads telling nothing of our lives to those who passed by but a name, a date of birth, a death.

Chapter 34

Christmas shoppers and the usual crew packed the Café Saturday afternoon. I shoved bags of gifts under my table and collapsed in the chair to wait for Lee. That morning she'd hatched a plan that might douse Roland's obsession with the letters. I wasn't so sure.

I wrote a lunch order and opened my date book, frowning at the packed cleaning schedule ahead of me, the last job not until five o'clock Tuesday, Miss Fizzi's house.

Hilda swooped down and snatched up the order, not a word. Not herself. I squinted at the kitchen door window, hoping for a glimpse of Garland, but she was nowhere to be found. I closed the date book, crossed my legs, and sat back, my eyes skimming the room while I waited for Lee to show up.

Pieces of conversation rose and fell at each table like drifting confetti — amazement at Joey coming out of the coma; Was the accident a brake failure or brake tampering?; Who broke into my house and Lee's? Teenagers? (And in a murmur) Roland?; Who would want to hurt Miss Fizzi?; Would Screamin' Larry (as dearly hoped) get away with gutting C.C.

and Leonard's happy home?

There sat Pal and the Eggheads, in between talk of Joey, voices rising in a crescendo over the best brand of kitty litter. There sat Larry, consuming his three lunches, looking all the world as guiltless and guileless as a choirboy on Christmas Eve. There sat Tina, Melody, and Margaret, debating all the latest gossip plus the questionable taste of Tina's new fashion purchase and the success of her latest diet. There sat Officer Lukzay, smirking at me over his menu as if he knew something I didn't. There sat Marlene, glum and morose, her artsy, rich friends vamoosed. She sighed heavily, more a groan than a sigh, distracting the Eggheads.

"Hey, Marlene," one of them yelled, "where's C.C. these days? Conferring with her decorator?" The two sniggered into their shirtsleeves and Larry let out a little whoop.

Marlene huffed and clanged a spoon around her teacup, eyes boring into Larry. She recognized his handiwork when she saw it, but bowed to the protective, impenetrable veil the community wrapped around their vigilante DJ hero.

"No plans to rebuild? Nice property. Handsome view. Gonna sell the property, are they?"

"You can ask Mr. Crosswell yourselves, morons. Here he comes now." Marlene sat up straight and brightened at the sight of her legal Galahad swooping into the Café.

Leonard, ever on his way to something more important, didn't bother to take his coat off

330

when he spotted Marlene and scraped a chair up to hers. She leaned eagerly toward him. I could practically see the dollar signs in her pupils.

Leonard, all business, got right down to it. He did all the talking in a discreet, high-priced attorney's voice. Marlene's face fell after the first thirty seconds and the dollar signs in her eyes visibly faded. She stuttered out a question or two and at the end of Leonard's speech, barely five minutes, her whole body seemed to shrink. I saw Leonard pat her hand paternally and pull out a fat envelope that he presented to her matter-of-factly, probably a bill.

As our Mr. Crosswell rose to leave, one of the Eggheads found the courage, based solely on incurable curiosity, to ask him if he and C.C. were, in fact, going to rebuild the house.

"No," he answered curtly, peering intently over his spectacles on the long, fox snout. "The house is history. The property will be sold."

Too stupid to realize he was pressing his luck, the other Egghead piped up, "You lose everything? Even your expensive Civil War collection?"

Leonard came to a halt midstep and slowly rotated, glaring at the entire room. You could practically hear his teeth grind when he said, "Yes. Everything. The collection was . . . irreplaceable. But I *will* start over." The black, canine eyes briefly caught hold of mine, and he disappeared.

A minute later, a whiff of cold air blew in and I turned to see Tom in the entranceway, stomping ice and dirt off his boots. He wasn't anywhere near, yet a rush like warm, mulled wine raced through my limbs and left me nearly drunk. He glanced up just as I felt the need to peel off a layer of clothes, and appeared at the table in time to help pull one arm out of a coat sleeve.

"Thanks."

He plopped into the chair beside me. "Always willing to help a lady undress."

I hadn't heard from him in a week and trying to read the man was wearing me out. "Well. What have you been up to, counselor?"

Roland slid behind the register close by, helping himself to a customer's money. Tom removed his coat, leaned forward, and whispered, "There's something you need to know."

"There's something you need to know, too. Lee is going to give Roland the letters."

He cocked a brow. "Oh?"

"Not the originals. She's keeping those at the Historical Society as a Civil War exhibit because they really were written by J.E.B. Stuart. But she ran off some copies this morning and she's bringing them in any minute. Her theory is once Roland reads the letters himself and sees what they're all about, he'll lose interest and we won't hear anymore lawsuit talk. Also," I peered beyond his shoulder into the street, "we're in luck today. Leonard Crosswell made his exit a minute ago."

Tom rubbed two index fingers down the bridge of his nose, thinking. Finally he said, "Good. That's a smart thing to do. Stem the tide and quell the fire. I suggest you do the same with the Bell Bible."

I scowled at him. "What are you talking about?"

"Lee has a point. Give Roland what he wants — or at least a modified version thereof — and his fire will burn itself out. Give him a copy of any personal writings, family memorabilia, whatever is in that Bible. Let him have it." He leaned back, problem solved. "Why do you look so shocked?"

I shook my head. "No."

"No? No what? You don't want him to even have a copy of what's in that Bible?"

"No, *Leona* didn't want him to have what's in that Bible. And frankly, I'm not so sure Lee should hand him copies of the Stuart letters because no male in the Bell family has ever seen them and there must be a very good reason for that."

"Perhaps at one time there was. But, Flip, we're talking about something that occurred over a hundred and thirty years ago. What possible difference could it make now?"

My stomach tightened. "I don't know. I don't know." He was making me so mad and disoriented, I turned on him abruptly, "What are you doing about Miss Fizzi?"

"Miss Fizzi?"

I hissed, one eye on Roland. "About you-know-who's attack on her! What the hell have you been doing about it?"

He dropped his voice, keeping the tone quiet and soothing as though speaking to a mental patient. "We still don't know if you-know-who is the culprit. My investigator had a look at the site but could draw no conclusions, and Suggs has been less than cooperative. No surprise there. I might also add, Pal said that when he went to the Frederick garage to check on the Cadillac, they told him it had been ordered to the scrap yard, apparently a day or two after Miss Fizzi's fall."

My glance flew to Officer Lukzay. That's what he knew that I didn't.

Tom continued. "But . . . as a precaution, I went to Garland and told her everything. I laid it on the line, told her Roland was a prime suspect and may need some kind of help soon or he'd end up in jail. I gave her a week to come up with viable suggestions."

"You're kidding." The idea of the rabbit snaring the wolf didn't cut it.

"No, I'm not kidding and you'd be surprised at Garland's good sense."

"What did she come up with?"

"Family counseling with Reverend McKnight. He came for Sunday supper at their home two weeks ago with Hilda and Ferrell T. present. It didn't go well. Roland was in complete denial."

The image crossed my mind: a hulking six

foot six Reverend McKnight hovering over Roland, the minister's fiery hair on end.

Our foreheads practically touched now as we whispered behind Roland's back. Tom leaned even closer. "What I meant when I said there is something you need to know is this — that first Sunday of family counseling was the last. The Friday after McKnight came to the house, Garland made headline news at the tree lighting ceremony for giving away Roland's 'hard-fought earnings.' He got her home and beat her to a pulp."

"Oh, my God." I spied Hilda across the room, face drawn, concentrating hard on work. "That's why Hilda's been acting the way she has. She told me her mother wasn't feeling well."

"She doesn't even know where her mother is. Garland did what I thought she'd never do. She left Roland a week ago."

Like a horror movie, the memory of Roland twisting my arm reeled through my mind. If he'd beat the hell out of his wife, why not twist the arm of a woman he really hated?

"How do you know all this?"

"Garland called me from a safe house in Baltimore. One of the Circle Ladies drove her down there."

"God bless her whoever she is. Does McKnight know?"

"Not yet, but I intend to tell him."

So. The answer seemed simple now. "When's Roland going to be arrested?"

Tom removed his glasses and rubbed dark eyes. "He's not. Garland won't cooperate."

My face fell. "Don't tell me that."

"She won't be persuaded. Believe me, I tried. She's going to let me know in a day or two what she wants done."

"What she wants *done?* Before or after the body count?" Hilda dropped off my lunch order and spun away. "And what about her? If he'd beat his wife, he'll go after the daughter soon enough."

"Don't you think I'm worried about that, too?!" All pretense at whispering fell away. Roland turned to stare at us.

Just then, a singsong voice chimed, "Oh, Roooolaaaand."

Roland's eyes swiveled to lock on Lee. "What the hell do you want?"

"I have something for you," she cooed. "Copies of the letters Leona left me. You know, the letters you've been so anxious to study for their historical value."

She stood there, a sticky sweet expression on her face and Sam behind her back. The hard glaze of Roland's demeanor melted into confusion. He jumped back when Lee offered him the papers.

"If you don't believe they're the same as the originals, feel free to check it out yourself down at Tom's office sometime — neutral territory."

"What is this?" he mumbled. "What are you trying to pull?"

"Nothing," Lee spoke loud enough for all to hear. "Absolutely nothing. This is no trick. These are bona fide copies of the Stuart letters."

"Read 'em, Roland!" Neither one of the Eggheads could keep still.

"Whudothey say? Whudothey say?"

I couldn't stand it. "Lee," I pleaded, "don't let *him* read them out loud, for God's sake!" The image I bore at that moment was of one of my mothers, Leona, stretched out on the floor of the majestic Bell house, telling me where to find these beautiful, almost sacred letters.

The second Lee caught the look in my eyes, she knew. She dropped the cavalier style and faced the audience who gathered round. This was their history, too. It was time to gift the letters to the town of Solace Glen.

Sam took a seat next to Tom and me. Lee waited for people to quiet down. Everyone opened their ears.

"Some time ago, as you all know, my Aunt Leona asked Flip to retrieve some letters for me that she said were written by General J.E.B. Stuart. I didn't think that possible, since all three letters were signed 'K.G.S.' Sam here helped me find an expert at the Smithsonian who examined the contents and paper. All the tests checked out."

Somebody called out, "If Stuart wrote them, what does 'K.G.S.' mean?"

"Knight of the Golden Spurs." Lee held up one of the copies and pointed to the signature.

"Stuart used to sign his personal letters like that after an unknown lady from Baltimore sent him a pair of golden spurs. Pretty romantic, huh?"

"Who's the woman he wrote to, Lee? Did the expert know who she was? Was she from Solace Glen?"

"Was she a Bell?" snapped Roland. "Because if so, I'm filing suit tomorrow. *Was* she a Bell?"

Lee held a rein on her temper; I don't know how. "No clue. This is the only known correspondence between the two of them, no mention of her to his wife or friends — big surprise. No mention of her by anyone else associated with Stuart at the time. I'm not familiar with the name, and the expert said we'd have to research local records of births, deaths, marriages, church membership, that sort of thing, to find her. It would take an awful lot of time." She shook her head at the letters and sighed. "I don't know if it's that important we know who she was."

"Not important?!" I had to throw in my two cents. If Lee chose to divulge the Bell women's secret, we ought to at least try to find all the pieces of the puzzle. "Of course it's important. Leona said so herself. These letters make Solace Glen important. Historical. Here is a famous Civil War general — dashing, brave, known for his daring cavalry escapades, raids into enemy territory, unbelievable escapes. The love his men had for him. The plumed hat. His reputation as a ladies' man."

Lee stuck a hand on her hip. "I think you should run the Historical Society."

"Seriously." I addressed my comments to everyone. "Find out who that woman was and we find out why, for more than one hundred and thirty-five years, the Bell family women passed these letters down to one another and shared the secret with *no one*. How is that not important?"

Forehead creased, Lee picked up the first letter and began to read. No one in the room made a sound.

September 9, 1862

Dearest Ellby,

Only two days ago I first set eyes upon you, strolling arm and arm with your friend, Miss Marsh, down the main thoroughfare of Urbana. I admit to you now, I had never seen a face so stirring. If the wind had not blown your bonnet off at that precise moment, I do not doubt that some other twist of fate would have conspired to join us together. Yet, I despaired, for no sooner had I presented you with the miscreant blue bonnet than duty called, and I was forced to part without introduction, carrying with me only the memory of your russet hair, your sunlit face, and your thanks. I thought never to see you again. How kind the Fates in our regard! The very next night, at the ball I gave in the female academy in Urbana, imagine my unbounded delight when your cousin presented you and you left his arm and took mine for the Virginia reel! I regret my little party was twice interrupted, once by a skirmish at the pickets, and again, by the wounded carried into the vacant academy rooms at dawn. You and the other ladies in your white dresses were only a little less than angels, administering to the poor fallen.

As Blackford, my adjutant, says, "One hour's acquaintance in war times goes further toward good feeling and acquaintanceship than months in the dull, slow period of peace." Could I have imagined an attachment and admiration so instantaneous and yet so deep, the poetry I deign to write would have taken quite a different turn in my youth. I dare say, I would have given up all early attempts entirely, knowing pure poetry walked this earth, and one day I would have the joy of dancing the Virginia reel with her.

Think me not a trifling man, Ellby, given to rhapsodies at the sight of any pretty face. I am, I assure you, in earnest. Yet time flows in a narrow stream for us, condensed to boundaries too paltry and contained.

Allow me to call on you and your cousin tomorrow in Solace Glen.

I lay my heart before you. Only you, dear Ellby, know the weight of it.

Your Most Obedient Servant,
K.G.S.

Lee handed me the second letter to read out loud.

September 11, 1862

My Darling Ellby,

When we stand before our God, we can but confess that among our many tiny sins, our great weakness was brought about by over-powering human emotion, for nothing base passed between us. I know this as I know my life and your heart. You remain a Lady of Esteem and I, your worshipful admirer.

We both painfully acknowledged the paths of our circumstances. My road is clear and laid out before me, a road I must advance upon, regardless of personal complaints or satisfactions. I take no satisfaction, though, Ellby, in leaving you. I know not when or if we shall meet again, except the sureness of our facing the same Maker and answering identical issues.

Know that I loved you, a deep, profound, and sorrowful love that tore the firmaments and ripped the recesses of my being.

I had known only faithfulness before you. Now I meet in combat, not only a mortal enemy on the field of battle, but the ghostly foe of my Immortal Soul, and each day and hour I must face the contest.

Will we, dearest Ellby, look upon our time and denounce it or cherish it? Will you confine the memory of me to the chamber in your being designed for guilt and regret? Of that, I pray not. For you will hold that kind place in my heart where only the most beautiful things of this earth reside. But you, dearest Ellby, will shame all other beauties and shine — the brightest jewel in my crown of remembrance!

Your Most Obedient Servant,
K.G.S.

Lee ironed the last letter with the palm of her hand and read.

November 1862

Dearest Ellby,

I thought my last letter to you before Sharpsburg would be the final correspondence between us, but I find myself turning urgently to one who knows my heart. Ellby, I fear the Almighty is a harsh judge, indeed, to punish mortal man in such a terrifying fashion as He has admonished this lowly servant. Dearest Ellby, my firstborn, my darling little daughter, Flora, has been taken from us. I could not, because of duty to country and to all our mothers and children, leave my post on the field of battle and hasten to the mother of my child to comfort her. Nor could I share in that grief in the final hours when the angels transported our little one, but five years old in September, to the heaven where she belonged.

I have a son, little more than two years of age, and I pray my wife and I will have the blessing of more children, but the loss of this one goes hard with me, Ellby. I cannot help but believe this is a punishment for our weakness and I have sought forgiveness at every turn.

I write to tell you of this affliction and to ask your own forgiveness for a sin I know I am solely responsible for, though you have protested that account. You need not write in response. What words leave your lips in silent prayer will reach the One who requires such an answer. Pray for me and keep this repentant soul alive in that kind chamber of your heart where the beautiful things of this earth reside and are remembered for their honor and their worth.

> In Humble Gratitude,
> Your Obedient Servant,
> K.G.S.

Lee folded the copies of the three letters together and handed them to Roland.

"You're right," she said to me quietly. "It is important to know."

When I arrived home that night after a long afternoon of work, two messages blinked on my answering machine. The first voice was Tom's, assuring me we'd have no further trouble with Marlene and adding, wouldn't it be a great idea to let Garland and Hilda stay in Louise's house? I grinned and clapped my hands together at his brilliance. Then I heard the second voice.

"Flip Paxton, Keeper of the Flame. Don't think this stuff Lee did with the letters will satisfy me. So what if the Bell women saved a bunch of stupid love letters written to some fool friend of theirs. You have a Bell original. An original. J.E.B. Stuart and his soppy love drool can go to blazes for all I care." He added in a loud farewell, "Don't you forget me at Christmas time, you hear? Because I won't forget *you*."

Chapter 35

I worked so hard the next three days that Roland's blatant threats hung in the shadows, but on Tuesday, with Christmas fast approaching, the message he left on my machine replayed in my head louder and louder. By the time I arrived at Miss Fizzi's house late Tuesday, my vacuum and I had covered almost every floor in Solace Glen, and Roland's voice traveled with us. Three days of bleach and ammonia clung so tight to my skin that the aroma of Miss Fizzi's fresh lemon chess pie could barely get through. I stood over a hot pie and breathed deep, the next best thing to a spa treatment.

The road to recovery neared the end for Miss Fizzi, and she hobbled around her heavy, dark antiques with newly minted hair, sprayed to the hilt with stuff the EPA probably banned years ago. With Sally, all was fair in love and hair. Miss Fizzi's bright pink lips dipped into a glass of sherry on the kitchen counter now and again.

"I baked one specially for you," she crowed, proud as a peacock.

"You are a wonder." I set my carryall and

vacuum on the kitchen floor. "You look ready to run the Preakness."

"Less than five months away! I'll be there with bells on!" She twittered and sipped at the sherry. "Flip." A sparkle lit her beautiful eyes. "You'll be happy to hear I remembered something."

"That is news. What did you remember?"

"I remembered the story Leona told me. The Lucy story."

"You did?" She had my full attention.

Miss Fizzi backed into a Windsor chair, so old its mahogany skin peeled, and propped her healing feet on a stool. "Years ago, Leona and I got hooked on that game, Clue. We couldn't get enough of it. Played every spare moment until we got hooked on Spades."

"Uh-huh." What all this had to do with the Lucy story, I could only guess.

"One rainy afternoon, we were going at it, guessing how the character got killed off, with what instrument, in what room, and we got on the subject of secrets."

"Secrets."

"Yes. And we agreed to tell each other our most private secret. I went first." She blushed. "I told her I was in love with Jake, had been for years, but if I couldn't have him, I was glad she was the one."

"When was this?" It touched me to think of Miss Fizzi carrying a torch for Jake all those years.

346

"Oh, I fell in love with him in my teens, even though he was a couple of years younger. I waited and waited, through my twenties, into my thirties. We maintained a lovely friendship, but one day he came back home from his traveling job, was sitting in church, and he spied Leona, about twenty years old. The thing hit him like a tidal wave. They married within a year."

"Goodness. And you never met anyone else who interested you?"

She sighed sweetly. "No one could compare to Jake."

"Was Leona surprised when you told her?"

"Not at all. Knew all the time, she said. Big deal. Do you want him now, she asked me, because the fool gave me a bird dog for my birthday. They named him Ruckus because that's what Leona raised with Jake. She'd wanted a diamond brooch."

I remembered Ruckus, a completely untrainable Springer. Leona used to hurl her fine china at him. "And what was Leona's secret?"

Miss Fizzi's robin's egg eyes widened. "An illegitimate child."

My head jerked back in surprise. "Leona had a baby before she married Jake?"

"Oh, no, dear heart! Bite your tongue! No." She shook her white head emphatically. "It wasn't Leona's baby. It was Lucy's baby."

I drew closer. "Lucy who?"

"Lucy Bell . . ."

"Paca Tanner."

347

"Yes," she bobbed her head. "That's right. You remember from the Bible. And the man was . . ."

"J.E.B. Stuart." The Knight of the Golden Spurs writing to Ellby. Lucy Bell. L.B.

She beamed at me. "Isn't that something? And all those years later, the Bell women still kept the secret, handing down letters, she said, that proved the affair."

"That's right. Leona's letters. She left them to Lee." I shook my head. "What I don't understand is why keep the secret for so long, and in such a way, with only the women in the family knowing."

"Consider the Bell men, Flip." We exchanged a knowing glance. "You know, only very recently has illegitimacy taken on a kind of vogue. I find it deeply disturbing and bizarre," she fluttered a little hand up to her heart. "But during the Civil War, such a circumstance warranted not only the ruination of a woman, but her entire family. Lucy Bell apparently made some excuse and left town before the birth. She gave up the child to friends for adoption."

I pictured the whole family tree in my mind with the empty parentheses under Lucinda Ann's name — the baby Lucy gave up. "Lucy must have confided in Gretal and Gretal's daughter-in-law, Florence Openheim. It was Florence who got the letters when Lucy passed away in 1912."

"And they've been handed down by the Bell women ever since."

"That's right." So Florence inherited the secret and passed it on to Katrina Chapelle Bell who gave the letters to Penelope who gave them to Leona who left them to Lee. "But I still don't understand why Penelope and Leona kept the secret all those years later."

Miss Fizzi shook her head. "I don't know, either, but what an unusual testament to the love Lucy inspired. Gretal and Florence must have held her in very high esteem. As did, of course, the General."

"Who never knew he'd fathered a child," I said sadly, thinking of his letters to Lucy and the loss of his little daughter, Flora. I'd read that he did have another child with his wife, a girl, less than a year after Flora's death, and five months later he was wounded at Yellow Tavern and died. "Lucy didn't tell him. He never knew."

"She didn't tell the child either."

I wrinkled my forehead. "I guess not since she gave the baby up for adoption."

"But the girl knew Lucy was her mother."

I stared at her. "How do you know that?"

"From the letter she wrote Lucy. The granddaughter wrote one, too, I remember."

"What letters?"

"The letters Lee has. I have no idea what is in them. Didn't you read them?"

I gaped at her. "Lee only has three letters, all from Stuart to Lucy."

Her face went quizzical and one shoulder lifted. "I know Leona said something about the

349

girl writing Lucy after she married and had a baby, then the baby grew up and wrote Lucy when she married." Miss Fizzi concentrated, tapping a finger against pursed lips. "Maybe those two letters are in the big house somewhere. Where would Leona have put them?"

The answer knocked me erect. I flew out of the room and into the car so fast, Miss Fizzi must have wondered what came over me and if I ever intended to come back for the carryall and vacuum left lying on her kitchen floor.

It didn't hit me until I saw his face that I'd run right through an open front door and into a house that had been locked tight. Ferrell T. stood in the center of my kitchen, the Bell family Bible in his hands. The basket of Spanish moss lay on the floor, Tom's gifts spilling out.

I screeched to a halt in the doorway, breathing fast, eyes fastened on the Bible. "What do you think you're doing, Ferrell T.?" Through my mind raced four things: Joey's car crash, my torn-apart house, Lee's break-in, Miss Fizzi's horrible fall. Was Ferrell T. really capable of such crimes?

"What's it look like? I'm collecting Daddy's Christmas present a little early, that's all." He stuck the Bible possessively under one arm and slid his hand into a pocket, a defiant grin spreading across his face.

He might just as well have ignited the pages

for the effect that small gesture had on me. The names of every Bell woman swept through my being, but the most important names were the two I did not know. The letters they left behind lay almost within reach, under the arm of a Bell man not five feet away. "Over my dead body."

He sniggered. "That's your choice, Miss Paxton."

From his pocket, I caught the gleam of something shiny and instantly grasped Ferrell T.'s capabilities. His father's son, after all.

"Roland put you up to this."

"Like I can't do anything on my own. Guess again." He snapped the blade open with the flick of a wrist and jabbed the knife in the air, close to my throat.

I flinched, surprised. "You wouldn't dare."

"Call my bluff, then. I'd just as soon carve you up as a Christmas turkey to keep what's rightfully mine."

One choice causes one domino to fall; another choice downs them all. My choices lined up against me in a wall so tall and thick, I had no inkling which one to knock over.

Ferrell T. stood there, grinning at my indecision. I took so long, he snapped the blade closed again. "Jeez. I don't have all night." He slid the knife back into his pocket, convinced I posed no threat. "Anyway, it's not like you don't have another Bible."

"But I don't have a *family* Bible, Ferrell T. Don't you get it? Leona left that Bible to me so

I'd feel like I had a family. She left it to *me*. Not Roland. And certainly not to you."

He huffed. "This isn't your family. It's mine. It's *my* inheritance, like the house and the car and the letters — everything. It was all supposed to go to *me*. I'm the rightful heir, and if I can't get it all back, I can at least get this back." He turned toward the door.

"No!" I sprang forward and wrenched the Bible out of his arm. Dried flower petals, scraps of paper, small envelopes floated to the floor.

Ferrell T. whirled around, grabbed the book and jerked it away. "It's mine!"

"No, it's not!" I lunged for the Bible, but a fist struck me dead center in the chest. I reeled backward onto the floor, breathless.

Two arms seized my waist from behind, yanked me off the floor and stayed securely coiled around my body. A large form flashed past and in one sudden motion, Ferrell T. lay stretched out, unconscious.

"When he comes to, I hope he gives me a crack at the other cheek." Reverend McKnight bent over his parishioner, wiping his huge paws.

"Don't soil your knuckles again." Tom slowly uncoiled his arms from around my waist and led me to a chair. "Are you all right?"

I nodded, unable to speak, gasping for the breath Ferrell T. knocked out.

Anguish drenched Tom's face. "I wish we'd gotten here sooner."

Ferrell T. groaned and rolled to a sitting position.

"If you thought I lit into your father a couple of weeks ago, wait'll you hear what's in store for *you,* heathen." Reverend McKnight plucked Ferrell T. off the floor as he might a stringed puppet. "You're coming with me and we're going to straighten you out down at the Frederick police station. And by God, if you don't get in line and make a good confessional, you'll not see the light of day till the next millennium."

Ferrell T. staggered out of my house at last, his minister shepherding the path ahead.

My lungs gradually took in air. "How did you know to come?"

"We dropped by to check on Miss Fizzi and found her with the two police officers you and Lee talked to. They'd traced the order to scrap Pal's car to Lukzay who admitted to doing a favor for 'the Bell boy.' When they couldn't find Ferrell T. at home or at my office, they headed to Miss Fizzi's for safety's sake. She told us her only visitor today was you and that you'd bolted away after discovering something about the Bell's. So we came here, thank God, with the police right behind us." Tom pulled up a chair and sank into it. "Also, Garland called Sunday, and yesterday McKnight and I picked her up in Baltimore. She's at Louise's house with Hilda. All Roland and Ferrell T. know is that Garland left and Hilda disappeared last night."

I rubbed my chest. "So they're safe. I hope they stay that way."

He placed a gentle hand on my knee, but every muscle in his face tensed. "If I'd acted sooner, maybe I could have kept you safe, too."

I wanted to take a fingertip and iron out each tight place along his jaw. "I don't know that he would have killed me, but I know now he's capable of it, Tom. And all he wanted was this."

I reached down and picked up the Bell family Bible. Tom bent to retrieve the dried flower petals, scraps of paper, and small, yellowed envelopes scattered across the kitchen floor. He placed the stack on the table before me and I lightly raked three fingers across the pile, spreading everything out. Two envelopes addressed to Lucy Bell Paca Tanner jumped out at me. I opened the first one, overwhelmed with curiosity, and began to read.

September 2, 1893

Dear Madam:

Although I have always known, since ever I could remember, that my kind parents adopted me, only of late did my mother reveal to me the name of that lady who showed me into this world, and through her own unhappy circumstance made my parents' situation most happy and complete. I know my mother, an old friend of yours from childhood, promised you from my birth that she would send news of my upbringing and did faithfully record my modest achievements, sending you brief accounts over the years. I know, too, that you destroyed those letters, having told my mother you would do so.

I have set before me two tasks, the reasons I write to you today. One is quite painful for us both. My mother, your dear friend, died not one week ago, and it was while she lay at death's door that she divulged your name and implored me to send this note. The second task is one of great joy and I only wish my mother had lived but a little longer and she could have shared in it, also. She, and you, have a granddaughter.

My fondest wish is that this child grow to be the adoring mother my own sweet mother was to me, and I have you to thank for placing me in such capable and loving arms.

I hope, Madam, this letter finds you in good health.

I am, most sincerely yours,
Flora Ellby Stockard

Flora Ellby. Flora, for Stuart's dead child. Ellby, for the secret name he gave Lucy. Lucy herself must have named the baby before handing her to the friend to raise. The poignancy of it brought me close to tears.

The second envelope, postmarked from Balti-

355

more, addressed Lucy in a different hand. The date at the top of the letter was only a few days before Lucy's death.

March 10, 1912

Dear Grandmother,

I hope you do not mind me calling you Grandmother. Mother assures me you will not. I only recently learned that I have a living grandparent. Mother explained everything, now that she says I am old enough to understand and will be marrying in a few weeks.

The purpose of my note is to invite you to my wedding. You would not have to reveal the relation if you do not wish to. We could simply refer to you as Mrs. Tanner from Solace Glen. Your presence would mean the world to both me and Mother, and I am quite positive my deceased grandmother, your good friend, would smile down from Heaven at the sight of us, all three, reunited. The wedding date is May 12 of this year. Please try to come. We both look forward to your response, as does my fiancé, Mr. George Reed.

Lovingly, Your Granddaughter,
Lila Ann Stockard

My heart leapt into my throat. I knew little of my father's family, even less of my mother's background. But I did know the names of her parents, my grandparents.

George and Lila Ann Reed.

Chapter 36

She respected the decisions and feelings of the women of her past; she respected the right of another generation to know the truth. To accomplish both ends, Leona bound Lee and me together, each with a part of the secret, each with different pieces of the puzzle. Without Lee's letters, I never would have grasped the whole picture. Without the letters in the Bell Bible, Lee may never have discovered the identity of Ellby, and I would never have known my true heritage.

> I leave this Bible in your care, Flip, knowing your deep appreciation of books, your love of this community and its history, and your own aloneness since the loss, so many years ago, of your family. May this old book, with its words of wisdom and inspiration, its pages filled with Bell family mementos, give you what I believe you long for most.

Leona Bell Jenner indeed knew what I longed for most. Family was her gift to me.

Leona knew, and her mother Penelope knew. It was Penelope who put it together, who befriended my mother, Julia Reed Paxton, when she arrived in Solace Glen as a twenty-four-year-old bride in 1948. She and Leona probably even met my grandmother, Lila Ann, before she died in Baltimore ten years later. Penelope harbored the letters, holding the secret dear, not for the sake of Lucy Bell, resting in peace, reunited at last with daughter and granddaughter, but for the sake of my mother who, if the truth were known, would have been stigmatized even then, most especially by the Bell men, for sins repented of long ago.

The sins of the mother, equal to, if not more grievous, than the sins of the father.

Chapter 37

Christmas Eve's dusk glowed as pink and rosy as Miss Fizzi's favorite lipstick. I dropped off her present, the botanical pie dish, and drove to Louise's house to deliver a special gift: the painted plant pot with a fresh poinsettia planted inside. Louise could no longer enjoy it, but Garland and Hilda would appreciate a touch of brightness in their lives this Christmas, especially after the sickening revelation of Ferrell T.'s evil acts. Following a confession that he later recanted, he sat in the Frederick County jail awaiting trial on brake tampering, breaking and entering, burglary, and the attempted murder of Miss Fizzi.

Garland and Hilda invited me in and we shared a cup of eggnog. Garland exercised her funny bone, laughing in a free and easy manner that lit her face bright and reminded me of her wedding and the old ladies talking about how pretty she was. Even Hilda relaxed, comfortable in the new setting of Louise's modest rancher, so different from the crowded, cramped Victorian house she'd grown up in, crammed with things, things, things.

Before I departed, Tina, Melody and Michael, Margaret, and Sally converged on the house bearing gifts and pure-from-the-heart laughter. I closed Louise's door behind me, Garland and Hilda chattering with their guests about silly, happy, mundane things, scrounging through suitcases to get at proper clothes for the evening church service.

Tom, Sam, Lee, and I devoured the whole enchilada for Christmas Eve — twenty minutes at each of the four Solace Glen church services — Catholic for Sam, Methodist for Tom, Episcopalian for Lee, and Presbyterian for me. We began our rounds at the tiny dollhouse of St. Francis of Assisi of Solace Glen, where from five o'clock to five-twenty, we knelt and crossed ourselves and got mixed up between prayer books and hymnals. Then we ran two blocks down the street to Tom's Methodist Church and listened to Reverend Grayson deliver a children's sermon that nobody could hear for all the screeching and wailing and shouting of the children. After that, we whisked into the Episcopal Church and bobbed like corks in the water up and down on our knees again. Finally, we capped the marathon off with the Presbyterian service, my favorite part, where the whole congregation lit candles, held them skyward, and sang "Silent Night, Holy Night" until every eye watered.

"I'm feeling extremely forgiven," declared Sam as we walked arm and arm back to Lee's house to get good and snockered on hot spiced wine. "If I keeled over dead right now, I might actually find myself in heaven."

"Dream on," Lee jabbed his chest. "It'll take more than an hour and a half of Christmas carols to usher you through the pearly gates."

Lee had decorated the Historical Society to beat the band — greenery, flowers, red apples and cranberries, popcorn, lemons. Even Plain Jane wore a festive air, her tomato red hair sporting a halo of baby's breath, a pair of papier-mâché wings crowning her shoulders.

"She's my guardian angel." Lee tweaked a wing. "Isn't she pretty?"

We dipped into the wine and settled around the old pine table to listen to Tom and Sam trade lawyer jokes, but the joking stopped when I drew the two yellowed envelopes out of my pocket that completed Lucy's saga and read them. Lee started to cry.

"I can't believe it." She stumbled to the kitchen sink to wipe her eyes on a dish towel. "Those women."

"So what all this boils down to is," Sam set his wine cup on the table and pointed at me, "you are related to Roland Bell."

"Thank you, Sam," I said. "Thank you so very, very much and Merry Christmas."

Tom sat quietly, a bemused expression across his face.

"Merry Christmas to you, too," said Sam, popping up. "But it won't really be merry until I present Miss Jenner with her Christmas present."

With that, Sam disappeared outside for a few

minutes. When he returned, he carried over his shoulder what looked like a dead body. He flung it into a chair beside Plain Jane. "Plain Jane," he announced proudly, "meet Dear John!"

Lee crept from the sink to the life-size doll. His hair matched Jane's, tomato red. He donned black boots made from blown out tires, pants stitched from tobacco burlap, a belt of bottle caps, a shirt of roofing shingles, Mickey Mouse-sized cotton glove hands, a mouth made of rubber worms, and a nose of bottle glass. And the eyes, the eyes stared back at us neon green. Neon IUDs.

"You outdid yourself." Tom wore a lopsided grin.

"No," Sam replied. "Not quite yet."

He moved behind Dear John and raised the cotton glove hands. "John has something to say. He's a talkative sort." He maneuvered the dummy to kneel down in front of Plain Jane and cleared his throat. "Jane, my darling angel. Will you marry me?"

Lee hopped behind Plain Jane, her mouth broad. "John, you mad, impetuous fool. This is so sudden. I have to consult my personal psychic."

"OK," said Dear John, "but I don't want to lug this thing back to Connolly's Jewelry Store, so would you wear it until your personal psychic can figure out the future?"

"Sure thing," burbled Plain Jane. "A doll can never have enough jewelry."

"So I'm told," said Sam, and he took a shiny object from his shirt pocket and slipped it on Lee's finger.

"Omigod. You're serious." Lee sputtered and started to cry again.

An elbow gently nudged my ribs and Tom and I slipped gracefully out of the Historical Society, Dear John collapsed in a heap on the floor from his big dramatic scene, Plain Jane slumped in her chair in shock.

I balanced myself on top of the kitchen counter and pulled the basket off the cabinet, pushed the Spanish moss aside and took out the Bell family Bible — *my* family Bible — the wrapped CD and the tie. I handed the gifts to Tom.

"Merry Christmas."

He helped me down. "You didn't have to do that."

He must not have gotten me anything. "Oh, it's not much. Just a little something for the trouble I've put you through this year."

"Is that what you've done?" Those eyes could melt a steel door. "A client/lawyer gift?"

"Well. Not exactly. A business lady/lawyer gift."

He unwrapped the presents, delighted with both. He threw the tie around his neck. "I bet you think I didn't get you anything."

"No!" Too much protest. "I mean, I hadn't thought about it. It doesn't matter."

He paused, smiling, then said, "I couldn't find frankincense and myrrh, but . . ." From a very deep pocket in his overcoat, Tom withdrew a sparkling, gold-ribboned bottle of Taittinger champagne. From another pocket, a gold half-pound box of Godiva chocolates met the kitchen light and gleamed. Glittering. Gold. Blinding.

I had to turn away. My eyes rested on the Bell family Bible and remained there, focused on the familiar, worn leather binding.

Behind me, a voice in my ear, his breath on my hair, then the rush of the warm mulled river of wine heating every vein in my body. "If you don't want the champagne and the chocolate, what do you want?"

A smile broke across my face and I slowly turned to face him.

"I want you," I said, inching my way along untested territory, "to ply me with wit and champagne, fruit, bread and cheese, a box of Godiva." I took the bottle and the box from his hands and set them on the counter. "Then I want you to recite one of your favorite poems. Something by Walt Whitman would be nice. And I want you to kiss me. Lightly. Insistently."

The dark eyes drew close, clasped onto mine. He placed one hand on either side of my face and slowly, quietly, softly, gently lulled me into his world.

Are you the new person drawn toward me?
To begin . . .

Postscript

The ladybugs leave in the spring, disappearing as suddenly as they appeared in September. The ceiling in the corner of my bathroom is bare, like the rest of the house. Bare, cleaned, culled of nearly twenty-five years of living alone, collecting the things one person collects.

I gave a lot of my little trinkets to Hilda to use in her dorm room in college in a year or so, knickknacks, old kitchen utensils, big sweaters never worn. She loves getting gifts, as if she never got any growing up. More important, she and Garland are both discovering each other's gifts.

They live in the same town as Roland, Ferrell T.'s most ardent supporter — the family split into two gender camps — attend the same church, shop the same grocery store, stop at the same stop signs. But that's where it ends. Garland opened her own restaurant, Garland's Bistro, which serves beer and wine, a first in Solace Glen. All of Roland's kitchen help switched to the other side of the street and his business, like his life, is falling apart, nothing left soon but the Victorian house packed with relics from the past.

Marlene stomps through the days of the week, adding Garland and Hilda to her list of people to blame for her problems, glaring holes into Louise's house with cold, fish eyes whenever she drives by.

Miss Fizzi, healthy as the racehorse she put her two dollars on at the Preakness, took center stage at her eighty-fifth birthday bash in May and danced a jig. The Eggheads stood by, ready to administer expert assistance if she jigged off the platform and broke a hip, but Miss Fizzi disappointed them and they got into a big argument with each other and Pal about the best car stereo systems. They tried to drag Screamin' Larry into it, calling on his fame as a radio personality to settle the issue, but he yawned in their faces and sauntered off, draining another longneck beer.

The next big event was Sam and Lee's wedding, and Louise would have loved the flowers. Tom and I stood as best man and best woman and Miss Fizzi sat in the front pew of the Episcopal Church as honorary grandmother, Plain Jane on her right, Dear John on her left. I glimpsed her at one point in the service, whispering a secret in Jane's ear.

The pear trees outshone themselves this year, along with the cherry and peach blossoms. They pepper the O'Connell property, and every window in the new house going up contains a view of a spring or autumn tree.

Trees are important, Tom says, and he plans

to plant more around the house and down the drive. In twenty or thirty years, when we sit rocking on the porch, those new trees will be tall, their branches sweeping out to shelter Tom and me. Only to shelter.